WHEN A SCANDAL THREATENS THE PRESIDENCY, HER TRUE COLORS ARE REVEALED.

RED, WHITE, and BLUE

LAURA HAYDEN

TYNDALE HOUSE PUBLISHERS, INC.,
CAROL STREAM, ILLINOIS

Visit Tyndale's exciting Web site at www.tyndale.com

Visit Laura Hayden's Web sites at www.suspense.net or www.EmilyBenton.com

TYNDALE and Tyndale's quill logo are registered trademarks of Tyndale House Publishers, Inc.

Red, White, and Blue

Designed by Julie Chen and Dean H. Renninger

Published in association with the literary agency of Alive Communications, Inc., 7680 Goddard St., Suite 200, Colorado Springs, CO 80920.

Library of Congress Cataloging-in-Publication Data

Hayden, Laura.
Red, white, and blue / Laura Hayden.
p. cm.
ISBN-13: 978-1-4143-1940-7 (sc : alk. paper)
1. Women presidents--Fiction. 2. Political fiction. I. Title.
PS3558.A8288R43 2009
813′.6—dc22 2008038151

Printed in the United States of America

15 14 13 12 11 10 09
7 6 5 4 3 2 1

To Pam, Karen, and Angel
for keeping me sane.

To my dad
for his strength, his patience,
and his faith in me.
(And all those neat genes
that let me figure out
how to construct and deconstruct.)

ACKNOWLEDGMENTS

As always, I couldn't do this series without the assistance of Denise Little, who helps me keep Kate and Emily alive and kicking.

KATE ROSEN SAT ON THE EDGE of the stage, the large hotel ballroom stretching beyond her, long emptied of people. The only things left behind were the detritus of a grand night of celebration—balloons skimming over the carpet, trampled paper streamers, discarded signs, and swags of limp bunting that sagged against the walls.

No more cameras, no strobe lights, no cheering throng. The exuberant but exhausted audience had finally faded away hours earlier, the journalists following suit shortly afterward. America had finally gone to bed, either celebrating or lamenting the fact that that they'd just elected their first female president.

Kate cherished the silence. She needed someplace where she could collect her thoughts, which had been shattered tonight. She'd discovered things she could hardly believe even still about her best friend. And she'd been disillusioned in a way that nobody, even a politician's top aide, was prepared to be. Her headache and heartache had been made worse by the oppressive crush of supporters commemorating their candidate's—her candidate's—triumph. Once Emily and her entourage, minus Kate, went upstairs, the party had finally broken up and the ballroom's capacity crowd started to stream home for their own private celebrations.

But Kate's ears still rang with the sound of more than a thousand people cheering, screaming their support of their candidate.

"Benton! Benton! Benton!"

Emily Rousseau Benton, former governor of Virginia, Kate's best friend, had been elected president of the United States, in no small part due to Kate's hard work. Emily's race for the White House had dominated both of their lives for the past four years. Everything Kate did, every action she took as Emily's campaign manager, had been done solely in support of her friend's bid for the presidency.

And now that Emily had won, Kate was alone, horrified at the prospect that she might have made a terrible mistake.

She slipped down from the stage riser and kicked idly at the balloons in her path, creating a slight rippling effect across the bubbled mass of them. An occasional balloon still floated down from the ceiling, a day late and a dollar short.

Kate's most recent revelation had been like that, one day too late. . . .

"Hey, Kate."

A lone voice penetrated the silence. She stiffened in surprise and raised her hand to shade her eyes and get a better look at the person standing on the balcony. Her mood lightened and her shoulders relaxed when she realized who had spoken.

"Hey, Wes."

"Y'all all right? Need some company?"

She nodded.

It was a classic Southern salutation, and the familiarity of it was oddly comforting. Then again, Wes Kingsbury always knew what to say—he was equal parts her friend and her spiritual mentor. Disappearing into the shadows, Wes emerged a few moments later from the staircase leading to the balcony box.

Kate glanced at her watch and stifled a yawn—3:46. That was a.m. Too early to be called morning, too late to be called night. The true dark hours of the human soul, when body rhythm and spirit were at their lowest point.

"I can't believe you're still here," she said. The man had a wife and a small child, a real world and home to which he could return. He hadn't closed his life down to a single obsessively sought goal. That had been her mistake.

"And I can't believe you're not upstairs. M's still up in the suite, partying hearty."

She kicked at a balloon, stirring up a small whirl of color. "I know. I'm not in much of a party mood."

"So I see." He fell into step next to her. "What's going on? I would have thought you'd be thrilled. This was the goal, right?" He pointed to an abandoned placard: *Benton/ Bochner '08*.

"It was. It is." She couldn't help but shiver. "It's complicated."

"It's Emily. It's always complicated." He chuckled, then sighed. "Okay, what has she done *now*?" At Kate's hesitation, he added, "It's got something to do with Talbot, doesn't it?"

Charles Talbot had been Emily's opponent in her race for

the White House. As such, he'd pulled out all the stops to find all the dirt he could on his challenger. Kate, as Emily's friend and ally for more than twenty years, had been positive there was no dirt to be found.

She'd been so wrong. . . .

Talbot's investigators discovered that Emily's family had illegally won important highway construction contracts in Virginia while Emily was the state's governor.

When Kate learned his camp was prepared to release this information, the only way she could stop him was to explain to him exactly the unsavory facts that her own investigations had uncovered on him—details she'd kept out of Emily's hands.

The last thing Kate had wanted was her friend to strike an ill-timed and unnecessary first blow—using a nuke when a nudge would have worked just as well. She'd learned the hard way that Emily, though a talented politician, wasn't exactly good at being subtle when she had a bigger weapon handy. But when Talbot made his big, bold move to not only discredit Emily but take down her family by attempting to dismantle the entire Benton legacy, Kate had intervened by threatening to use her opposition research.

Talbot had killed . . . and Kate felt that she had no choice but to remind him of the lengths to which he'd gone to cover up his own crimes. She had the bloody proof that he'd been criminally negligent, if not morally responsible, in the grisly death of his college girlfriend. Talbot might have maneuvered his way out of the scandal, but Kate had the goods on him—incontrovertible evidence.

If released to the public, her evidence would have been sufficient to end his campaign, destroy his reputation, and possibly land him in jail for a long, long time. Talbot saw the light and backed down from his threats.

So Talbot had been stopped. The situation had served to cement Kate's resolve that Emily Benton would make a far better president than her opponent. Emily was a policy wonk who knew her stuff, she was talented at getting things done, she worked hard for the people she represented, and she was charismatic enough to persuade even those who opposed her to allow time for her ideas to have a chance to work. In other words, Emily was the best politician of her time.

However, Kate soon learned not only that her actions had made Talbot her enemy for life, but also that no one ever wins in a competition of "who has the best blackmail" because the games like that never end. She'd felt sickened, soiled, and finally betrayed.

Kate drew a deep breath. "Emily found out."

Wes straightened for a moment. He'd been one of only two confidants who knew the sins of both candidates, other than the candidates themselves.

"About . . ." Wes paused and glanced around as if gauging the likelihood of being overheard. Even though no one was in sight, he kept his voice low. "About the ammunition you had? How?"

"I told her I'd stopped Talbot, but I refused to tell her how. I didn't think she needed to know. So in the middle of the night, my best friend M sent one of her protégées to 'borrow' the report from me."

"'Protégées'?" Wes's gaze narrowed. "Maia," he said in a flat voice.

Kate nodded. "Our very own iron ingenue in training."

She stared across the vast ballroom, watching a piece of bunting as it slipped from the balcony railing and wafted gently to the floor. "Though apparently she's more iron maiden than ingenue. Scruples don't seem to concern her. I rip my heart out every day, trying to find the right balance between my Christian convictions and loyalty to my country and to my friends—especially Emily. I want to make a difference in the world, make people's lives better. I don't always like how I do it. Yet Maia didn't have a second thought when Emily asked her to steal the reports from me in the middle of the night. She made copies, then replaced the originals so I wouldn't know. Then Emily had Maia contact Talbot with what you'd call a very thinly veiled threat."

Wes read between the lines. "Destroying any hope of the campaign staying out of the gutter."

"Yeah. But then came the weird part. It did—stay out of the gutter, I mean." A shiver coursed up her spine and she crossed her arms in an effort to combat it. "Buttoned up tighter than Fort Knox. Maybe my way wasn't effective enough. Maybe Emily's decision to send him a second threat was the only real way to stop him." A second tremor joined the first, and Kate knew it wasn't because she was cold. "Maybe I was wrong. Or maybe I'm in the wrong business. Or maybe I'm simply overreacting."

"Or maybe not."

They took several more steps through the remains of the revelry before Kate stopped. She reached down and rescued a placard bearing Emily's likeness.

"In any case, I don't know . . ." She hated how her voice broke when she spoke. "I don't know if I can stay. If I can continue working with her. She lied to me, stole from me.

Maia actually expected me to be impressed by their cleverness. Emily knew better. But she set it up anyway." She studied the picture plastered across the placard. Emily's resolute smile looked effortless despite the fact it'd taken the photographer over two hours to capture the perfect expression.

"You have very high standards for your behavior." Wes took a few more steps, then stopped, pivoting to face her, his hands jammed in his pockets. "Emily's a lot more flexible; she's a big proponent for 'the end justifies the means.' You know that. I know that. The question is, can you tolerate that? Jesus himself said, 'Render unto Caesar that which was Caesar's.' But there have to be consequences when a person crosses the line. Nobody's above the law, not even Emily—though she'd probably argue that point. The big question you have to answer here is what is the right thing for your faith and the right thing for the world. Think hard about that and then move forward. I'll pray for you. I know it's going to be a tough decision."

Kate looked up from Emily's compelling expression, the look in her eyes that said, *You know you can trust me.* "A decision I was hoping you'd help me make."

To her utter surprise, Wes shook his head. "Nope."

"But—"

He raised his palm to stop her. "Hear me out. I'm always willing to offer advice, lend a hand or even a shoulder, but when it comes to something like this, you need to work with a higher authority." He pointed upward.

Kate managed to conjure up a tight smile. "Somehow, I don't think you mean President-Elect Benton in the penthouse suite."

"Nope. A lot higher."

★ ★ ★ ★ ★

They rode up the elevator in silence. It wasn't until they reached the door to the suite, flanked by Secret Service agents, that Wes hesitated.

Kate fought the urge to say, "You're going in with me, aren't you?" She realized she needed to speak to Emily in private. If any of the campaign entourage still hung about, Kate would have to bide her time, smile, make nice with the natives, and wait for her chance after all the hoopla finally ended. It had been relatively easy to have the candidate's ear in private, but getting the attention of the next president would be more complicated.

She practiced her smile on the two agents, whose names she needed to learn. Then she stopped herself.

Or maybe after tonight it wouldn't matter.

"This is where I say good-bye." Wes leaned over and kissed her forehead. "And good luck. Let me know what happens."

"Thanks. I will," she whispered. Drawing in a deep breath, Kate reached for the doorknob, but the agent on the right beat her to it.

"Allow me, Ms. Rosen." He opened the door.

It was a testament to the construction of the hotel that she heard little in the way of sound from the suite until the door opened. Then a cacophony of laughter and voices met her, the celebration evidently still in full swing. The crowd had dwindled some, but an impressive number of folks still lingered, including several of Washington's biggest power players, senior members of the party, a large assortment of Benton family members, and some of the key campaign staffers.

Kate didn't see Emily at first but finally spotted her in

a corner of the room, holding court. They made eye contact and Emily raised her hand as if saying, *Over here* and motioned Kate over. In response, Kate began to pick her way through the clusters of people. She was stopped every foot or so to be congratulated, hugged, and offered a drink.

She felt odd accepting the accolades, but she had no trouble waving off the libations. The last thing she needed was the muddle of alcohol. She could only hope that Emily had kept a clear head as well.

Before Kate could reach Emily's position, she bumped into a rather solid male form. Before she could recover her balance, a hand grasped her elbow and she was hit in the face with a cloud of whiskey breath.

"Katie-girl!" Emily's old family adviser Dozier Marsh pulled her into an awkward embrace. He might have looked like someone's sainted grandfather, but it was as far from what he really was as the North Pole from Antarctica. He was the ultimate political fixer—a devious, dangerous old power broker with a fondness for hard liquor and Emily, though not always in that order. And right now, he was acting like a lecherous uncle.

Great-uncle.

"Where you been, darlin'?" he wheezed. "Hard to have a party without Emily's right-hand gal!" He tried to swing her around. The move would have made them both fall over had the young aide standing next to him not reached up and steadied him.

"Sir, perhaps you'd rather sit," the aide said.

Dozier gave Kate a grin and leaned heavily against his aide. "I suspect you're right, Percy. The room is definitely leaning to one side." He dropped heavily into the nearest chair, managing to spill two drinks that were abandoned on the nearby end table. He stared blearily at the mess. "Would you be a dear, Kate, and get me a couple of cocktail napkins so I can clean up behind my sorry, drunken self? I'd ask Perry here, but he's playing a key role in supporting me."

"Now, Dozier . . ." Emily's voice knifed neatly through the chatter, instantly commanding the attention of the room. "You're not asking the future White House chief of staff to be your fetch-it girl, are you?"

Dozier's ruddy complexion deepened. "Of c-course not, Emily. . . . I mean . . ." He pulled awkwardly to his feet, away from his aide, and managed a small stiff bow without falling over. "Madam President."

The room went silent, no one quite sure what direction Emily's response might head next.

"I've never really liked being called 'madam.'" After a tense millisecond, Emily allowed a smile to spread across her face. "But I guess I'll get used to it, if *president* gets to follow."

Dozier, freed from the sharp conversational hook on which he'd impaled himself, offered a weaker version of her smile and lifted the drink he'd never lost grip of. "Hear, hear."

With the momentary tension broken, the room went back to its earlier state—celebrating people clustering in small discussion knots. Dozier's aide, a young man whose name was neither Percy nor Perry but Zack, distracted Dozier with something shiny, giving Kate a chance to escape. Once again, Emily gestured for Kate to follow her and led to the bedroom portion of the suite.

Once the door was closed behind them, Emily gave her a warm hug. "I was starting to get worried about you." She gave Kate a close scrutiny. "Honey, you look like the weight of the free world is still on your shoulders. But the campaign's over. We won. You can afford to relax now."

"No. I can't." Kate said. She bit her lip before her words started pouring out, uncontrolled and bitter. She wanted to be completely in control of her emotions before she confronted Emily.

Emily sighed, obviously ignorant of the battle brewing inside Kate. "I know. I feel the same way. Campaigning is hard work, but nothing compared to running a country." She dropped to the bed. "If I allowed myself a chance to stop and think about what I'm taking on, I'd probably run out of this hotel screaming like the Madwoman of Chaillot.

"Remember when we went to New York on spring break back when we were in school? How we jumped on our beds at the Waldorf-Astoria hotel and had a pillow fight? Mom was horrified, but Dad told me that he hoped I'd never get too old to bounce on the bed."

"Yeah," Kate said. Decades of memories came crashing down upon her. Room service, going to plays, Emily's genuine pleasure at sharing the treat with her friend. The phrase "Never get too old to jump on the bed" had become an inside joke, a motto for that trip and later, the watchwords for those times when the responsibilities of law school—and beyond—threatened to drag them down.

When Nick and Emily got married, their gift to each bridesmaid included a sterling silver box engraved with that motto. Kate still had that box sitting in a place of honor on her dresser.

"Well?" The next president of the United States, the Honorable Emily Rousseau Benton, took off her shoes and took a few experimental bounces on the bed as if to test the bed's recoil potential.

"Not today." Kate tried to smile, desperately wanting to recapture that same sense of giddy accomplishment that Emily evidently felt. Kate had indeed expected to feel a sense of joyous triumph when thinking ahead to this day. But now her heart was too heavy, her mind too burdened with the difficult decision that lay ahead of her.

Emily stopped jumping, the bed undulating in her wake. "Why not?" she said. The confusion that initially filled her face dissolved into an expression that Kate couldn't quite understand. Then it passed almost immediately to a tight, guarded smile. "You have a point. I need to be dignified. Somehow, I don't think the White House curator is going to let anyone jump on the bed in the Lincoln Bedroom. Not you. Not even me."

"That's not what I meant."

Emily locked eyes with her for a moment. Then she turned away, unable to hold the contact for long. A Benton never crumbled under pressure. A real Benton dodged it. The president-elect slid off the bed, pulled on her heels, and straightened her skirt. She didn't meet Kate's gaze.

"You're right. We're both exhausted. You've always dealt with exhaustion in different ways than I do. Why don't you take off a—"

"I'm exhausted. But that's not the problem. I'm confused. Angry. And I'm disappointed in you." Kate's heart took the extra beat it always did when she made the final decision to confront her best friend. "You didn't need to send Maia to steal the files from me. You should have talked to me about it."

"Oh." Emily spoke in a low, even voice. "You found out about that?"

Kate nodded.

"I didn't send her," Emily said. "She did that on her own, trying to curry my favor."

Kate didn't know whom to believe. She knew Emily better than she knew herself in some ways. Emily was brilliant, capable, the best person imaginable to have around in an emergency. She was a born leader. But part of that leadership tool kit was that she would also stop at nothing when she wanted something. Of course, Maia was cut from the same cloth. Emily's words were plausible. "So did the favor currying work?" She tried to keep any emotion out of her voice. "Did she make a big impression on you?"

"Yes, but it was a mixed bag. I thought Maia showed a remarkable amount of initiative, but I told her that she'd chosen the wrong person to cross."

"But that didn't stop you from reading the reports, did it?"

"Of course not. I'd have been a fool to lose that unexpected opportunity. I'm no fool. You know that."

"Yes, I do. And I guess that's why you instructed her to send the threatening e-mail to Talbot. Were you just taking advantage of another unexpected opportunity?"

"Sure. It seemed the wise thing to do at the moment. He was a loose cannon. He needed to be locked down."

"And now? Are you still glad you did it?"

Emily collapsed on the bed, her ice queen facade shattered. A single tear trickled down her face, leaving a glistening trail through her perfect makeup. "No. I regret it more than you'll ever know." She bent her head, trying desperately to hide the additional tears, but a sob tore through her, making her shoulders shake.

Kate almost gaped at her friend. She'd seen Emily's crocodile tears before. But they didn't look anything like this. This was the real thing.

Real emotion. Real regret. . . .

Emily continued. "Mind you, I didn't hate what I did to Charles Talbot. He's a pariah, an abomination. A murderer. He should never have been able to get away with driving that car while drunk, and leaving that poor girl behind, still clinging to life, to take the rap for his actions. Had he gotten her help at the time of the accident, she might have survived the crash as something other than a vegetable. But no, he had to save face, run away, pretend nothing had happened. He left her to die in that car. It took hours for anyone to discover the wreck. Then he had the audacity to bribe and threaten people into giving him an alibi. He had to make everyone think she'd been the one driving while intoxicated, even if it killed her. He's the lowest of scumbags. I won't apologize for pricking whatever fragments he has left of his conscience. I'm pretty sure all I did was dent his enormously bloated and unconscionable pride."

Emily's flare of anger dissipated quickly, as if she suddenly felt guilty of failing to be remorseful for her own actions. Kate knew that, for Emily, anger was an emotion easier to understand and embrace than remorse. Especially when she felt that anger was righteous. Emily could move mountains when she had on a full load of righteous anger. Kate had seen her shame an entire state legislature into voting for health insurance for disadvantaged children, all because she'd vented her anger into a biting five-minute speech to them.

Kate gave her friend a steady stare. “What he did and what you did are separate issues. And you know it.”

“I’m sorry.” Emily’s voice dropped to a whisper. “You’re right. When Maia gave me those copies, I did exactly what you were afraid I was going to do.” She looked up, naked emotion filling her face, tears rolling down her cheeks. “I allowed my need for revenge to overwhelm my sense of honor. I’m so sorry.” She stood, her arms at her side. Her voice broke in a show of raw emotion that Kate had never seen from her before.

“Kate, can you forgive me?”

Kate felt tears forming in her own eyes.

Could she forgive Emily? Of course she could. Christ was clear on the responsibility to forgive a repentant sinner. Kate could do no less.

But could she trust Emily enough to continue working for her? That was another question entirely.

For now, she reached over and hugged her friend. The two of them cried together for what seemed like hours.

But the big question—whether Kate would stay on after this—hung over them. No matter how often Emily asked it, Kate refused to answer.

Finally Emily said, “Take some time, go home, cool off, and then we’ll talk.”

As was often the case, Emily was right.

ROBERT FROST ONCE SAID something to the effect that home was a place where, when you go there, they have to take you in. He never mentioned anything about what to do when home is no longer home.

Ever since Kate's parents had moved out of the family home where she'd grown up, she always felt a little out of place in their retirement house, even though she knew she was welcome there.

It was . . . different. Yet there were still reminders of her childhood home—like her grandmother's armless rocking chair in her parents' bedroom. On the coffee table sat her father's humidor, which had never held a single cigar but instead a constantly changing collection of pens and pencils. Just like before, her mother had hung the family photographs in the hallway leading to the bedrooms, the pictures chronicling the growth of Kate and of her brother, Brian, from childhood to adulthood.

Kate studied how her mother had balanced the diametrically opposed lives of her two children. Brian's pictures included his wedding portrait and both formal and casual shots of Jill and Brian. Her brother's pictures often showed him in uniform. The lives of his three kids, their parents' only grandchildren, were also carefully chronicled, with a place of special honor given to the pictures of the new baby.

Kate's collection of photos lacked a husband and children but included her multiple graduations and shots of her various roles in life—lawyer, assistant to the lieutenant governor, assistant to the governor, and manager of Emily's presidential campaign. Kate knew it was her mother's way of showing that she had just as much pride in Kate's accomplishments as she did in Brian's. The photographs even included a few snapshots of Kate standing next to Emily, aka "our adopted daughter."

And that was true. As much as Emily loved her fellow Bentons, she lovingly called the Rosens her "wonderful normal family." Holidays at the Benton manse had always been magnificent affairs with twenty-foot trees decorated by Martha Stewart herself, meticulously wrapped presents in color-coordinated paper, and gourmet meals cooked by some of the finest chefs in the world. The opulence both entranced and repelled Kate the few times she had joined in the grand festivities.

A Rosen family Christmas included homemade ornaments—some of them embarrassingly bad childhood craft projects from long ago—Christmas cards pinned to a piece of yarn stretched across the fireplace mantle, a Crock-Pot steaming with apple cider all hours of the day, and Christmas Eve services at church where no one minded if Kate was somewhat tone-deaf when she sang with gusto.

But it wasn't Christmas.

It wasn't even Thanksgiving.

Kate went home, nonetheless.

Her parents lived in a small town in the center of Virginia, just far enough from Richmond and D.C. not to be considered a distant bedroom community of either city. When her parents retired, they both wanted to escape the rat race known as commuting from outside the Beltway into D.C. No wonder that they chose a sleepy little town with enough amenities to support their hobbies but not enough traffic to fry their brains.

Due to the driving distance, Kate didn't arrive until late afternoon. At her parents' insistence, she crashed in the spare bedroom right after she said hello to them. She'd had no sleep in the last forty-eight hours.

When she woke up, Kate was momentarily disoriented. Then she finally recognized her surroundings—her parents' guest room. She felt a familiar warm pressure against her back.

"Move over, Buster."

Her dog, Buster—half beagle, half poodle—cracked open one eye, yawned, stretched, and fell back asleep with a grumpy but satisfied sigh. Her parents had been babysitting Buster for the past two weeks leading up to the election since her job as campaign manager meant packing thirty hours of work in twenty-four-hour days. Working harder than a dog herself meant she had little time to devote to him. A little vacation in the country seemed the ideal way to make sure he wasn't neglected while she toiled.

Kate told herself that Buster was the reason she came back, but she knew it was far more complicated than that.

She needed a sympathetic ear, a sounding board. There were no better listeners in the world than her parents. They might have escaped the political rat race by moving to the middle of nowhere, but that didn't mean they didn't still understand the rats.

Glancing at the bedside clock, she realized that, to no surprise, her afternoon nap had turned into a very long night's sleep. Nothing had interrupted her. No anxious phone calls. No text messages. No demands on her time.

Glorious.

She rolled tentatively from the bed, stretched, and followed the aroma of hot coffee to the kitchen. Her father, long since retired, still woke up early on the weekends to prepare a full breakfast. Although her homecoming was in the middle of the week, he had taken the lead in the kitchen in honor of her return.

She walked into the kitchen and saw all the ingredients for a big breakfast pulled out on the counter.

"Oh, good." Her father turned and beamed at her. "You're up. I figured once you hit the sack yesterday, you might not get back up until this afternoon. No wonder, considering how hard you've been working lately." He used the spatula in his hand to gesture to the carton of eggs sitting beside the refrigerator. "Do you want your eggs fried or scrambled?"

"Scrambled, please."

"You got it." He turned back to the stove, calling over his shoulder, "For the record, Buster likes his scrambled." The dog had wandered into the kitchen behind Kate and took up his station on the floor next to her father's feet.

"I bet you've been spoiling him. Rotten."

"Yep." Her father expertly flipped a bit of cooked egg from the pan and Buster caught it without effort before it hit the floor. "Either my aim or his catching skills are getting better." Her father nodded toward the counter, where the coffeemaker had just completed its last *glug*. "Coffee's ready. Fix me a cup, please?"

Kate padded over, chose two mugs from the dozen hanging on the wall, and poured coffee for herself and her father. They both liked it the same way—two sugars, one cream. But in this health-conscious household, that translated to two packets of sugar substitute and a splash of 2 percent milk. Her mother managed the three Cs with an iron glove—calories, cholesterol, and caffeine.

He accepted the mug and took a tentative sip. "Your mom's sleeping in."

"Hard night last night?"

He nodded. "I keep telling her that retirement is supposed to mean she should work less. But she's so wrapped up with things at the center that she's putting in twice as many hours as she did when she taught school."

"What kept her up last night? Worrying about something?"

"One of the girls from the center called her last night, crying, and your mom stayed up talking on the phone to her for at least two hours. You know how keyed up she gets after one of those calls."

Her mother volunteered at a local shelter that took in abused women, mostly from D.C. Since her mom possessed a good heart, a level head, and a loving soul, she spoke with a quiet maternal authority that offered strength to the weak and faith to the lost. The shelter was thrilled with her work.

Not to mention her mom could charm donations from the stingiest CEOs around.

Kate's father handed her a plate of bacon, which she dutifully placed on the table. "You don't need to cook for me, Dad."

"I'm not," he said, turning back to the stove. "I'm cooking for me. If I happen to cook enough for . . . oh . . . let's say three people—" he catapulted another morsel of egg that Buster intercepted in midair—"and one dog? Then so be it."

Kate reached over and kissed him on the cheek. "So be it." She busied herself, ferrying plates, napkins, utensils, and condiments to the table. She hid her smile as she contemplated the jelly jar, knowing her mother had soaked off the label so that her father wouldn't know it was sugar-free.

Of course he knew. It was for that same reason he always found an excuse to use her mother's car to run a weekend errand and return it freshly washed and with a full tank of gas.

They delighted in taking care of each other.

At the not-so-tender age of forty-four, Kate knew her odds of finding someone like that to share her life were diminishing, minute by minute. There had been what her grandmother had always described as "a few near misses, but no misters." But Kate didn't regret one moment of energy or time she'd put into her life. What she *did* regret was that she might have to alter her goals in midstream and walk away from the political structure she'd worked so hard to build with Emily at the top and with Kate in an advisory rung just below. If she left that life, had she wasted her youth on a mistaken cause?

Kate resisted the urge to sigh. Instead, she waited for

her father to finish cooking so she could carry the eggs and grits to the table. As a pièce de résistance, he pulled a pan of homemade biscuits from the oven and plopped two each on their plates.

"Let's eat."

Once seated, they bowed their heads as he recited the prayer that had accompanied every meal she'd ever eaten with her parents.

"Lord, thank you for these and all our many blessings. In Jesus Christ's name, amen."

Simple and heartfelt. She couldn't help but smile. That described her father as well—an uncomplicated man who understood the value of hard work and, as he always put it, "the love of a good woman." Kate's mother usually gave him a good-natured swat whenever he said it.

Although Kate wasn't terribly hungry, she helped herself to a little of everything, if for no other reason than to pacify her father, who would give her a heartier helping if she didn't plan and institute an effective countermeasure. After a few bites, she stopped, the food turning to lead shot rolling around in her stomach.

Her father eyed her plate. "I'm no gourmet chef, but I know breakfast isn't that bad."

She tried to muster a look of enthusiasm but failed miserably. "It's great, Dad. Really. It's just that I'm not all that hungry."

"So I noticed." He continued to eat. "Otherwise you'd be in D.C. celebrating Emily's election instead of coming here to hang out with the old folks. You know you didn't need to drive all the way down here. We'd have been glad to bring Buster back to you." He split a biscuit, the steam rising into the air. "I figure when you're ready to talk, you'll talk."

It was a tactic he'd employed ever since she could remember—a sense of calm patience. He knew that by simply stating he was willing to wait until she thought it was time to talk, she'd soon break open like a bad piñata and spill out what was bothering her.

But Kate did take several moments to ponder her next words. Her mother and father had always treated Emily like a daughter from the day they met her, perhaps sensing that she needed love like theirs. More importantly, Emily returned their affection, perhaps with more sincerity than to her own family.

Kate swallowed hard. Confiding her concerns about Emily to her father felt like ratting out her sister.

After several false starts and abrupt stops, she finally boiled everything down to the mildest of explanations. "There were a couple of situations that happened toward the end of the campaign that really bothered me."

"Situations?" He paused, his coffee cup halfway to his mouth. "You mean like . . . campaign irregularities?"

She nodded. "And because of them, I need to reevaluate my—" she struggled for the word—"c-commitment to Emily's administration."

He whistled, then scratched his chin, leveling her with a steely gaze. "But you'd rather not tell me all the gory details, right?"

Up to that moment, Kate had expected to tell him everything. She wanted her father to tell her she was the good daughter who'd made the right decision keeping the information away from Emily. And that Emily had been the bad daughter who succumbed to the temptation of using the ill-gained knowledge.

But he was right. He didn't need to know all the gory details. He only needed to know the generalities. Good fathers of adult children let them make their own decisions, and he was one of the best, managing to probe beneath the surface of a problem without getting under her skin or making her feel as if she were in the crosshairs.

"Don't worry, sweetie." He slathered his biscuit with something that at least looked like margarine but probably had no fat, no calories, and quite possibly, no taste. "Your mother and I have always been aware of the possibilities that M's basic nature might win out occasionally. She's used to getting her way. We just hoped that your influence would help keep her on track."

Kate gaped at her father. Her parents' insight never failed to amaze her, but seldom did it take her by surprise quite like this.

"Don't look so shocked. Neither your mother nor I have ever doubted your dedication and involvement. This need to serve God by helping others—it's been a part of you all your life." He released the familiar sigh of unfailing paternal insight. "But Emily? She's another matter entirely. She's . . . wired differently. She's had different influences in her life, especially from her family. Then again, she's been your friend for over twenty years. Some of *you* has rubbed off on *her*. Your values. Your morality. And we consider that to be a very good thing. For Emily. And for the state and now the country."

Kate stared out the window at a thicket of trees, the branches stripped bare by winter. "You've never been afraid of the reverse? that I would pick up some of her . . . bad habits?"

She pivoted in time to see him lift one shoulder in a shrug. "Not really." He turned back to his food, stirring his eggs and grits together. "Don't get me wrong," he said, gesturing with his fork. "She's got good habits too. Emily Benton's been good *to* you, good *for* you, in many ways, and she's always treated your mother and me with a great deal of respect and—dare I say it—love. But the bottom line is that she does it because she needs you."

"Needs me . . . ," Kate repeated flatly.

"Sure. Emily grew up in the lap of luxury, her every whim catered to, her every wish fulfilled. I'm still amazed that she's not some spoiled little heiress princess afraid to chip a nail. Instead, she's a very astute political schemer who's not afraid to roll up her sleeves and dig right in if it means she can figure out how to successfully use people to advance her own position."

She gaped at her father.

"Think about it," he continued. "Could she have become president without your help?" He didn't wait for an answer. "Of course not. It took your vision, your talents, your advice, your self-control, your hard work to keep her out of trouble, on the right path, and always bathed in a flattering light in public. How many times did you stop her from shooting herself in the foot or shooting off her mouth? How many times did you have to remind her of the underlying issues, not just the ones that put her in the limelight? I could give you chapter and verse, but I don't have to." He pushed back in his chair, away from his plate, but kept his coffee close at hand. "You were there. You know exactly what incidents I'm talking about. And I bet there are dozens more that nobody knows about beyond you two."

Kate swallowed hard. How could her father have seen this so clearly when she hadn't?

He looked up over the rim of his coffee mug. "Hitting too close to home for you?"

She nodded.

"Your mother and I have talked about it a lot. Worrying that Emily was dominating too much of your life and that you were concentrating too much on the big goal, working only to see the bigger picture."

"But you didn't say anything."

"Of course not. You're an adult. The last thing you need is for your parents to rag on you about your choice of friends. And it's not as if we don't honestly like Emily."

"So you think I should stick with her."

He stalled by taking a long, contemplative swig of his coffee. "I didn't say that. I can't and won't tell you whether you should stay or go. I can see good reasons to support either outcome. But only you can make that decision. What I will say is that with your help, I think she could be a very effective president."

"But without my help?"

He shrugged. "I'm not so sure. That could go either way. She's got undeniable talent for the job. I'm concerned about who might influence her if you're not there. Emily will change this country—for better or for worse." He put down his cup, laced his fingers, and leaned forward. "But you're my daughter. That means my interests are a lot more narrow than most people's would be. I want you to be happy. The bottom line? We don't want you to forget who you are and what you believe in simply because you've gotten used to standing in her shadow."

Kate couldn't help but bristle a bit. "She's offered me the White House chief of staff position. That's not exactly a place in the shadows."

"You're right. It isn't." He sighed. "Honey, I have no doubt that you'll do great things in that office. But what you have to ask yourself is, will you be doing great things with Emily's help or in spite of her?"

Kate put her head in her hands. Her dad had, as usual, put his finger on the heart of her problem. And her answer?

That's the problem. I don't know. . . .

IN THE BACK OF KATE'S MIND, she wondered what would happen if she didn't go back to work. She had her laptop in the backseat, her overnight bag in the trunk, and Buster the Wonder Dog asleep on the heated passenger's seat of her Volvo. The weather was cold but sunny and she had a full tank of gas. What if she simply e-mailed in her resignation and took off for parts unknown?

Even though her thoughts were full of wanderlust and escape, she automatically headed north when she reached the interstate. But just north of Richmond, she made a last-minute decision to take the long way home. In fact, it wasn't even the long way home, but the wrong way home.

But I'm not running away, she told herself.

She couldn't even call it the scenic route, but there was something along this particular detour she needed to see. Hopefully it would help her make up her mind.

During her term as governor, Emily had spearheaded a

highway program that resulted in the much-lauded I-995 Tollway, bypassing the always-clogged I-95 corridor through Washington, D.C. Using the toll road, Eastern seaboard traffic could avoid the worst of the Beltway traffic and connect back to I-95 closer to Baltimore.

When a barge broke loose a couple of months ago and clipped one of the bridge supports, federal inspectors realized that substandard materials had been used in the building of the bridge. Charles Talbot, Emily's opponent in the presidential race, had probed deeper into the problem and uncovered the fact that most of the companies who had won the various highway construction bids had been owned by one or more holding companies controlled by members of the Benton family. The disclosure had shocked Kate, who had known nothing about the Benton involvement in any construction contracts.

This was the ammunition Talbot had planned to use to destroy Emily's campaign, until Kate explained to him how the American public might be much more appalled if they knew the extent of the cover-up he himself had created.

When it came to comparing a few contract irregularities to a cold-blooded murder, it was like comparing apples to bowling balls.

And now Kate was driving her car on the very evidence of Emily Benton's guilt.

When she reached the first tollbooth, Buster didn't wake up until the woman at the window commented on what a good-looking dog he was and returned a Milk-Bone with Kate's change. That got his attention. At the second tollbooth, Buster sat up in great hopes of a treat and was rewarded with yet another biscuit. By the time they reached the tollbooth for the bridge, Buster strained against his doggy seat belt in hopes of pushing past Kate to reach the expected treat.

Any other day, she might be annoyed by his antics, but today, the normality of his reactions helped to alleviate some of her tension. He was a wonderful constant in her life, demanding affection, returning it with equal vigor, and only requiring a few snacks along the way to keep him happy.

When they reached the bridge stretching across the Potomac, she pulled off the road and parked at a scenic overlook. She'd been there many times before, soothed by the lapping waters of the river, the underfoot crunch of mussel shells lining the shore, and the deep throaty whistles of the passing barges. Until she'd been slapped in the face with Emily's nepotistic connection to its construction, the toll road and bridge had represented the height of Emily's success. It was a project conceived, coordinated, and completed in a very short span of time, its success flying in the face of those who said it could never be done. Not only had the project been executed in an incredibly short length of time, but it had come in early and under budget.

Now, though, Kate looked at the bridge with a much more jaundiced eye. Exactly what other under-the-table deals had Emily participated in to make this bridge happen? Had she applied undue pressure on the Maryland officials to secure their cooperation? maybe a little blackmail or a few greased palms in the right places? What else had Emily managed to do without Kate even knowing?

Everything else or nothing more?

She and Buster followed the beaten path from the parking lot to the river's edge. A cold wind pushed against her as if trying to propel her back up the slope and away from the cold water.

Glancing down the picket fence of bridge supports, Kate easily spotted the newly repaired pillar, its surface whiter than the others. She couldn't help but remember Emily's breezy explanation of why she'd secretly sidestepped rules against nepotism and allowed her family to bid and win many if not most of the highway construction contracts.

"See what happens when you hire a subcontractor outside of the family? We subbed out to a smaller firm and they're the ones who substituted cheaper materials and pocketed the difference."

But it was Emily's second statement that revealed the heart of her family's agenda and gave hope to Kate: *"Had we known, we would have taken it over ourselves. We would have gladly lost money rather than build an unsafe bridge, especially on Virginia soil."*

The evidence, as Kate understood it, seemed to bear out Emily's statement.

Buster struggled against the leash, trying to tug Kate toward the water.

"Forget it, Buster. It's freezing cold." She shivered, her thin jacket providing little protection against the wind whipping off the Potomac. A barge whistle sounded, causing Buster to gleefully howl as if returning a call of friendship.

Kate scooped up the dog, brushed the damp soil from his feet, and trudged back up the slope toward her car. It had been a mistake to come here, she decided. She already knew that Emily had no problem with doing the wrong thing for the right reasons . . . for what *she considered* the right reasons.

Kate worked slowly up the slope, battling a sudden gust of wind, slippery footing, and a struggling dog who wanted down—*now*. On top of everything, she felt the cell phone in her pocket vibrate.

As she juggled Buster, the lock remote, and the car door, she decided to let the phone go to voice mail. By the time she finally got both Buster and herself into the car and out of the elements, the phone had stopped vibrating.

A moment later, it chimed, indicating she had a voice mail. She punched in the code and put it on speakerphone.

Nick Beaudry's accent was a bit deeper than usual, probably because he'd been back home in Louisiana for several weeks.

"Um . . . hey, Kate, this is Nick."

A shiver coursed through her and she had no idea whether it was pleasure or apprehension.

"I was just calling to congratulate you and M. I know how much stress y'all been under the last few days or so." He paused to laugh. "Stress. That's a pretty mild description of what's been goin' on, isn't it? Well, anyway, I wanted to talk to you because I've received a job offer and . . ." He hesitated and his accent waned a bit as if he made a conscious effort to slip back into a Washington mind-set and tongue. "Well . . . I'd like to talk it over with you, get your take on it, if possible. If—if you don't want to call me back, that's okay. I know you're going to be really busy these next four years and . . ." There was an audible sigh. "Call me back if you have time, and if you don't, I'll understand completely. Completely," he repeated with emphasis.

Kate stared at the phone. Should she call him back or forget she ever got his message? Part of her whispered that he was trouble.

No, not trouble. Untouchable.

First off, he was Emily's ex-husband, and to say the Beaudry-Benton union had been acrimoniously ripped apart was putting a positive spin on their breakup. Kate had never seen a more vitriolic dissolution of a marriage. Nick had made a drunken spectacle of himself in the governor's mansion at a big event; Emily called his bluff despite the very public setting; and then he'd celebrated the news by participating in a debacle that ended in his arrest for DUI, assaulting a law enforcement officer, two counts of lewd conduct, and two charges of solicitation of prostitution.

Second, he'd been Charles Talbot's deputy campaign manager, pulled into the oppositional camp solely because Nick knew all about the various Benton secrets and hot buttons.

But despite all that, the newly sober and reborn Nick had played fair. Having rediscovered his faith and renewed his sense of honor, he never dipped into his past with Emily to pull out any dirty laundry or cheap tricks. Even when Charles Talbot secretly planned to release damning evidence about the Benton family involvement in the highway construction bids, Nick alerted Kate so, at the minimum, the Benton camp wouldn't be caught unaware.

But as if the indignity of being fired wasn't enough, he received a beating at the hands of unidentified attackers sent by Talbot as a warning to others who might "betray" the campaign.

However, after what he'd done to play fair and even help Emily, he deserved Kate's thanks if not her friendship. What had helped to cement her acceptance of his change of heart and soul had been the wide inconsistencies her investigators turned up in the reports of his drunken escapades. The facts strongly suggested that the charges had been manufactured by one or two overly enthusiastic officers, eager to please close friends of a very angry governor of Virginia.

A woman scorned . . .

Kate hit the redial option.

Nick answered promptly. "Hello?"

"Hey. It's Kate. Sorry, my dog, Buster, wouldn't let me get to the cell phone in time to answer it."

"Thanks for calling back. Is this a good time? I mean if you're busy, or—" he softened his voice as if not wanting to be overheard on either end—"if *she's* around . . ."

"No, it's okay. I'm not in D.C. I'm on the road back from seeing my parents, but I'd stopped so that Buster could go kick a tree." She glanced at her dog, knowing he wouldn't mind her slight embellishment of the truth. He was busy, checking the seat for Milk-Bone crumbs. She didn't want to tell Nick exactly where she was or admit to the muddled state of her conscience.

She conjured up a false sense of cheer. "So what's going on?"

"Like I said, I just wanted to congratulate you . . . and Emily. After witnessing how low Talbot was willing to go, I really do believe the better candidate won."

She couldn't help herself from automatically rising to the bait. "Better candidate, but not right candidate?"

"Time will tell. But from what I hear, the one thing that everyone agrees on is that she's chosen the right chief of staff. Congratulations for that. You'll be great."

"Thanks." Rather than let him dwell on a tender topic, she deftly changed the subject. "You said something about a new job. Are you going back into state politics?"

"Not quite."

"Going back to practice law, then?" She suddenly had visions of Nicholas Beaudry, gentleman attorney, standing in some steamy Louisiana parish courthouse and imparting legal wisdom in a big, booming voice.

His deep South upbringing slipped into his words. "That neither. I was hoping maybe we could talk about things. I need some advice. I don't want to get caught up again where someone thinks they can use me to upset or shake up or otherwise distract M."

"You have a job offer?"

"Yeah, and a pretty good one, I think. What's the chances of us getting together and talking?"

"When?"

"What are you doing tonight?"

"You're back? In D.C.?"

He released a sigh. "Yeah. I decided I wouldn't let Talbot run me out."

She thought about the time she'd spoken to him right after he'd been attacked by someone from the Talbot camp. Nick had tried to gloss over it, but she later learned the beating had been more severe than he'd let on, requiring overnight hospitalization.

"Is that wise, Nick?"

"Probably not. But now I have friends in high places."

Since he couldn't possibly mean Emily, Kate realized he meant her. That is, if she accepted the position. . . .

After a minute of discussion, they decided that a private meeting would be better. There was no use in deliberately feeding the Washington rumor mill. Kate squeezed her eyes shut when she made what she considered either a very brave or a very foolish offer.

"Why don't you just come to my house? That is, if you don't mind Buster hanging around us. We'd have more privacy there than if we met someplace in town."

"True. Sounds like a plan to me. Tell you what—I'll bring dinner. You like Chinese food? Better yet, does Buster?"

Sudden apprehension filled her. How had their simple powwow transformed into a dinner date? This was *so* not a good idea. But she was unsure how to back out of it. Left with no other choice, she assured Nick that she loved Chinese food and gave him directions to her place. Hopefully she had enough time to get home and clean up before he arrived.

Once she disconnected the call, she tossed the cell phone on the seat next to Buster.

"Next time, you answer it, okay?" Then she leaned her head against the steering wheel and sent up a brief but heartfelt prayer.

"Lord? Please don't let me make a big mistake."

KATE COULD HEAR the phone in the kitchen ringing as soon as she hit the bottom of the staircase leading from her garage to the main floor of her house. She'd purchased the tiny bungalow in Annandale years ago with the idea of fixing it up for resale, but she'd never had the time or energy to devote to the project. Her fixer-upper still needed a lot of fixing-upping.

Buster raced ahead up the stairs as if saying, "I'll get it!" But all he succeeded in doing was to tangle his leash around Kate's feet, preventing her from reaching the phone before the answering machine kicked in.

She heard a beep; then the only sound after that was the momentary buzz of a dial tone, which quickly cut off. Whoever had called, they hadn't left a message. Glancing at the answering machine, she realized she had eighteen messages.

All from Emily, I bet.

Kate's sense of duty warred with her sense of fatigue. If

Emily—or anyone else for that matter—had a critical concern or timely message, they would have called Kate's cell. So any messages left on the answering machine were more likely "Just checking to see if you're home. Call me back when you get this" or "It's time to see your dentist for your annual exam."

Kate glared once more at the machine and then turned her back on it. She still had a decision to work through, and until she made up her mind, she didn't want to talk to Emily.

Or her dentist, either.

Kate's gaze shifted across the counter toward the digital clock in the stove. Two hours left before Nick arrived. She needed that time to spruce up the place. Vacuum, dust, hide the mountain of junk mail she hadn't gone through in the past month. Do some of the things she'd let slide while running a presidential campaign.

"We should have gotten weekly maid service," she said to Buster, who was lapping his bowl as if he hadn't seen water in hours. He ignored her proclamation and zipped out the doggy door to her postage stamp–size backyard.

Two hours later, she'd still managed to ignore the awaiting phone messages and, instead, had spent her attention and time taming the piles of controlled mess in the public areas of her house, removing the remains of chaos from her living room and kitchen.

At seven sharp, her doorbell rang.

When she looked out the peephole, she was suddenly transported back to a time long ago when Nick would show up on their stoop in Georgetown to court Emily, a bottle of expensive wine in one hand and flowers in the other. After the perfunctory greetings, Kate, the proverbial third wheel, would manufacture an excuse to leave the two of them alone.

The courtship eventually turned into an engagement, which became a big society marriage, which dissolved into a hostile divorce. The flowers might have wilted, but the bottle of wine never left his hand for long during any phase of their relationship.

But now, he carried no bottle. He still juggled the requisite bouquet of flowers—albeit tastefully small—and two brown paper sacks.

Their greeting was awkward, but no less than the last time they had seen each other, a clandestine meeting at Dulles airport, where political revelations had exposed heretofore secret flaws and weaknesses of both presidential candidates.

"I couldn't remember if you liked spicy food or not." Nick hoisted one of the sacks filled to the brim with small, white take-out cartons. "So I got a little of everything: sweet and sour, Szechuan, Hunan . . ."

Kate led the way to the kitchen, where she put the flowers in a small vase. He had indeed brought enough food to feed a platoon and even remembered to get some chopsticks, so all she had to do was provide plates and napkins. Buster danced in anticipation of a handout, so Kate temporarily pacified him with a rawhide bone. He snatched it from her hand and then ran with his plunder to his bed in the den.

Once their pot of hot tea was ready, she and Nick settled at the kitchen table. After closing her eyes and saying a silent grace, she looked up, surprised to see Nick doing the same thing. It was reassuring to know they had more than just Emily in common. The politicos in Washington were usually more at ease with religion as a broad concept rather than as a personal display of faith.

Once they started eating, their conversation hopscotched from general niceties—weather, old acquaintances, and such—to finally landing on the real topic of concern.

Kate dug into the fried rice. "So tell me about this new job offer."

"It's as a lobbyist for the Better Energy Alliance. You heard of them?"

She shook her head. "No, but there are like thirty thousand lobbyists in the District."

"If not more. Anyway, they're a new firm being formed to work with Emily's energy-exploration campaign platform."

"They're not wasting any time."

"Nope. They want to be up and running by the time she gets into office. You know as well as I do that she's going to push that program into place first."

"True." Kate thought about her next statement, debating on how to make it not sound like an accusation. "So they believe you'll be an asset when it comes to dealing with her administration?"

He shrugged. "I know. Sounds like a long shot to me too. But here's the funny thing." He leaned forward and his voice lowered as if they could be overheard. "The person who asked for the interview said they got word 'under the table' that someone reportedly high up in the Benton camp had recommended me for the position."

He took a moment to search her features, making her wonder if she was blushing and didn't know it. Then he sat back in his chair, looking somewhat crestfallen. "And judging from the look of surprise on your face, it wasn't you who recommended me."

"No. I didn't know anything about it."

He shrugged and turned his attention to the next carton of food, opening it and using the chopsticks to guide a generous amount onto his plate. "Well, it sure couldn't have been Emily. The only job she'd suggest me for would be as a tester for an electric chair."

They ate in silence for another minute, but Kate could see that he was still mulling over the identity of whoever recommended him.

He pretended to be absorbed by the act of eating, but finally he dropped his chopsticks to his plate, unable to keep up the ruse. "So . . . you think maybe Dozier had a change of heart? He and I always got along fairly well. And he knows my background was in geology and petroleum law. We talked about it, more than once."

"Possibly. But for Dozier to have a change of heart, he'd have to demonstrate he had a heart in the first place."

Nick snorted.

At first glance, Dozier Marsh looked like an old man who believed in old-school politics. It hadn't taken Kate long to see the truth once he became her campaign colleague. Over the years, he'd carefully cultivated a jovial, sometimes even harmless-looking, facade as a ploy to cover up his sharp political mind and his sharper tendency to go for the jugular vein of anyone who got in his way. And yet Kate realized his unwavering support for Emily wasn't simply because she was her father's daughter—even if Dozier had admired her father way back when and become one of the man's close political cronies. Dozier's type of old-school opinions usually went hand in hand with classic misogyny. But for all his politically incorrect behavior, Dozier backed Emily totally. Her gender didn't complicate or weaken the strength of his convictions and willingness to be a senior member of her campaign staff and eventually a senior presidential adviser.

"Nah . . ." Nick cocked his head and corrected himself. "Probably not him. After the divorce, he wouldn't give me the time of day. Not that I really blame him." Nick wielded the chopsticks like a pro as he returned his attention to his meal, attacking the piles of chicken and vegetables on his plate. "Good ol' Doze. The Speaker of the House you'd most enjoy sitting down with to share a pint. And then if he had to slit your throat immediately thereafter, he'd do it without hesitation."

"That's our Dozier. I get along well with him too. Maybe because he thinks I'm good for Emily. Maybe it's his formal manners or maybe the fact that he just can't quite figure out what my agenda is."

Nick paused dramatically, the food suspended halfway from his plate to his mouth. "*You* have an agenda?" he asked with mock horror.

She smiled and took a sip of her tea.

He laughed. "Forget I asked that. So someone on your side of the coin thinks I could be an effective lobbyist."

"They're right."

He looked up, surprise lightening his features. "Thanks. Good to hear."

"Well, it's true. There's nothing wrong with using your knowledge of what makes Emily tick to help a good cause."

"As opposed to a bad cause, like Talbot," he added darkly.

She ignored his comment. "Besides your legal background, you come from oil people, don't you?"

"Not really." Nick shook his head. "Oil people are the ones who own the oil rights. My family just worked in the industry—in the oil fields and refineries. I have first, second, even third cousins who are toolpushers, motormen, floorhands. . . ."

At her confused look, he grinned. "Working stiffs. They all think I'm a lazy good-for-nuthin' because I'm the first one in the family who doesn't work with his hands." His voice softened perceptibly. "And as my father used to say, I don't work much with my head, either."

Kate remembered meeting Mr. Beaudry, a salt-of-the-earth type with the same cocky grin as his son. She knew the man had passed away since the divorce. "You miss him? your dad?"

His grin faded slightly to something more sentimental. "Yeah, I do miss him. Every day. Mom too." He busied himself with his meal, not making eye contact with Kate as he spoke, obviously from the heart. "I only hope they can see how I turned things around for myself. After Mom died of cancer, he wasn't the same man. It was like someone had drilled a hole in him and his life was slowly leaking out. He was pretty much gone after the first stroke, but his body held out for longer than any of us boys thought possible. Most of the changes in me occurred *because* of what happened to him. So I feel a bit guilty that I didn't have a chance to show him I straightened out and up."

Kate reached over and patted his arm. "I'm sure he knows."

It was a simple gesture, born out of what she could only classify as sympathy in light of their growing friendship—a kindness she would show to anyone else expressing such a sentiment. But why did it feel like something else? Why, when he looked up and her gaze met his, did he hold her attention a moment too long?

Why did she feel a connection with this man?

She withdrew her hand slowly, knowing that a quick movement might betray the confusion she was feeling. Maybe they could both just forget anything had happened.

Maybe . . .

She turned her attention to the containers of food that decorated the table. "You didn't have to buy every single item on the menu."

He seemed grateful for the distraction. "You know how it is when you stand at the counter, staring at that big menu on the wall and then look into the take-out kitchen, where the guys are tossing everything into big woks. Everything smells so good. You think—'One chicken, one beef, one pork, one veggie, maybe something hot . . . oh and soup, too, and maybe some shrimp puffs and crab rangoons.' It's hard to stop."

She grimaced. "Back to the topic. The job offer. So what's the problem? If it's a good offer in a field you know well and presumably like, then why not jump at the chance?"

He contemplated the remains of his meal. "I'm not sure. Something's just not quite right about it. I was hoping to find out that you made the recommendation because then I'd know it came without any strings attached."

"You're expecting strings?"

He pushed his plate away. "This is Washington politics. I'm expecting ropes. Chains, even. After what I've been through, getting tied up with Talbot, I need to be more careful so I don't make that kind of mistake again."

Kate glanced at the small scar near his hairline. She gestured to his head. "Is that from . . . ?" She couldn't find the right words.

He reached up and probed the spot gingerly. "A souvenir from the beating I got? Sure is. I'd still like to get my hands on the slimy ba—" His face flushed and he stopped midword. "I'm sorry, Kate. As you can tell, it's still a sore point with me. And the funny thing is, I don't think Charles Talbot ordered—for the lack of a better word—the hit. It's not his way."

"Then who do you think did?" She went through a mental lineup of Talbot's senior campaign staff. "Ron Wooster?" Kate might not particularly like Talbot's campaign manager, but she didn't think he'd resort to such violence.

"Rooster? No." Nick's tight grin lacked any humor. "It's not necessarily the people above you that you have to watch out for. It's the ones who want to move up into your spot who can be the most dangerous. You know . . . ascension via assassination, character or otherwise. Sometimes they're willing to get their hands dirty—or in this case, bloody—if it means a chance to curry the favor of a higher-up."

"I know exactly what you mean." Kate couldn't help but be reminded of Maia Bari. The young woman had hoped to create a more permanent position for herself in the Benton administration by doing Emily's dirty work. Even worse, Maia had mistakenly thought an admission of her guilt to Kate would end with a reward for such honesty. "I've run into a few . . . people like that, too." She tried to ignore the little voice in the back of her head that said, *You might be working with and for people like that.*

Kate didn't realize she'd stopped talking until she heard Buster bark outside in the yard, breaking a heavy silence.

"You look like something's bothering you," Nick said in a quiet voice. "Can I help?"

Could he?

Kate didn't doubt his sincerity. When he broke allegiance to Talbot because of the candidate's dirty politics, Nick took a big step toward proving he'd risen above any resentments and lingering animosities he had as Emily's ex-husband. It was obvious his newfound faith had helped him make some very good choices.

If anyone could understand the difficulty she was having in picking a path that allowed her to walk in God's will and be Emily's friend and adviser at the same time, it might be Nick Beaudry.

It was worth a shot.

"Actually I *would* like to talk. It's about Emily." She glanced down at the remains of their meal, suddenly aghast at how much food she'd eaten. As delicious as it had been, it now sat in her stomach like a rock. "Would you like to sit in the living room?"

"Sure." He stood, and before she could shift, he'd moved to her chair to hold it for her as she rose. Ever the Southern gentleman . . .

He followed her to the living room, where they sat in the wingback chairs that flanked the fireplace. He waited until she got settled before drawing a deep breath.

"Okay. What has she done *now*?"

WES KINGSBURY HAD SAID the same exact words to Kate, only Wes's voice reflected both amusement and exasperation. In Nick's case, the words held more wariness than anything else.

Kate dove headfirst into her tale, telling him every gory moment.

"To cap it off, Emily managed to make a copy of my file without my knowledge. It detailed all the proof I had—which was damning—and she used that information to send him a threat of her own."

Nick's whistle was one of universal sympathy. "Man, oh man. . . . How did she get the file to make a copy? Bribe your investigators?"

"No." She drew a deep breath. "This is the point where I have to choose which person to believe. I'd refused to tell Emily any particulars concerning Talbot's problem because I knew she'd be tempted to go after him with both barrels blazing. But we both know how mudslinging can backfire on you. So she promised to respect my decision to keep the evidence secret and agreed to not pry into the details, as long as I took care of the problem."

Nick crossed his arms. "At least she *said* she wouldn't pry."

"Yeah. That's the problem." Kate nodded. "That night, only a few hours later, someone sneaked into my hotel room, stole and copied the evidence, and returned the originals without me realizing it. I only learned about it weeks after the fact."

"Your very own Bentongate." He made a face. "I know that had to hurt. So who broke in? More importantly, did Emily send him?"

Kate almost corrected him by saying, "Her, not him" but decided that exposing Maia Bari's role wasn't necessary to tell the story and get the much-needed advice.

"That's one of the big questions. Emily says no, she sent nobody. The thief says yes, that it was a direct request from Emily."

"Hmm. How would the thief know the files existed in the first place or that you had them with you unless Emily told him?"

"She certainly could have overheard Emily and me talking about the situation. She's smart. And she was around at the critical times." Kate realized she'd slipped up and identified Maia's gender. Maybe Nick hadn't noticed. She continued. "The big problem is that when armed with the evidence—whether by design or by happenstance—Emily broke her word to me. She did exactly what I was afraid she'd do: she used that knowledge against Talbot. No finesse. No subtlety. She went straight for the kill—politically."

He remained quiet for a moment, contemplating Kate's

story. Finally he spoke. "Did you confront M? Did she admit to it?"

"Yes, I confronted her. And she admitted to having sent Talbot a threat. And then she . . ." Kate hesitated. Somehow, admitting to Emily's emotional breakdown seemed a betrayal of sorts.

Nick crossed his arms, obviously anticipating something bad. "What'd she do?" he prompted with a sigh of exasperation. "Said it was too late now? water under the bridge?"

Kate remembered the rare look of anguish on her friend's face. The tears. The voice that had cracked as Emily spoke. It had been honest emotion. It had to be. . . .

Kate had a hard time controlling her own emotion. "Emily broke down. She cried like her heart was breaking." Kate looked up to see his disbelief melt into astonishment. "She admitted that she'd succumbed to temptation and made the wrong decision. She . . . she asked for my forgiveness."

He stared at Kate, obviously stunned by the revelation. "Our Emily?" His face flushed. "I mean *your* Emily. She's not been mine for . . . years. She cried . . . real tears? not the usual Benton crocodile variety?"

"Yeah. Real tears." She didn't want to admit she'd never seen anything but the fake ones before from Emily and those had been rare at best. "It was real. I saw gut-wrenchingly honest emotion on her part."

He stretched forward to warm his hands in the heat from the fireplace. "I have to admit . . . I've never thought she was capable of something like that. She didn't cry when I asked her to marry me, she didn't cry during the wedding, and she sure as heck didn't cry when we got divorced. She stuck with getting even."

"I know." Kate had been present for all those times and more. There had been occasions when Emily conjured up convenient tears for her public persona, but Kate had never seen her cry behind private doors.

At least not since Emily's father died, taking an assassin's bullet meant for another president.

Not until now.

Doubt flickered in Nick's eyes. "And she asked for forgiveness? She used those exact words?"

Kate nodded. "I gave it to her. But I haven't agreed to take the chief of staff job yet. She's going crazy waiting for my answer."

They sat in silence, words failing them both. They listened instead to the soothing pop and crackle of the fireplace.

Finally Nick spoke quietly. "What are you going to do?"

Kate shrugged. "I don't know. I can understand why she was tempted to do what she did. But I don't know if I can work in her administration. I don't know if I can risk it happening again. I'll never be able to forget what happened. What if she's tempted again?"

"It's going to happen. Power's like that. The more you have, the more temptation is scattered along your path." He pushed his chair back, left the warm fireplace, and walked to the window overlooking the street. "Trust me, I know a lot about temptation. It was tempting for me to pick up a bottle of wine to go with dinner tonight. Harmless, right? And if I remembered you weren't much of a drinker, then that meant more for me. Temptation," he repeated, still staring out the window. "I struggle with it every day."

He braced one hand against the windowframe. "When I got into AA, one of the important steps I had to take was to take ownership of what I'd done—to admit that I'd hurt a lot of people, especially those I loved, and to make amends to them if possible. I tried to call Emily, but you know she wouldn't give me the time of day. Of course, I understood her reluctance." He corrected himself. "Her animosity." He turned back toward Kate but avoided eye contact by pretending to study something in the dancing flames. "So I wrote her a long letter, owned up to all my bad behavior, and sincerely apologized."

His voice went flat. "Her response was classic Benton. She sent me a bottle of bourbon and said if I ever got in her way again, caused her another minute of concern, she'd make sure this bottle was my last one." He managed a hollow laugh. "The woman always had a way of coming up with the perfect threat. The queen of double meanings, one masking the other."

"I'm sure she didn't mean—" Kate stopped. What was she sure of?

"We're talking about a Benton here. As long as you ride along with them, you're fine. The moment you get out of the car and stand in their way, you discover you weren't standing in front of a limousine but a steamroller. And you're no match for it."

He turned away from the fireplace, obviously trying to gloss over his brief emotional moment by hiding his face in the shadows. "So what did she do to Talbot? Threaten to splash his guilt in the headlines of every newspaper in the world with accompanying eight-by-ten glossies of the bloody evidence?"

"No." Kate had a hard time finding her voice. "No, she sent him a reminder—the date of his college alumni meeting. And a packet of copies of the evidence."

Although Nick stood with his back to the fireplace, he shivered. "Wow. That was more restrained than I would have expected. I thought she'd at least make it look like it came from the girl he murdered. Is there any way he can trace that back to her?" Before Kate could answer, he waved his hand in dismissal and flopped down into the other chair. "Of course not. Emily's callous, not careless."

His brow knit in concentration; then suddenly his eyes widened in revelation. "I doubt Talbot even knew it came from her. He probably figured it was a reminder from you."

The concept took Kate by surprise, making her breath catch in her throat. "You know, I hadn't thought of it like that," she admitted after swallowing hard. "I bet she did just that."

Silence filled the room as he seemed lost in conjecture and Kate's mind filled with the maelstrom of indecision and worry. If Talbot thought the threat came from her, would he try to retaliate? Surely not. But what if . . .

Finally Nick broke the silence.

"But she apologized to you," he added as if needing to be reassured once more. "A real, honest apology. Not her usual halfhearted, get-you-off-her-back excuse."

"Yeah." Kate nodded, relieved to turn her thoughts from Talbot back to Emily. "Absolutely authentic."

"Well . . . if it's any consolation, I don't think she's ever apologized to anyone. Ever. I think . . . I think maybe it's a good start."

"A start to what?"

"Maybe this is what we've both been looking for. For Emily to take that first voluntary step on the path to enlightenment. Maybe even a closer walk with God. That walk starts with humility—something Emily has never been good at. Maybe this will open her up to Christ's influence."

It was an optimism Kate wanted to share but couldn't quite fathom. "Asking forgiveness from me is nothing like asking forgiveness from God."

"Of course not, but it's an important first step. She has to learn to answer to someone besides herself. Maybe this will help her realize she has to place her faith in a higher authority. It's something I knew in my heart when I was growing up, lost once I got into politics, but then relearned when I joined AA." His smile was strained. "Too bad there's not a Politicians Anonymous."

"Then you think I ought to stay in her administration." It was more of a statement than a question.

"I didn't say that. You have to do what you think is right, go where God leads you, which may be someplace other than—"

The phone rang. Kate sighed and excused herself to the kitchen, where she read the caller ID—*No data*.

"Hello?"

"Finally. I wondered when you'd get home."

She didn't recognize the male voice. "Who is this?" she challenged.

"You don't know me. But I worked for Chuck Talbot."

She wondered if the better part of valor was simply hanging up. "Why are you calling me?"

"Because I wanted you to realize someone knows what you did. I know."

Valor was about to win. "I'm going to hang up now. Don't call me again."

"Wait, wait! I'm not trying to threaten you," he said quickly. "I'm trying to *thank* you."

Kate recognized the trick. If she accepted his "thanks," then she was confirming her actions and her role in playing the "who has the better blackmail" game.

"I have no idea what you're talking about."

"Yeah, yeah, I get it. Plausible deniability. In any case, you need to know that many of us agree that what Ms. Benton did with the bridge is nothing compared to Talbot's crimes."

Another trap. Or another blackmail attempt? In either case, her best response was to continue her denial.

"I still don't know what you're talking about, and quite frankly, I don't care. Don't call back."

"But—"

She disconnected the call.

"Telemarketer?"

"No." Kate looked down and saw that she was still clutching the phone in a near death grip. It took much of her self-control to replace it gently in the cradle rather than slam it.

"Kate?"

Vaguely she heard Nick's voice above the rushing of blood in her ears. But it wasn't until he touched her shoulder that she responded.

"That was someone from Chuck Talbot's campaign staff. At least, that's what he implied."

"Upchuck still trying to pull strings?"

"I don't know." She finally turned away from the phone and faced Nick, who stood next to her at the kitchen counter. "He called to thank me for stopping Chuck."

"That's . . . unlikely."

"Exactly. I think he was either fishing for more information or he already knows the details and this was a veiled threat. I really don't think it was the simple thanks it appeared to be."

Nick leaned against the counter, his arms crossed. "What would Talbot have to gain? The election is over, but he still has a career in politics. Word is he'll probably get reelected as the governor of Ohio."

"Maybe it's not Talbot but simply someone on his staff who wants to leverage what he knows."

Nick nodded. "That's a possibility. Unfortunately he's probably a month too late. You and I both know that as soon as Emily learned about the blackmail attempt, she covered her trail, had all the records expunged, removed every last shred of proof that connected any Benton to that highway project. I'm just surprised she went into the campaign without doing that first."

"True. So either this was a seriously stupid fishing expedition or . . ."

Nick finished her thought. "Or someone—besides me—in the Talbot camp had a conscience and is now dealing with his remorse."

"Maybe." She glanced at the kitchen table, covered in white take-out boxes, many still full. "Did you get any fortune cookies?"

"Of course." Nick's infectious laughter was another of his attractive qualities. "What's Chinese food without fortune cookies?" He rustled around in one of the bags and produced a double handful of cellophane-wrapped cookies. "They must have thought I was feeding an army. Take your pick."

As Kate reached to select one package, the phone rang again.

"I'm not answering it," she said quickly.

"Want me to?"

"No, I'll just let the machine pick it up. We'll hear the message and even record it."

"Maybe I can identify his voice."

They both stared expectantly at the machine, but Kate never expected to hear Emily's voice instead.

"It's me. Listen, I'm not trying to rush you, but—"

Kate had only two courses of action—answer the phone or find the control on the answering machine to lower the volume so neither she nor Nick could hear the rest of the call. She fumbled, trying to find the control.

Emily's voice continued to boom. "Something else came up the other day and I wanted to mention it now. Conrad Schertz called me yesterday—unofficially of course—wondering if I could recommend anybody with experience in petroleum law."

Kate glanced at Nick, who had dropped any pretense of not listening to his ex-wife's voice. "Conrad Schertz is the guy who offered me the position," he whispered to her, as if Emily might overhear.

Kate pulled her hand back, allowing them to continue to hear the message as it recorded.

"Con didn't say what firm he was hiring for, and I didn't ask. It's safer to not know these things. Anyway, I know it sounds weird, but I mentioned Nick."

He hung his head. "Here it comes. So long, job offer."

Kate reached again to cut off the speaker, but something told her to leave it on.

"Okay, okay, I know. Bad blood and all that, but you made me take a second look at him, especially in light of all this big stink with Talbot. Nick helped us, so it seems right that we do something to return the favor. He does seem to have straightened himself out, and even I have to admit he has the right background for the oil lobby—if indeed that's what Con's looking for. So maybe I need to get my head examined, but I recommended Nick for the position.

"But here's the thing." Emily lowered her voice. "I told Schertz that the recommendation couldn't come from me—it needed to come from you. There's no way that Nick would believe I'd do this for him. Not after our commitment to open and everlasting animosity. But I do believe in paying my debts, and I probably owe him big-time for alerting us to Talbot's plans. But if you ever tell him that, I'll deny it. I'll go back to loathing the very air he breathes. Give me a call when you get in. We need to talk." She hung up.

When Kate turned, Nick's mouth hung open in total shock. Finally he spoke. "I wouldn't have believed it if I hadn't heard it myself. She really is turning over a new leaf. I can't imagine what it took for Emily to do that."

"M-me either," Kate stammered.

"And here I thought I'd gotten the offer because of my credentials, my ability, and my shining personality."

"You did. Even Emily said so. She had to concede to your credentials and ability."

He dropped back into his chair, obviously deflated. "So, what do I do? Do I take the job? I thought I went into the job with Talbot with my eyes open, and look how bad that went."

"I don't think this is the same sort of situation."

He contemplated the fortune cookie he still had clutched in his palm. "Wouldn't it be nice if you could just crack open a cookie and get an answer?"

"Maybe this is your answer." Kate nodded toward the answering machine. "You have a lot more information now about the job than you did before."

"Yeah. And even if I'm not sure what to do, maybe this is the burning bush *you* need when it comes to working with Emily." His face lightened perceptibly. "Look what you've done. Not only did you prick her conscience and cause her to show real remorse for what she did to you, but it brought about this . . . this change in attitude toward me." He grinned and corrected himself. "Okay, this *momentary* change in attitude toward me. Can you imagine in your wildest dreams that she'd ever do something like that?"

"No."

"I'm not telling you what to do, but at least you need to put this one in the plus column. If you managed to pull off both of those things with your influence, imagine what you can do now that she's president. . . . You may be able to help her achieve great things."

Was this the sign she'd been waiting for? Kate closed her eyes, sending up a quick prayer for guidance. A sudden calmness settled over her, making her churning stomach settle and her racing heart slow down.

"I trust you and you trust me, right?"

He answered her without hesitation. "Yes."

"Then believe me when I say I think Emily was being honest about repaying you. I also believe she needs me as her chief of staff to guide her. Why don't we both take these job offers and find out what we can do to shape history, together? You watch my back. I'll watch yours. And I'll be in a position to make sure there are no strings to pull you when Emily needs something."

He took a deep breath. "You got a deal."

EVEN IF KATE HADN'T accepted the position of White House chief of staff, she would still have had duties to perform as Emily's campaign manager, even after the election. One of those tasks was to oversee the dismantling of the Benton campaign war machine.

Benton campaign headquarters across the nation were pulling their signs and shutting their doors. The national headquarters in Alexandria would be the last to close, becoming a transitional administrative office during the interim. But even with a continued mission of transitioning to the White House, Kate still needed to shrink the workforce.

Some personnel would make that highly sought-after transition from campaign worker to White House staff. It was no secret that many people had volunteered for the campaign in hopes that they might benefit from the trickle-up hiring.

During the campaign, both Emily and Kate had been careful to make only a few conditional promises to key longtime staffers who had already proven themselves as irreplaceable and indispensable. They'd identified those people early on and begun grooming them for bigger and better things along the campaign trail.

The first person Kate knew she needed to tap was Miriam Smart, Emily's master scheduler. Miriam not only had valuable campaign experience dealing with the minutiae of a candidate's scheduling requirements, but she had worked for Emily's uncle, President William Benton, as a young assistant in the scheduling department. The woman brought her familiarity with Emily's personal and professional preferences plus experience with the White House scheduling office to the table.

Although David Dickens, their deputy campaign manager, had all the chops necessary to be named the next White House press secretary, his ultimate goal of becoming a network news anchor had already come true, and he was about to join CBS on the track to the eventual position of nightly news anchor.

Instead, both Emily and Kate had their eyes on another senior staff member, Harold Morelli, who—prior to being the campaign's director of communications—had been a former head of CNN's West Coast operations as well as an East Coast journalist. With his dual qualifications of print and broadcasting and his familiarity with the Washington scene, he was the ideal candidate.

But for every Miriam and Harold, there were dozens of other staffers—both paid and volunteer—who were packing their things and bidding a fond farewell to the office and each other. Rather than let most of them slink away without fanfare, Kate had decided to throw a big going-away party.

She glanced across the bull pen at the festivities. They'd rented a large home in Alexandria to serve as the national headquarters, and the huge living room had been refitted with well over a dozen desks as their chief call center. But now the desks had been shoved together to form a giant buffet line, which Kate had filled with food catered by the collective staff's favorite restaurant, Poco Rio.

Kaleesa King, phone answerer and chief Buster-sitter, held up a glass that contained far more punch than it did rum. "You sure know how to throw a farewell party!" She giggled. "Do you know how glad I am to see decorations in colors other than red, white, and blue?"

Kate had pulled down the patriotic campaign colors and replaced them with fiesta colors of gold, orange, and purple streamers. After living and working in a world of red, white, and blue for so long, Kate had also longed for a different color scheme, even if only temporarily.

Mario Medina, their deputy communications officer, abandoned the buffet table long enough to lean over and give Kate a chaste kiss on the cheek. "The food is fabulous. Just like Momma used to make." Judging by his plate, he'd concentrated on the basics, mostly tortillas, beans, and homemade salsa. "Maybe even better. But don't tell her I said that."

Although this was a farewell party, the group's general spirits were high. The point of the campaign had been to put Emily Benton in office, and that triumphant goal had been realized. Other than a select few, everyone involved in the campaign efforts would be returning home to their families, their former lives and jobs, rightfully filled with a sense of shared success.

Those who had no prior positions to return to or no future employment in the Benton administration weren't forgotten either. Kate made sure that anyone needing a job had ample opportunity to interview with several large companies in the area, mostly thanks to the Benton family's widespread connections. Plus, each job seeker possessed the highest of personalized recommendations, written by Kate and signed by Emily herself.

It wasn't every day that a file clerk or a receptionist could apply for a job with a written recommendation from the president of the United States.

Being around the high-spirited group helped Kate feel better about her decision to accept the position in Emily's administration. It felt right.

And speaking of morale boosters, shouldn't Emily be through by now? Kate glanced at her watch. There had been an unavoidable last-minute meeting with party officials on the Hill that Emily had to attend. But she promised to end it promptly so that she could get back to Alexandria in time to join the farewell bash. It would probably be the last time most of the staffers would be able to walk up to their president unimpeded and strike up a casual conversation or have her ear for a moment.

When the first wave of Secret Service agents entered the building, Kate knew Emily wasn't far behind. She signaled Steve, their resident audiovisual specialist, and he timed it so that "Hail to the Chief" played right as Emily walked into the room.

Applause and cheers filled the building, echoing from wall to wall and making the windows visibly vibrate. Emily waited until the noise died down before she spoke.

"You know when I got up this morning and looked at my schedule for the day—and a fine schedule it was; thank you, Miriam—I saw two major blocks of time marked out. One said 'Party Officials,' and one was marked 'Official Party.' I thought this was truly going to be a full day of celebration."

The room erupted in laughter.

"Boy, did I have a rude awakening when I sat down at the first meeting and all they had was a pot of coffee and a plate of stale cookies."

"What? No chocolate chip cookies warm from the oven?" a voice chirped from the back of the room.

Emily was infamous for her love of chocolate chip cookies. It had been her honest preference, but the infamy was manufactured by Kate, who realized the search for the "perfect chocolate chip cookie recipe" was an ideal way to humanize the candidate, no matter where in the U.S. she campaigned. Each cookie stop photo op allowed Emily an opportunity to be a "regular" person, to show a slight weakness that Americans could identify with and not-so-secretly appreciate.

"It just makes me that much happier to come here to M Central, where I can meet with you all, thank you for your efforts, and where we know how to throw a real party!" She looked at the impressive array of food. "Not only do I see the world's best chocolate chip cookies—thank you, Louise—but nachos, fajitas, burritos . . ." She glanced at Kate, a gleam in her eye. "Poco Rio?"

Kate nodded.

Emily smacked her lips. "My favorite too." She splayed a hand across her stomach. "Do you guys mind if I eat now? And speechify later? I'm starved!"

As a result, Emily headed to the buffet accompanied by a roar of laughter and a backslapping crowd of enthusiasts pushing her onward. A few minutes later, Emily sat at a card table with a full plate and a big glass of iced tea, enjoying her meal. The casual seating had been rearranged so that her table was the unofficial head of a large circular gathering of office chairs and extra folding chairs brought in for the occasion. People abandoned their own makeshift table surfaces in order to move closer to their presidential boss, even if that meant they had to balance their plates in their laps.

"Are you looking forward to living in the White House?" one brave staffer asked.

"I am," Emily said between bites. "I've been living out of suitcases for the past two years. It'll be nice to have a room I can call my own, even if American taxpayers own it."

An anonymous voice from the back of the room called out, "Is it big enough for you?"

Emily grinned. "It's a little small, but I'll make do."

Kate heard a noise behind her and saw Buster nudge open the door from her private office. She'd stashed him there with a selection of rawhide treats to keep him out of trouble. He spotted the food, then saw Emily, and something very close to human indecision reflected in his eyes. After a moment's hesitation, he scampered toward Emily, ears flopping, tail wagging.

Emily greeted him and managed to slip him a chip before Kate could haul him away from the table.

"Are you going to let Buster into the Oval Office?" someone else asked.

Emily grinned. "I don't know how to keep him out. You know how he is with doors. He and I have an agreement.

He can lie in front of the fireplace as long as he doesn't poop on the big presidential rug—" she gestured with her fork—"which I get to design, by the way. I'm thinking of doing it in the same colors as his fur so it won't show if he sheds."

"Are you going to get your own dog someday?"

"Only if I could get Son of Buster. Or Daughter, as the case may be. But I'm afraid that might be a moot point. I'm pretty sure our Buster isn't going to ever sire any little Busters or Busterettes. His owner's the most responsible person in politics."

Laughter erupted throughout the room. Buster had been a campaign fixture in the headquarters, an unofficial mascot of sorts, another humanizing element.

Our president loves chocolate chip cookies and dogs. . . .

The impromptu question-and-answer session continued, lighthearted and wide-open. Emily already knew which people she was going to integrate into her administration. She made time for a private word with them. She also asked about the plans of the others. Even if she was no longer campaigning, an air of "we take care of our own" permeated the conversations. Kate couldn't have been more pleased with Emily if she'd staged the whole scene herself.

But it wasn't staged. Or rehearsed. It was just Emily demonstrating some of the lessons she'd learned after two and a half long years of campaigning. Kate had worked hard to help give Emily Rousseau Benton of the Virginia Bentons a better grounding in the ways of the Everyman and Everywoman in the office—their concerns, their interests, their needs, and their dreams. It wasn't that Emily had lived in an ivory tower all her life and didn't know about life on the streets, but she had to be reminded when she first started pressing the flesh how to seek out a sense of commonality with others.

Kate watched as Emily reacted warmly with the volunteers. More importantly, she paid attention to their reactions to her. These people were well-versed on Emily's stance on major issues, so they didn't need to pepper her with questions concerning the policies and changes her administration would bring. No one challenged her or her plans because those were their plans too.

The calm before the storm . . .

Every now and then, Emily would look up and catch Kate's attention, and the fleeting look in her eyes would say, "I'm doing good, aren't I?"

What should have been a statement came across more like a question, her need to be reassured that Kate approved.

It had been like that ever since Kate had sat down with Emily and laid out the conditions for her return and what it would take for her to accept the position of White House chief of staff; Emily had been more cautious and more introspective than usual. Kate likened it to the aftereffects of a near brush with death. When someone sidestepped a potentially disastrous situation and thought, "There but by the grace of God go I."

Emily had come perilously close to losing Kate's friendship, her counsel, and her trust. Now Emily realized it. But they both knew that they had to minimize speculation from others and not let anyone else know that there had been a major earthquake that threatened Camelot.

Still, even though she'd made the decision to stay, Kate was finding it hard to recapture the tone of their public relationship. Loretta Keene, Emily's primary traveling assistant, sidled up to Kate while everyone else centered their attention on Emily's discourse on cookie recipes.

"You okay, Kate? You look a little under the weather."

The lie came too easily. "I'm fine," Kate said in her breeziest tones. "I'm still recuperating from all the election excitement. I keep forgetting I'm not twenty anymore. All-nighters are taking their toll on me."

"Yeah, right. That will satisfy most people, but not me." Loretta maintained her smile as if they were having the most pleasant of conversations. "You forget. I work on the other side of the wall."

That was the euphemism they'd coined long ago for seeing and sharing the everyday life of the candidate in mid-campaign. On the other side of the wall, you saw the good, the bad, and sometimes the ugly of a politician after the cameras turned off, the microphones were stowed, and the doors were closed. In Emily's case, the ugly reared its head when she was too tired, too frustrated, or too angry to cope by herself. Unfortunately, more often than not, Loretta caught the brunt of it.

Loretta had played equal parts hairdresser, clothier, washwoman, masseuse, concierge, and any other role affecting comfort or style that Emily needed fulfilled while she lived on the road. The fact that the woman hadn't quit two or three . . . dozen times during the campaign was a miracle. It also meant Loretta had a more realistic, if not slightly tarnished, view of Emily than most of the volunteers. Then again, most volunteers hadn't interfaced with a grumpy coffee-craving candidate on a strict travel schedule that allowed her only three hours' sleep before heading off to yet another rally or speech or dinner.

"I know why Emily needs you—she couldn't do this without you. But I'm still surprised she wants me around," Loretta said quietly.

"Why would that surprise you? You've been a key player in her success."

Loretta offered Kate a small smile. "I thought sure Ms. Exotica was angling for my job and was likely to get it."

There could be only one Ms. Exotica—the enigmatic Maia Bari. A protégée of Washington's most lauded political image consultant, the exotic-looking Maia had captured Emily's favor by bringing some freshness to her wardrobe and style at a key point in the campaign. As a result, Emily had embraced the young woman, pulling her into her inner circle of advisers.

There for a while, Loretta's job *had* been in jeopardy. But Kate had recognized the hungry gleam in Maia's dark eyes and, as a result, had performed an in-depth investigation into the young woman's background. It revealed that instead of being an ageless beauty from some far-off land, Maia had been born in Bahrain but raised in Hoboken. She'd managed to use a deceased aunt's identity to create her own mysterious and somewhat hazy background.

No matter if Maia decided on her own volition to steal the Talbot file or whether she'd been sent by Emily, Kate knew the young woman represented an unnecessary liability. There had been no way on God's green earth that Kate would allow the young woman to work in the White House.

Kate placed an arm around Loretta's waist to give her a quick hug. "Are you kidding? No way. You were the first person I knew we had to get on the White House team. I have to have somebody at Emily's right hand that I trust and who I know will be able to handle the day-to-day stuff."

"Meaning you don't trust Mata Hari."

"Meaning I don't trust Maia Bari."

Loretta released a huff of relief. "Thank heavens. I was afraid you'd fallen for her charms like most of the people around here." She made a pointed effort of glancing at Chip McWilliamson, who stood in the corner of the room, taking pictures. "At least he's been smart enough to look and not touch. Can you imagine *him* trying to juggle two women at the same time?"

Kate bit her tongue. It was one thing to commiserate with Loretta over a perceived threat to her position. It was another thing to gossip about Emily and the relationship she might or might not have with the younger man.

The *much* younger man.

Loretta took another sip of her drink. From the aroma, Kate realized the beverage, unlike Kaleesa's, had more rum than punch.

"If Mata Bari decides to show up here, I just might have to take her aside and tell her a few things. I'm pretty sure she's the one who made a mess of my makeup case." A rare look of pure spite crossed Loretta's face. "And I'm also certain I have *her* to thank for some straight pins that appeared in one of Emily's hems after I'd fixed it. I know I took the pins out, but when Emily sat down, one jabbed her in the back of her leg. Of course she assumed I'd been careless and left it behind."

Loretta muttered a less than flattering word, which Kate assumed was meant for Maia, not Emily. "I could have wrung that girl's neck, Kate, for trying to sabotage my position so she could take over." She drained her drink, then wobbled, grabbing Kate's arm to brace herself. "Tell you what, if she tries it again, she's gonna be really surprised."

And I'll be really surprised if you remember this conversation in the morning, Kate thought as she extricated herself from Loretta's grasp.

Loretta looked at her hand, her fingers curled as if still clinging to Kate's arm. "Oops. Am I getting loud and saying and doing things I shouldn't?"

"Close to it."

Loretta looked at her empty drink. "I guess I didn't put this down in time." She gently placed the plastic cup on the closest flat surface, misjudging the distance and dropping the empty cup a few inches shy of the table. She gave Kate a bleary look. "We have coffee, right?"

Kate nodded. "In the break room."

"I need some." Loretta turned and took a step toward the kitchen, then stopped and called back over her shoulder. "Don't worry. I took the Metro here." She dug into her sweater pocket and produced a small ring of keys. "See? House keys only. No car keys." She stumbled toward the awaiting coffee.

"Thank you, Lord," Kate whispered after she was out of hearing range.

The voice in her ear almost made her jump.

"I've never seen her snockered." Emily stepped next to Kate. "And trust me, I've given her plenty of reasons to want to drink."

"I can imagine. I'm just glad you want to keep her as a personal aide."

"She's still young enough; she's sharp; and so far, she's done a really good job." They both watched Loretta carefully pour herself a cup of coffee. "Then again, she's not the only one suited for the position. I did consider Maia, but—"

she raised her hand before Kate could protest—"that was before our issues with her. However, we might have a small problem."

The muscles in Kate's back froze in place, the nerves screaming in pain. "What kind of small problem?"

"Since this is a farewell party and we're saying farewell to Maia, I invited her." Emily nodded toward the entryway to the headquarters. "She's standing in the foyer."

Kate knew she should have realized that when practically every man in the place turned his head and automatically took a step toward the door; it meant Maia had arrived.

She wore a deep red dress that went well with her olive complexion and dark hair. The woman always looked as if she'd stepped out of a magazine—no hair out of place and with the perfect accessories. She moved with the fluid grace of a dancer, charming her way across the room. It was evident her main objective was to get to Emily, but to do it, she had to find a way to subtly maneuver through a gauntlet of male admirers without making them feel slighted.

Judging by their rapt looks, it appeared as if Maia appeased them all along the way as she plotted a straight line to Emily.

"I don't want to talk to her," Kate said, looking around for an exit strategy.

Emily released an unattractive snort. "For heaven's sake, pull up your big girl panties and stand your ground." Emily raised her hand. "Maia!" she called out as if so very pleased to see the young turncoat. "Over here."

Maia seemed imminently thrilled to have been singled out and used the excuse to plow faster through her crowd of admirers.

"I hate you," Kate whispered.

"No you don't." Emily switched seamlessly from sotto voce to her polished politician's voice. "I was just telling Kate that I hoped you would make an appearance."

They did the usual European air-kiss thing, evidently also the popular greeting for girls from Hoboken. At least Maia didn't have the audacity to meet Kate's flat gaze.

She simpered nicely in her pseudo English-as-a-strong-second-language manner. "I just wanted to stop and tell you how much I appreciated being able to work with you. It was indeed a dream come true. As Miss Marjorie said, it was the sort of experience that comes once in a lifetime. I'm so very lucky and thankful that I was allowed such an opportunity."

"Miss Marjorie" was Marjorie Redding, older than dirt but the foremost authority on image consultancy in the U.S. political arena. She claimed no political affiliations; she had worked with members of both major parties to retool their public images—changing hairstyle, clothing style, manners, and even speaking voices to make them more universally attractive and respected. When Marjorie got through with a client, they looked, sounded, and acted at the top of their game.

Maia, her protégée, had been sent to help Emily when Marjorie had a family commitment and couldn't help during the debate preparations. Whether Kate liked the young woman or not, she'd done a good job of making Emily look every inch the perfect presidential candidate. And when the final count was tallied, enough people agreed that Emily was the right choice.

That had been the bottom line, at the time.

But now Maia was a liability—either a loose cannon indiscriminately smashing up the campaign deck or an ICBM in the hands of a master missileer like Emily.

Kate reached deep inside and found a smile that didn't reek of insincerity. "We appreciate all the effort that went into helping refine Emily's image."

Now say good-bye and excuse yourself. Kate wasn't sure if she was trying to instruct herself or influence the young woman.

In polite response, Maia offered her usual enigmatic smile and her hand to Emily. "It was my pleasure."

Emily didn't hesitate to accept the handshake. But when Maia turned to Kate, Kate not only curbed the instinct to reach out but found the fortitude to make eye contact with the young woman and say, "You'll forgive me for not shaking your hand."

No excuses. No explanations.

The young woman faltered for a moment, then pulled her hand back. "I'm . . . I'm sorry." She pivoted smartly and made a hasty exit from their small conversation group.

Emily made a clucking noise once the young woman was out of earshot. "Was that entirely necessary?"

"To me, it was. She got the message, don't you think?"

They both looked at Maia, who seemed to have survived the slight and was bestowing her considerable charms in the direction of Dave Dickens, Kate's second in command.

"I don't know about getting a message, but if I were to judge, I'd say you've probably made her an enemy," Emily stated in a rather matter-of-fact voice.

"Probably have." Kate feigned interest in a basket of Mexican wedding cookies, ignoring her stomach, which seized at the thought of eating anything now. "But I can handle her."

Emily stepped next to her at the table. "How?" she asked pointedly.

Kate picked up a cookie and sampled its powdered sugar edge. "Pardon the pun, but I stole a page from your playbook. She knows that I know her biggest secret."

"Which is . . . ?"

"If I told, it'd no longer be a secret, now would it?"

ALMOST SIX THOUSAND POSITIONS. Theoretically that was how many jobs could be up for grabs at the changeover from the Cooper administration to Benton control. The first thing Kate did was hire an experienced personnel staffer to manage the sudden wave of job applications that flooded their office. As the number of applications grew, so did the size of the personnel office, eventually topping two hundred people making contacts, checking references, cataloguing, and filtering through the paperwork generated by nearly two hundred thousand job seekers.

But before they could start filling positions, Emily, Kate, and the transition team had to determine which personnel connected with the current administration would stay and which would go. In theory, Emily could replace everyone from ambassadors down to the White House waitstaff, but that sort of explosive housecleaning was unnecessary. In practice, it would be highly detrimental to the smooth running of her new administration.

So she and her staffers had to operate like surgeons, keeping the good, removing anything that looked like trouble. Kate didn't have it easy. In the days between the election and the inauguration, she caught meals on the fly and slept for only a couple of hours each night. It was the price she paid for doing what few if any campaign managers had ever done—moving immediately from managing a presidential campaign into the role of incoming White House chief of staff. Although it eased any friction between the campaign staff and the transition team, it gave Kate no downtime between critical roles.

Working from their transitional offices, she and Emily put into play the first level of plans that their inner circle had been working on in secret since the convention.

Their initial concern was securing those people who would fill the senior White House staff positions and become President Benton's key policy advisers. The goal was to identify the designees as early as possible so that their FBI checks and economic disclosure reviews would be completed in time to give them transitional ramp-up time as well. They too had to hire their own staff and needed as much time as possible to do this before taking their official positions.

Emily had strong opinions about who should be among her inner circle of senior advisers. Working with their campaign's advisers, a dream team of sorts had been assembled on paper shortly after Emily won the party's nomination. Kept secret, this document became the initial blueprint of the Benton administration, and as the White House chief of staff designee, Kate's job was to make it happen.

But if coming up with the dream team had been hard, making it a reality appeared to be nearly impossible.

Considering they had only eleven weeks to assemble, vet, and flesh out the skeleton of the White House staff and then the cabinet, Kate, Emily, and their growing staff spent their collective energies contacting, negotiating, and sometimes reworking the elements of their plans.

As a result, Thanksgiving was lost in a blur. Kate remembered being slightly annoyed that government offices were closed that Thursday, and it wasn't until someone brought leftover turkey into the office that she realized how much she had missed the traditional gathering at her family's house.

While the main personnel office—led by Pria Shangalia, who would eventually head the Office of Presidential Personnel—handled the bulk of the work, as chief of staff, Kate ran a separate personnel unit responsible for coordinating everything necessary to ease over six hundred people into their new positions and prepare them for new responsibilities. Many appointments couldn't be made until Emily actually took office. Other appointments would have to wait for Senate confirmation before becoming set.

By the time Christmas rolled around, Emily made everyone take a mandatory couple of vacation days, saying that if they didn't take a break, her first act as President Benton would be to institute a national week of sleep. In any case, they were stymied in their efforts to keep the bureaucratic ball rolling at the same speed since many government agencies were short-staffed around the holidays.

By the time they reached Inauguration Day, most of the positions had been filled, the selectees vetted and ready to pack their boxes and move from their transitional offices to the real thing in the White House after Emily took the oath.

In many cases, within the hour.

Ah yes . . . the inauguration. Kate thought about it with a fair amount of excitement and equal part dread. She looked forward to the traditional pageantry, the official pomp and circumstance which would start that day and continue for four years—eight, if they were lucky. But it was the carnival-like atmosphere that began five days prior to the actual swearing-in ceremony and the four days afterward she wished she could avoid.

She stared at the latest version of the ambitious schedule that the Presidential Inaugural Committee had drawn up. Parties, concerts, official presidential balls (nine of them), unofficial balls, receptions, candlelight dinners, brunches, luncheons, a parade . . .

It made her tired just to read it.

That's just your fatigue talking, she told herself. It would be a once-in-a-lifetime experience, something she'd never forget and would probably tell much too often in the old folks' home. Sure, she'd been to her share of Washington parties, even an inauguration ball or two, but she'd never spent much time seeing the behind-the-scenes preparations.

So when the day of the inauguration finally arrived, Kate had already survived five days of events, including three concerts, a half-dozen receptions, and the Black Tie and Boots Ball. As she sat in St. John's Church, one row behind Emily and Vice President–Elect Burl Bochner and his wife, Melissa, Kate sent up a prayer of thanks for the brief respite.

The next four years working at Emily's side in the White House would likely be exhausting, exhilarating, and exasperating. But for the moment, Kate drank in the comforting silence of sitting on the far end of the president's pew in the hushed church, waiting for the rector to take his position.

Kate didn't have to be Episcopalian to find a sense of comfort in the rector's words, his admonition to pay attention to the needs of the world around them and how it influenced the legacies of leadership.

"High above us is a steeple, and in that steeple is a very historic bell that still rings to this day. You probably heard it earlier this morning. The bell was installed up there in 1822, only a few months after being forged by John Revere, the son of famed patriot Paul Revere. I guess you might call it a legacy of freedom. As we witness the passing of the presidential torch later today from one administration to the next, I can't help but think this is an excellent example of the American legacy of freedom in action, a legacy that knows no color, no gender, and no limitations."

Kate glanced over at Emily, who seemed to listen with rapt attention. A sense of guarded pride grew inside Kate, not for herself, but for her colleague, her employer, her friend. Even though becoming the first female to achieve that lofty position was a singular accolade, Emily hadn't won the office because she was a woman. She'd won because she had been the best candidate in the field, gender aside.

And Kate was going to do everything in her power to make sure the legacy Emily left behind was one of leadership, compassion, and strength.

Two hours later, at high noon, Emily Rousseau Benton stood on the steps of the Capitol's west side, her right hand on the Bible and her left held aloft.

"I, Emily Rousseau Benton, do solemnly swear that I will faithfully execute the office of President of the United States, and will to the best of my ability, preserve, protect and defend the Constitution of the United States."

There was the slightest of pauses as if she faced either a moment of indecision or she wanted to give more emphasis to her next words.

"So help me, God."

A shiver slid across Kate's shoulders. It had been Emily's sole decision to add the phrase, which wasn't technically part of the official oath.

Later, as they stood for the first time together in the Oval Office, Emily offered an explanation.

"Why? Because I figured I needed all the help I could get."

"Seriously," Kate chided.

Emily ran her hand over the edge of the famous Resolute desk that she'd opted to use as so many presidents had before her. "I knew it meant a lot to you, and therefore, it means a lot to me. Sometimes I don't see the big picture, and there's no bigger picture than God, right?"

Kate hugged her friend. "Absolutely right."

That night, as Kate left the White House, she had her driver—who had introduced himself as Edward—stop outside of the iron fence that separated both Joe Tourist and Joe Terrorist from the White House grounds. She gave the grand old lady of a building a lingering look, containing far more awe than pride. "It's hard to believe I work there."

Edward nodded. "Yes, ma'am. I can imagine."

She'd driven past the building a thousand times, even visited it a half-dozen times or two. But working there . . . she was still trying to wrap her head around that one. After one more look, she said, "Okay. Let's head home."

Edward pulled out into traffic, expertly finding a place between a cab and a double-decker tour bus full of people gawking at the sites.

Kate settled back in her seat, rolling the window up. "I guess you hear that a lot about the White House."

"Yes, ma'am. At the beginning, at least."

"And later on?"

"Not so much. The newness wears off. But that's normal."

Normal. Somehow, she didn't think she would be able to use the word to describe her life over the next four years. Just today, she stood at the right hand of the most powerful leader in the free world. Later on, she ran a meeting of the newly installed White House senior staff. Some of them she knew personally, like Dozier Marsh; some she knew in passing; a couple she knew only by reputation. No matter whether they were men, women, older, younger, they would funnel their concerns, their programs, their communications through her to reach Emily.

Kate would now be the official gatekeeper to the president. Nothing would get to Emily, no one would step through the door of the Oval Office, without Kate's knowledge or approval. It wasn't a position to be taken lightly or more importantly, harshly. Kate had studied her predecessors in the job and intended her version of the position to be one of influence rather than control. She learned long ago that Emily would be receptive to the former and bristle, if not openly rebel, against the latter.

Once Kate reached home, she had a little over an hour to get ready before heading out again. What else would cap off her first day at work better than attending an official ball or two?

She remembered the first presidential ball she'd attended—in the far lesser capacity as assistant to the governor, when Emily held that post in Virginia. It had been crowded and hot, the food disappeared long before she reached any serving table, and once the president finally arrived, he and his wife had danced for exactly one and a half minutes before waving their good-byes and pushing off to the next in a string of patriotically named balls that sounded more like battleships than parties.

Liberty. Constitution.

However, this time, Kate's party-going experience would be different. She had her selection of balls to attend and decided to go to two of the many—the Constitution Ball, the first one Emily would hit on her circuit, and the Commander in Chief Ball, the last event on Emily's agenda, an event held exclusively for military personnel. Kate's brother, Brian, an air force officer, would be her escort only because her sister-in-law, Jill, had broken her foot the week before and didn't want to negotiate the crowds on crutches.

Ah yes, the sensitive subject of escorts . . .

The White House Protocol Office had approached both Emily and Kate weeks before, concerned at how the president-elect wanted to handle her unattached status when it came to social events such as the inaugural balls. Short of going out and dancing by herself, the president needed a suitable escort since there was no First Gentleman.

Emily and Kate had discussed options and finally settled on asking Emily's cousin Richard Benton, son of former President William Benton, to be her escort in social settings requiring one. He was a familiar face at such events and, more importantly, had four years of experience under his belt of dealing with press, politics, and protocol. His unattached state was legendary in political circles. He'd been nicknamed a most eligible political bachelor and had even made *People*'s sexiest men list a time or two.

Duties that would normally fall to the First Lady would be shared by another of Emily's cousins, Margaret Benton Shaiyne, and by Melissa Bochner, the vice president's wife. The dichotomy of the two—a stay-at-home mother and a career-oriented mother—meant they would bring an interesting range of experiences to the position.

But in all her haste to see that Emily had the proper support in those key areas, Kate had failed to arrange an escort for herself. That didn't mean her brother wasn't a congenial substitute, but it still made it pretty evident that her social life had come to a standstill over the last two years on the campaign trail.

All Kate could do was convince herself that this was simply a work-related function. "It's not a real party," she repeated to herself as she climbed into the limousine. When she stepped through the VIP entrance to the main floor of the ballroom, she tried to remind herself one more time, but as she looked out at the crowd of fancy dresses and tuxedos, she found it hard to tell herself otherwise.

A ripple went through the crowd, an unofficial fanfare announcing the arrival of Emily and her security entourage. Kate walked backstage and waited for Emily to appear. As Emily's campaign manager, it had always been Kate's self-appointed task to make one last review of Emily's appearance before she stepped onstage. It was a hard habit to break.

For both of them.

Emily's slightly pinched features relaxed when she saw Kate. "There you are! How's the dress look? Is it hanging straight in back?" She turned as if trying to catch a glimpse of herself.

Although Emily had the figure and the bearing to pull off an Academy Award–red carpet–worthy dress, she'd selected something a little more sedate from the spate of designers who offered their wares in hopes the president would give them some high-ranking exposure.

The gown she selected had simple, classic lines that accentuated her athletic figure without flaunting it and a neckline that displayed a tasteful hint of cleavage. The dress from an unheard of but soon-to-be-famous designer named C'Teris was a shade of deep crimson so dark that it verged on black but was livened up by small crystals woven into the fabric. With no precedence as to what a female president should wear to this function—or any other function for that matter—Emily had decided to write the rule book, using her own good taste plus an unerring sense of color combined with the talents of Marjorie Redding, image consultant extraordinaire.

Kate admired the finished product. "You look perfect." It was no lie. Emily absolutely glowed, looking both commanding yet comfortable.

"Thanks. Wish me luck."

Kate took her place in the front of the crowd right as four ruffles and flourishes, then "Hail to the Chief" echoed across the enormous room. Emily's arrival was preceded by an eruption of applause and cheers.

She spoke with her usual combination of elegance and ease, keeping it light. No heavy political speeches here. She offered her thanks and spoke more about the tone of her administration and plans rather than getting into details about the upcoming policy changes.

She quipped, "And now let's see if my cousin actually remembers anything from the dance lessons we took as kids." She and Richard took center stage as the orchestra struck up "Some Enchanted Evening."

Someone tapped Kate on the shoulder and said over the music, "She always *could* dance."

Kate turned, stunned to find Nick Beaudry standing next to her, impeccably dressed as always. "What are you doing here?" she mouthed.

He leaned closer so he wouldn't have to yell over the competing music. "Don't worry. I didn't crash the party. Security is too tight to do something like that." He grinned as he reached into his tuxedo jacket and pulled out an envelope and ticket stub. "I guess by the look on your face you didn't send this." He flushed a little as he laughed. "Seems to me I've said that to you once before . . . not too long ago."

Kate ran her finger across the raised letters of the return address—the White House.

"I guess I made another wrong assumption, which leads me to wonder . . ."

They both looked out toward the dance floor, where Emily and Richard twirled in rhythm to the music.

To his credit, Nick watched her with mild interest, betraying more a sense of nostalgia than unrequited feelings. "You don't think she's getting sentimental in her old age, do you?"

"Emily?" Kate sputtered.

He made a dismissive gesture. "Scratch that. I guess I forgot who I was talking about." He stuffed the invitation back into his jacket pocket. "This may be a signal that you need to take a closer look at the Protocol Office. If they can make a mistake like this . . ."

Kate waved away his concern. "Maybe this is just Emily's way of saying bygones are bygones."

He looked dubious. "Maybe."

They watched the lower dance floor begin to fill with couples. Emily and Richard still danced by themselves on a higher dais decorated with a large presidential seal on the stage floor.

Nick held out his hand. "Care to dance?"

If he were anybody else but Emily's ex-husband, Kate would have seriously considered saying yes. Nick Beaudry had transformed himself into a pleasant, intelligent, and well-mannered man. But beyond political ramifications, beyond social manners, the unofficial girlfriend's rule book said to never date your best friend's ex.

"Thanks, but—"

"No thanks," he supplied with a nod. "I understand. I should have thought before I even offered." He turned slightly away. "Uh-oh . . . she spotted us."

Kate looked toward the upper stage and caught Emily's raised eyebrow expression. In response, Kate lifted one hand to offer her friend a small wave.

Nick glanced at Emily, his expression growing sheepish as he turned away. "I knew this was a mistake. Coming here."

Kate continued to smile at Emily but spoke to Nick at her side. "You were invited. You have every right to attend."

He sighed. "I need a drink."

Sudden alarm filled Kate and she pivoted sharply. "No you don't."

His sheepish look faded into something much more reflective but controlled. "No, not *drink* as in alcohol. I need one of those overpriced sodas. You know—all ice and an ounce or two of Coke for five bucks. American free enterprise at its best. Or worst. Can I get you something?"

"I . . . I'll go with you."

His voice grew quiet. "I'm not going to get any booze, Kate. I'm not foolish enough to say those days are behind me—one day at a time, you know—but today? A pricey soft drink or tonic water will do me just fine."

Kate felt her face flush with embarrassment, but before she could apologize, Chip McWilliamson wedged himself between them. It was obvious that the young man was taking advantage of the ebb and flow of the crowd to expertly cut Nick off. After spending the better part of the last two years being in close proximity to Emily while on the campaign trail, he'd learned how to rescue her from overexcited supporters with a well-placed body block.

Only Kate didn't need or want any rescue.

"Sorry to interrupt, man," he called over his shoulder to Nick, whom he'd forced to step back. Then he turned to Kate, winked, and stated in a voice a little too loud for the situation, "Ms. Rosen, the president needs to speak with you immediately."

Kate glanced over and saw that President Benton, Emily's uncle, had cut in on his son Richard and was now dancing with his niece.

Two presidents, one former, one current, dancing together. The entire ballroom was lit up with camera strobes. It was obvious that Emily wasn't waiting to talk to Kate or anyone else at that moment. Nothing in the world would make the woman give up the limelight at the moment.

Kate tried not to look annoyed at Chip but knew she'd probably failed. If her self-appointed Rescue Ranger was going to make up an excuse, he certainly could have done a better job of it and made up something believable.

"Kate, I'll talk to—" Nick was jostled from behind by a woman, and as a result, he took a step closer to Chip, trying to regain his balance.

Before Kate could turn back to inform her would-be hero that everything was actually fine, Chip continued with his imaginary role, raising his voice. "Maybe you didn't understand me, but get lost, Beaudry. You're not wanted here."

A Secret Service agent, stationed nearby in the crowd, made eye contact with Kate, raising his hand to his ear in order to report the disturbance into his sleeve microphone. She made a small dismissive gesture with her hand to wave off his concern. He lowered his arm, acknowledging her command with a barely perceptible nod of his head. If she needed any real rescue, he would be the person to turn to, not some slightly inebriated soon-to-be semiofficial White House blogger who had the hots for the president.

Nick peered around Kate's self-appointed liberator who had placed himself between them and mouthed, *You need any help?* He obviously realized that Chip was no threat to her. When she shook her head, he shot her a small salute and mouthed, *Catch you later* and then was swallowed up by the crowd.

Chip peered over his shoulder at Nick's departure, then turned back, smirking in triumph over his apparent success. "Beaudry was the last person I expected to be here.

He's lucky I didn't have him escorted out." He puffed up his chest in a classic big-protector-of-small-women way.

Kate motioned for him to come closer, and he leaned down accordingly, probably expecting her undying thanks or, worse, a chaste kiss on the cheek.

The white knight syndrome could be so tiring. . . .

Kate kept her voice low and even. "If you ever pull a stupid stunt like that again, in public or in private, I will have every press credential you possess revoked and you will be banned from covering any and all White House events during this administration. Your official blogging days will be over. Do you understand me?"

He gaped at her and suddenly the twenty-year difference in their ages made him truly seem a generation away. Then he flushed with an unexpected flair of anger. "Now wait a freakin' minute, I thought—"

She met his ire with her own. "You didn't think. That's the problem. If you did stop to think, you would have realized that you do *not* insert yourself into private conversations, especially ones that show no signs of any discord or uneasiness. You don't get to run roughshod over any of my discussions simply because you've decided Nick Beaudry shouldn't be here."

"C'mon, Kate . . ."

Her irritation flash-boiled over into full-blown anger. It was probably a result of the building pressures of the past few weeks and the fact that she'd worked hard to find the right tone for her new position as White House chief of staff. The last thing she expected was to be forced to deal with backsliding among those senior campaign staffers who were being integrated into White House staff.

Perhaps what was really bothering her was that Emily had insisted on finding Chip a position that would put them in daily contact.

And probably nightly contact, if Chip had his wish.

"Let's get one thing straight, Mr. McWilliamson. We're no longer on the campaign trail, where we maintained less formal procedures out of convenience. I'm now Ms. Rosen to you, the White House chief of staff. I am your boss. And I will hold conversations with whomever necessary, whenever I deem necessary. If you can no longer control your impulsiveness or your alcohol intake, you will be removed from this event and all others if I deem necessary."

Although she knew she'd probably regret giving him a little dig, she succumbed to temptation and added, "And just so you know, Mr. Beaudry was invited—" she leveled him with an I-know-more-than-you glare—"by *someone* in the White House." She tipped her head toward the dance floor. "Understand?"

The young man's mouth dropped open. "You mean . . ." He watched Emily on the dance floor. "She and . . . Beaudry? Again?"

The color began to drain from his face, and Kate took a tiny amount of pity on him.

"If I were to speculate—and that's my privilege, not yours—I'd suspect President Benton may have wanted to make a pointed statement to her ex-husband. You know . . . 'Look what you gave up'? A little salt in the wound?"

Kate suddenly realized what she'd just done to the love-struck young man herself—found his weakness and exploited it. Realization left a bad taste in her mouth.

"Salt," he repeated in a flat tone. "Sure." He straightened. "Yeah." He was gaining some momentum now. "Giving him a front-row seat and twisting the knife a little." That seemed to satisfy his more bloodthirsty instincts, and he nodded in approval. "Pretty smart," he said in admiration, watching Emily as she displayed talents honed at more than one Virginian cotillion in her youth.

Chip tore his attention away from Emily long enough to stutter out a passable apology, and then he slunk away. But now Kate had questions eating at her. What was Emily doing? And more importantly, why? First, she helped Nick and excused that as a bit of quid pro quo. But then she sent him a ticket to an inaugural ball? Maybe Chip had it all wrong. Maybe Emily wasn't twisting the knife but inviting Nick back into the fold. Now that he was reformed—a model citizen of sorts—was Emily considering him as a possible First Gentleman?

[illegible] was [illegible] new [illegible] Corrie [illegible] the [illegible] she said [illegible] condition in her mouth.

The [illegible] her [illegible] long [illegible] an agreeable apology, and then [illegible] away. But now Kate had [illegible] What was [illegible] And [illegible] Nick [illegible] But then she sent him a [illegible] the Club [illegible] all [illegible] She [illegible] back into the [illegible] asked [illegible] him.

EMILY AND NICK, TOGETHER AGAIN.

Kate's mind conjured an uncomfortable image of the two of them, a charming portrait of two people smiling at an invisible camera.

The practical side of her rationalized that such a reunion would play well in the press and would likely appeal to the general public. The Prodigal Husband returns a renewed man, to reunite with the woman he loved but wronged. Then again, the more practical voice suggested that something like that would have been far more useful during the campaign. . . .

And if Kate thought about the idea, it was sure that Emily had already completely dissected the concept, investigated its individual parts, and perhaps reassembled it into something Frankensteinian in nature.

A voice intruded on her ruminations. "Ms. Rosen? I just wanted to congratulate you on your new position."

Her greeter became the first in a long stream of Washington

movers and shakers who firmly believed that an inaugural ball was the perfect time to remind Kate that they'd met her years ago or they hadn't had the chance yet to meet her or that they hoped they could get a meeting with her after she got settled in her new position.

Finally she managed to use Emily's imminent departure to the next in a long line of official balls to excuse herself from her glut of well-wishers, implying that regrettably, she too had to be part of the progressive ball program.

"Is it safe to talk?"

Kate turned at the sound of the familiar voice. "*Safe* is a relative term."

Nick held two small plastic glasses of soda and offered her one. "I figured you might be thirsty after surviving that rather impressive political gauntlet. I never thought I'd see the ranking member of the House Armed Services Committee stoop to such obvious brownnosing."

"Impressive, wasn't it? Thanks," she said, accepting the drink. "I guess it's all just part of the job description." True to Nick's earlier description, the cup contained more ice than anything else, but despite that, the soda was refreshing, if briefly so. Although it was a cold January evening, the ballroom was starting to grow warm thanks to the crush of people, not to mention the hot air they generated in true Washingtonian fashion.

"I thought you'd be headed off with Emily to the next big gala, along with what's-his-name, her puppy–slash–guard dog."

She hid a smile. Chip and Buster *did* seem to have more than one quality in common, particularly the strength of their bark in comparison to their "byte." "Don't mind Chip. He's harmless."

"He is now, thanks to the dressing-down that you gave him."

"You overheard us?" She hadn't thought anyone had; she'd tried to keep her voice under control. The last thing she'd wanted to do was attract any attention to their terse discussion.

Nick laughed. "Don't look so worried. I didn't hear anything. But I did get a puerile sense of enjoyment watching his expression as it changed. Whatever you said, it made him realize he'd stepped over a very big line and made an even bigger mistake." He paused. "Is it bad of me to have found a bit of pleasure in that?"

"Not bad. Just human."

"Then can this 'just human' offer to dance with you?"

She hesitated. Why, she wasn't sure. Too many complications, she decided. Whether he was simply in Emily's past or possibly in her future, he really had no business in Kate's present.

"I'd like to; I really would. But I'm late for the Commander in Chief Ball."

"Hot date?" he quipped.

"My brother."

Something that almost looked like relief crossed his face, then dissipated quickly. "That's right. I remember that he's . . . what? Air force?"

Before she could answer, Nick's body language shifted perceptibly, suggesting that something or someone unpleasant was approaching. Although he lowered his voice, he maintained his expression. "You won't believe it, but your rescuer has returned."

Sure enough, she felt a tap on her shoulder.

"Please pardon me for interrupting you, Ms. Rosen." The voice contained equal parts caution and respect.

Kate turned around, ready to read Chip McWilliamson the riot act again until she caught sight of his face. This was not a young man making a foolish decision but one with an honest message. He also wasn't alone. The man standing one step behind Chip wore his experience like the badge he probably carried in his pocket. Although suitably attired for a business meeting, his dark suit made him stand out like a beacon in the sea of tuxedos. Whether he was plainclothes police, FBI, or Secret Service, she wasn't sure. But he was definitely a cop of some sort.

Before the man could even speak, Chip blurted out, "Something's happened and I'm not sure if we should inform the president."

Only one day into the job . . .

"Chip, that's my decision. Not yours. And you are, sir . . . ?"

The man produced his credentials, which identified him as Special Agent Brown of the Secret Service. "Ma'am, I'm assigned to the command post here. We just got word from the Park Police that there's been an accident involving one of the president's former campaign advisers."

Kate's mind jumped ahead. *Dozier? Francesca?*

She motioned for them to follow—Nick included—as she led the way to a less crowded corner where hopefully they wouldn't be easily overheard. Once they were out of the mainstream traffic, she shooed Chip away. "Make sure we get some privacy." She turned to the plainclothes cop. "Who?"

Brown consulted a small notebook. "A woman named Maia Bari."

"What happened?" Kate might not have liked the young woman, but she would never wish Maia any harm. "Is she okay?"

"No, ma'am. Ms. Bari was the passenger in a one-car accident on the Rock Creek Parkway approximately one hour ago. I'm afraid neither she nor the driver survived the crash."

Any lingering dislike of Maia was swept away by the flood of sympathy that filled Kate's heart and mind. Her first thoughts were, *How horrible. . . . I hope she didn't suffer.* And then, *Her poor family . . .*

"An accident?" she asked.

"The investigators are still working the scene." The man wore an appropriately grim expression. "But high speed and alcohol are never a good combination."

"True."

Nick stepped closer as if to comfort her, but he didn't touch her. "Who was the driver?" he asked.

The agent responded with stoic silence. Evidently Nick was not on the need-to-know list.

"He's with me. Who *was* the driver?" she repeated.

The agent consulted his notebook again. "According to his ID, a man named Timothy Colton."

Kate had never met Tim Colton, but she knew he sat on one of the innermost rings of Charles Talbot's circle of campaign advisers. That meant Nick probably knew him. But when she turned, she saw no signs of recognition on

Nick's poker face and decided not to mention the possible connection.

His feigned expression might fool the agent, but it didn't fool her.

Although, technically, Charles Talbot and his cronies were no longer "the enemy," Kate couldn't help but wonder what brought Maia and Colton together across enemy lines. But perhaps the more curious question wasn't *what* brought them across the line between parties, but *when* had they crossed those lines?

And why? Was it purely personal? Colton always ranked high on the list of Washington's bachelors, and certainly Maia could be considered one of the most beautiful women in the District.

As pertinent and pressing as the questions were, Kate kept them to herself. She had other concerns at the moment. "Agent Brown, has this hit the local news yet?"

"No, ma'am. The identity of the victims won't be released until police contact their next of kin. Because it was on the parkway, the jurisdiction lies with the Park Police. The names of the victims won't be released until morning."

Did she tell Emily now, later tonight, or wait until morning? It wasn't a hard decision for Kate. "I don't see why we should interrupt the president's big evening with this news. As unfortunate as it is, there's nothing she can do. It's not like she can contact the family and give them her condolences before they're officially informed. This can wait until morning. Please tell the investigating agency to let my office know prior to broadcasting any news releases."

"Yes, ma'am. Thank you." The agent stepped back, disappearing into the crowd.

Chip stood several steps away and remained there a moment longer than he should before he excused himself. Kate made a mental note to thank him in the morning. To ease her conscience, she gave him a quick nod of thanks.

Once both men had left, she turned to Nick. "You know . . . knew Tim Colton, right?"

His face betrayed the emotion he withheld earlier. "Yes." A harsh light entered his eyes.

"So I gather he's not a friend?"

"Hardly." He leaned closer. "Remember earlier when we talked about people who rose through the ranks by eliminating those above them?"

She nodded, recalling the conversation over their dinner. "You mean . . . Tim?"

"I have no proof, but I always suspected it was him. He opposed bringing me onto the staff and wasn't afraid to say it. Often. I always thought it was nothing more than petty jealousy. Before I came on board, he was their big authority on Emily because he dated one of her cousins for a while." Nick sighed. "I guess I don't have to worry about him anymore." His expression suggested that not worrying was a good thing. Then he cocked his head, as if remembering there had been two victims. "I'm sorry. I'm being a bit insensitive, aren't I? The woman. She was a colleague of yours, right? I'm so sorry."

Kate said nothing, and it took Nick only a moment or two to read the right meaning into the silence.

"She's not the one who . . . The files?"

Kate nodded. "One and the same."

His posture sagged as if the news deflated him somewhat. "Your thief and my tormenter—in the same car together.

That's painting a picture I don't think I like at all. And both of them capable of everything from blackmail to character assassination to outright crime. I wonder what they were up to? And I bet we wouldn't like it if we found out."

"Me either. But now with both of them gone, we might never know if it was a conspiracy or not."

His gaze clouded over. "You realize that when this hits the news tomorrow, media speculations are going to run wild."

"No, they won't."

Nick seemed taken aback, and his unfocused gaze sharpened suddenly. "You're going to stop it from reaching the public?"

The thought had never occurred to her—that she might be in a position of such influence that she could exert enough pressure to alter a small stream much less dam a potential flood.

"No, no. . . . I mean that she works for Marjorie Redding. You know how careful Marjorie is about not aligning with any one political party. Her business depends on getting clients from both parties. Maia is . . . was . . . much too savvy to say anything to anyone—besides me—about wanting to work for Emily. Marjorie would have thrown her out on her ear."

"You never told Marjorie?"

"I thought about it, but I realized it might inadvertently give her insight into my weaknesses or, more importantly, Emily's."

Nick nodded. "Marjorie could just as easily become the image consultant for Emily's next opponent."

"Exactly. I'd figured it was safer knowing Maia was under Marjorie's watchful eye." She glanced at the watch peeking out from the sleeve of his tuxedo. "Is it nine yet?"

"Five till."

She reached deep into her portfolio of manners and tried to find an appropriate and diplomatic way to say good-bye. "I hate to leave, but I really do have to push on to the next event and catch up with my brother." She reached over and grasped Nick's arm. "I'm very glad we ran into each other tonight."

He patted her hand. "Me too. If you learn anything else about the accident, will you let me know?" He shrugged. "Curiosity, you know."

Kate thought the request was odd but reasonable. "I will. Take care."

After their somewhat congenial but no less awkward farewell, she exited through the VIP door, where her limousine waited, a perk that came with her elevated position.

Once she arrived at the Commander in Chief Ball, her evening as Brian's date proved to be much more easygoing and entertaining. The casual topics of the evening were just that—casual as opposed to political. No one wanted her ear to tout their own particular brand of political influence. No one wanted to make nice in order to pave a possible path to the Oval Office. They were more apt to talk planes, tanks, and ships at this all-military event.

Kate never anticipated being the belle of this particular ball, but until Emily arrived, Kate held unexpected court.

Brian was to blame mostly. Her affable brother made sure she didn't lack any dance partners, and when they weren't dancing, he told the most horrendously embarrassing stories about his big sister, Katie.

However, Kate got her revenge on him by telling an equal number of irreverent childhood tales of baby Brian, Boy

Scout Brian, and Brian the brain. But the pièce de résistance occurred when Emily arrived.

Tradition meant that first, the president would speak briefly, thanking the military members for their service to their country and then offering an additional thanks to the family members who stood beside them. Then the president would dance with a specially selected military partygoer.

At Emily's request, Kate arranged with the ball committee for Emily to dance with not one, but two military men—the first, a decorated sergeant newly returned from a long tour of duty in the Middle East and the second, Major Brian Rosen.

As Kate watched her red-faced brother fox-trot with the president of the United States, she knew that despite his apparent embarrassment, the episode would become the newest entry in his repertoire of great military adventures. It would give him a one-upmanship that he would exploit shamelessly as an "Oh yeah? Let me tell you what *I* did" tale.

Kate wasn't sure which was better: watching Emily and Brian on the dance floor or going to an inaugural ball that lacked the political jockeying of the others. In either case, it was the wonderful ending to a less than perfect evening.

And the lingering glow of satisfaction lasted until the phone call came in the wee hours of the morning.

"WE HAVE A PROBLEM." Emily's voice shot through the receiver like a bolt of lightning, jangling Kate's nerves.

"Most people say *hello* first. What problem?"

"Maia's dead."

"I know."

"You knew?" Disbelief faded to indignation. "And you didn't tell me?"

Perhaps it was because Kate had been awoken from a dead sleep and her usual filters weren't up. Or maybe she'd developed a new attitude to go with her new position. "You didn't have a need to know at the moment." She realized how harsh that sounded and softened it slightly by adding, "There was nothing you could do anyway. The Secret Service contacted me, and since it seemed likely it was an accident, I decided that you could wait until morning to hear about it." Kate squinted at her bedside clock. "Later in the morning."

"Are you sure?"

"C'mon, M. Don't start looking for conspiracies where there are none. You have to be in office for at least a month before you're allowed to do that." She stifled a yawn. "Of course it was an accident. A stupid mixture of alcohol-impaired judgment and high speeds. When I got the briefing, the victim's families hadn't even been notified yet. So I made a judgment call. As sad and as unfortunate as the news was, I didn't need to interrupt your evening with it. There simply wasn't anything you could do at the moment."

There was a long moment where Emily didn't speak.

Finally she sighed. "And I guess that's your job, right?" There wasn't a single drop of sarcasm in her voice.

"Yep. It is. Now go to sleep. We have a long day ahead of us tomorrow." The clock numbers swam in her vision. "Today."

"Yes, ma'am."

Kate hung up, rolled over, and buried her face in the pillow. *I think I'm going to like the job. But maybe not the hours.*

By noon that day, Kate felt as if she'd already put in an eight-hour day. A breakfast meeting with the senior staff led to separate meetings with each to clarify ongoing and new departmental policies and programs. In the midst of that, Kate's office received 146 requests from various government officials, business leaders, and congressional members, all wanting to speak with the president about a subject of utmost importance.

The trouble was *everything* was of utmost importance. Everybody had a reason, almost all of them good, to want Emily's ear. However, only a handful of those many requests would be granted.

Kate didn't see it as playing bad guy, per se. The twenty-four hours of Emily's day had to be carefully proportioned to get the maximum amount of work done—people seen, policies discussed, information received, information imparted. Plus, there had to be a little Emily time embedded in there as well. All work and no play would dull her razor-sharp mind.

After what seemed a lifetime on the Benton campaign trail, Kate knew better than anyone how to broker Emily's time and therefore her attention. Although, unlike many chiefs of staff before her, Kate would step away from actual policy making, she would, nonetheless, have a front-row seat for all policy meetings—domestic and foreign—tempering Emily's decisions with guidance and advice and, once those decisions or policies were made, charting a course to market those ideas to Congress and the public.

In some ways, it was just another campaign—to stay in office rather than attain it.

By Friday, Kate had settled into a basic pattern of meetings and schedule reviews. Even then, she realized how rare this would likely be—having a discernible pattern from one week to the next. It was as if the world were holding its breath until Emily got comfortably into office before exploding with a new earth-shattering event.

So far, Kate's lunches had all been working ones with Emily, but today, she had the opportunity to eat in the peace and quiet of her own office. It was a nice office, suitably designed for the needs of her position—a conference table that could seat eight, a sitting area for more intimate conversations, and a desk that blended fashion and function nicely. She'd already tested the leather couch and determined that it would make a suitable place for a purloined nap or an overnight stay, if world events made either a necessity.

But instead of world events intruding, it was a local call that interrupted Kate halfway through her salad.

She glared at her insistent cell phone, then succumbed to the need to answer it.

A pleasant voice hit her ear. "So how's the first almost week in office?"

Nick. She smiled, then flushed, surprised by her own reaction. "Pretty good. How's the lobbying business?"

"You know the drill. A lot of schmoozing. Curiosity is opening a lot of doors."

"Curiosity?"

"Sure. The president's ex-husband? Everyone's expecting a bit of gossip. Or at least the inside scoop. We'll see if it's a lot harder to get a second meeting after they've learned a smart divorced man tells no tales."

"You're definitely smart."

"And divorced. Listen, I know you're busy, so I won't keep you long. I was just wondering if, in light of the impending announcement of the oil independence program, I could get a few minutes of her nibs's time next week. Under the guise of ex-family, of course."

Kate hesitated. Lobbyists met with presidents all the time, but for propriety's sake, they didn't meet as lobbyists, per se. Nick had essentially given her the right official reason, but would Emily agree? Kate had never questioned Emily as to the reason behind his invitation to the inaugural ball. Maybe this was a good time to broach the subject. If nothing else, Kate needed to know if Nick was slowly becoming part of the picture again.

"Let me sound her out. Okay?"

"Great."

"I'll call back later after I've had a chance to talk to her about it."

"Thanks." A brief moment passed before he added, "Later, then."

After she hung up, Kate pushed back in her chair. *That was awkward*, she thought.

However, things grew more awkward only a few hours later when Emily called her into the office for an unexpected meeting.

When Kate entered, Emily was standing near the fireplace. A man sat with his back toward the door, and it wasn't until he stood and turned that Kate recognized who he was.

George Richfield, the director of the FBI, held out his hand as she approached. "Ms. Rosen, good to see you again." They'd met at least two times before in social situations. But this time, *social* didn't seem the right word to describe what was unfolding in front of her.

She accepted his handshake, trying not to appear too hesitant. "Director. Likewise. To what honor do we owe your unexpected visit, sir?" Her initial salvo had to be polite, but if she was going to protect her own position within the administration, she knew she had to play the control card immediately. It was a lesson she'd learned as a female carving out a position in a more male-dominated business. "I wasn't aware we had any meetings scheduled with you." Her tone said what she couldn't—*And I should have known.*

He shared a sidelong glance at Emily. "We have a possible issue, and I wanted to brief the president first."

Kate sat down without invitation. In the British monarchy, it would be considered the height of insult to sit prior to the queen taking her own seat. However, Kate did it for no other reason than to remind the FBI director and Emily that there was no royalty present. "Then please . . . sit. Tell me what's going on."

Emily smothered a small grin in response to the deliberate break in protocol. But any sense of veiled amusement vanished when she and Director Richfield sat on the opposite couch in a classic us-versus-you seating position. The director laced his fingers, propped his elbows on his knees, and leaned forward to lessen the harshness of their almost confrontational arrangement.

"No doubt you remember the tragic accident that occurred the night of the inauguration." He managed to rip all sense of emotion from the word *tragic*. "Timothy Colton and Maia Bari were killed in a one-car accident on Rock Creek Parkway."

How could I forget? "Yes, I was the one who decided not to interrupt the president's evening with the unfortunate details."

Emily shifted slightly. "I called Kate later that evening—actually in the wee hours of the morning—complaining about her decision, but what I should have done instead was thank her." She turned to Kate. "You were right, as always. Had you told me, it would have put an unnecessary damper on the evening. And like you said, there was nothing I could do until morning, anyway."

Kate acknowledged Emily's belated thanks with a quick nod and turned her attention back to the director. "So what seems to be the problem? The FBI isn't usually called in for traffic accidents."

"True. But in light of Ms. Bari's connection to the president and Mr. Colton's connection to Governor Talbot, the Park Police requested our assistance when they uncovered some signs of . . . tampering."

"Tampering? As in evidence tampering?"

Richfield shook his head. "No, as in evidence that the car had been tampered with prior to the accident."

"Are you saying this wasn't an accident?" Emily asked.

Something's all wrong about this, Kate thought. Here was the director of the FBI, involving himself in a case. Wouldn't he leave that up to someone with real investigative experience? Even given the high profile of the people involved?

Kate reached down deep into her reservoir of courage to find the right nonconfrontational tack to take. "Sir, before we go on, may I ask why you're handling this instead of a field agent?"

He managed a tight grin. "It's not a question I haven't asked myself. But considering the potentially sensitive nature of the situation, I decided to break procedure." Richfield continued as if his vague response were a real answer. "I was told that you received news of the wreck from one of the Secret Service agents working the command post at the ball, correct?"

Kate hesitated, then finally decided to play it his way. "Yes. An Agent Brown found me in the crowd. Evidently the command post had been monitoring all the various law enforcement frequencies, and someone recognized Maia's name as being associated with the campaign staff. After he briefed me, I made the decision to hold off informing the president until that next morning after the ball."

"I understand you weren't alone when you were briefed. Correct?"

Kate hadn't spent a huge amount of time in the courtroom but enough so that she knew how to maintain her facial expression and control her body language. "No, as it happens, I was talking with Nicholas Beaudry when the agent approached—" she glanced at Emily—"in the company of Chip McWilliamson, who was also aware of the situation. I believe he'd been instrumental in locating me in the middle of the crowd. He remained there and overheard the resulting conversation."

"McWilliamson." The slightest hint of distaste crossed the director's face. "That's right. The . . . blogger." He said the word with the same enthusiasm as one might say, "The mosquito."

The man regrouped and continued. "So in addition to Mr. McWilliamson, Mr. Beaudry also overheard the news of the accident and what few details you had at the moment."

"Correct."

"And he said nothing?"

"Who? Nick? No. I'm sure he knew it wasn't appropriate to enter into the conversation."

The director crossed his arms as if having uncovered a Scooby-Doo–size clue. "But he didn't step away and give you any privacy."

"No, but then again, I didn't find that odd. It was obvious that it wasn't a security matter where he might need a specific clearance. If it had been, the agent would have never tried to conduct a secure brief in the middle of a ballroom full of partygoers. Anyone could have overheard."

"So when Mr. Beaudry overheard the discussion, he didn't say anything about knowing Timothy Colton?"

"Not at that time. Once the agent stepped away, he brought the subject up. It wasn't like it was a secret. He knew I was aware of the hierarchy of Talbot's staff, including his own former position in that structure. With that in mind, it didn't take any great leaps in logic to presume he knew Colton, probably fairly well. They had to have worked together at some point on the campaign. As I recall, we exchanged sympathies since we'd both lost a—" she stumbled over the word—"colleague. He knew who Maia was and that I'd worked with her." Kate hesitated, then added, "She is—was the sort of woman that men always noticed."

"Indeed. She was quite a beautiful woman." The director nodded. "So, during your conversation with Mr. Beaudry, did he mention any animosity he might have had against Colton?"

Kate shifted, signaling an end to her willingness to be grilled. "Director, you're asking some very pointed questions that lead me to believe you have some suspicions about Mr. Beaudry's involvement in this terrible situation. Certainly you're not accusing him of having anything to do with the accident? Or tampering with the vehicle?"

Richfield shifted on the couch, sitting up a bit straighter. "We're making no accusations. It's simply come to our attention that Mr. Beaudry and Mr. Colton were not friendly coworkers—more like bitter adversaries, according to Governor Talbot."

Now things were starting to make more sense. If Talbot

had weighed in on the situation, no doubt he'd worked hard to cast Nick in the worst possible light. Their opponent had been none too thrilled to learn his plan to use Emily's ex-husband against her had backfired.

Kate folded her hands in her lap. "Mr. Beaudry said nothing to me to substantiate that." She worked very hard to keep *I already knew it was fact* from showing in her expression.

Richfield dug a little deeper. "So he had never mentioned to you that on the day he resigned from Governor Talbot's staff, he was attacked?"

Although this was no court of law and she'd taken no oath, Kate realized the truth was the only avenue she could follow at the moment. "Actually I knew about that incident shortly after it occurred."

Emily quirked an eyebrow. "You talked that often with him?"

The single look Kate shot her friend carried at least three messages—the most important of which was *You don't want me to go into this, not with the FBI or anyone else for that matter.*

She turned back to Richfield. "I spoke with him a few times, mostly coordinating issues common to both campaigns." She chose her words carefully. "I believe toward the end of the campaign, he'd gotten disillusioned with Governor Talbot, and that was why he called me—to inform me that he was resigning from his position."

"He didn't offer to sell or otherwise give you any secrets about the Talbot campaign?"

Kate couldn't help one gibe. "I didn't realize you also sat on the Federal Election Commission as well." She dismissed the supposed absurdity of her own statement with a wave of her hand. "No, he didn't. In any case, I doubt there was anything he could tell us that we didn't already know." She raised a finger. "Wait. I take that back. I remember that in the conversation we had about his resignation, he mentioned in passing that Talbot was planning to have a press conference the next day. However, I guess that shows you how out of the loop he truly was. As I recall, Talbot had no press conference that next day."

"Interesting. And you remember this . . . why?"

"Because, besides being proactive, part of my job was reactive, and I always monitored the actions of the other side." Kate sighed. "Director, I'm finding your questions to be . . . rather disturbing. Normally I would ask if I needed to have a lawyer present." She glanced at Emily. "But she's here already. So I'll continue to answer your questions. For now."

Richfield caught himself just short of issuing a harrumph. "I'm sorry, Ms. Rosen. I'm just trying to get the background on Beaudry. I only have a few more questions." He pressed on without pausing. "The night of the inauguration, had you made arrangements to meet Beaudry at the ball?"

Kate didn't have to look at Emily to know that she had turned her face away from the conversation, fearing her expressions might be telling.

"Absolutely not. I didn't even know he'd been invited. It seems *someone* from the White House made sure he was sent a ticket."

After a moment of silence, Emily raised her hand lazily in the air. "That would be me." She turned to face them and offered a shrug with her explanation. "What can I say? It seemed like a decent gesture. Goodwill and all that." She managed a small crooked smile. "Me burying the hatchet somewhere other than his skull."

The director spared Emily a quick glance as if mandated by law to pay attention to anyone talking about hatchets and skulls. He turned back to Kate. "Do you recall what time you first saw Mr. Beaudry at the ball?"

Although she'd already mentally taken the pieces and assembled them into an uncomfortable conclusion, Kate decided to voice her observation. "Before I answer that, let me ask you a question. Are you accusing the president's former husband of having something to do with the accident?"

He stiffened. "I'm merely trying to establish a timeline to aid in the investigation." He pressed on without even taking a breath. "When did you first see him that night?"

Kate knew who Nick had been in the past and who he'd become in the intervening years. She couldn't imagine either version of Nick being involved in something like this, not even during his worst drinking days. As her father always said, "Booze doesn't turn a good man into a mean drunk. It simply removes all the filters and self-controls he uses every day to control his temper and his tongue." Even fully intoxicated, Nick Beaudry had never been a mean drunk.

She faced the director. "I'm unsure of the exact time—I wasn't wearing a watch. But the first time we spoke was during Emily's first dance with Richard. I'm sure there are media files that will give you the exact time frame of the dance."

"No point prior to that?"

"No. That was the first time I saw him that night."

"And his demeanor at that time?"

"What do you mean?"

"Was he excited? relieved? distracted? Had he had anything to drink? Was he intoxicated?"

The last question got under Kate's skin, and she couldn't stop herself from firing back. "Next you'll ask me if I noticed the telltale sign of oil stains on his hands or some vital piece of a braking system in the pocket of his tuxedo."

The director shot Emily a glance as if the two of them were sharing some great revelation.

Kate closed her eyes for a moment, struggling to regain her composure, then stood, hoping it would get the message across that her patience had been stretched to its end. "Nick Beaudry was pleasant and even-keeled that evening, even when he encountered a less than polite member of our staff who wanted to throw him bodily out of the hotel. And he was stone-cold sober when I spoke to him and remained sober all night."

"For as long as you were there," the director corrected.

"True. And long after, I suspect. I don't know if you've spoken with him, but he appears to be very serious about and very dedicated to maintaining his sobriety." She met the director eye to eye. "Are there any other questions? I still have many meetings on my docket today." Her use of the legalistic term was deliberate.

"No, ma'am." Richfield stood as well. "I'm sorry to have had to ask them at all. But this way, I can spare you any other inquiries from agents assigned to investigate this."

"Then let me state that I sincerely doubt Nick Beaudry had anything to do with the deaths of Timothy and Maia."

He didn't offer his hand, and Kate wasn't sure she'd have accepted it had he made the gesture.

"I'm sure you're correct. Thank you so much." He turned

to Emily. "Madam President? Thank you for your valuable time." With a nod of salutation, he headed for the door.

Kate waited until the panel closed behind him before speaking. She pivoted sharply and glared at Emily. "What in the world has gotten into you?"

"Into me?" Emily wrapped herself in an air of innocence that smelled dank. "I should be asking you that question." A look of virtue transformed effortlessly to sadness on her face. "You and Nick? My ex-husband?"

Kate crossed over to the fireplace, hoping the dancing flames might chase away the sudden chill that settled on her. "Get real, Emily. There is no Nick and me. You're the one who sent him a ticket. Goodwill gesture? Like I believe that." She turned away from the fire. "Chip had it right. All you wanted was a chance to twist the knife a little in public. You dragged him there just to remind him of what he lost, to tell him, 'You could have been up here as First Gentleman if you hadn't been such a louse.'"

"That's not the way I meant it."

To anyone else, Emily's look appeared to be one of genuine confusion, but Kate saw something far less appealing in the shadows behind her eyes.

Emily continued, her words sounding theatrical at best. "I thought you believed in forgiveness. In letting bygones be bygones."

"I do. But the trouble is—I know you don't. Can the act, M. I know exactly what sort of trick you're trying to pull. And while we're at it, why did you give me no warning that the director of the FBI wanted to grill me?"

Emily dropped all pretense of confused innocence. "Trust

me." She stood, walked over to her desk, and perched on the corner of it. "I was doing you a favor."

"A favor . . ."

"Sure. One of George's minions could have called on you, raised a stink, asked you to make a formal statement. Formal statements mean public records. But instead, you simply told him the facts in an informal setting."

"The Oval Office is *not* an informal setting."

"More so than his office. Still, it's over. He'll pass the data along to a subordinate and that'll be that. He's not going to bother you again because he got everything he needed from your unprepared, off-the-cuff answers."

"And what is he going to do with my answers? Pursue Nick as a possible suspect in the deaths of two people?" Kate paused and raised one finger to make a point. "Wait, if it's sabotage, then it'd be considered premeditated murder." Indignation began to bubble up inside of her. "C'mon, Emily, you know he's not capable of that."

Emily crossed her arms, and a look of belligerence filled her face and her stance. "That's what we thought about Charles Talbot. When you started rooting around in his past, I bet you expected to find a few relatively harmless skeletons in his closet—not a dead girlfriend."

Kate said nothing. The rules of politics were similar to those of fight club—never talk about fight club or dirty politics. If you're overheard, you have to explain yourself. And neither she nor Emily wanted anyone wondering why they knew so much dirt about Charles Talbot but had never released their findings to the public.

If any media type caught wind of the stalemate between the erstwhile candidates, two sets of dirty secrets might still be pinned to the clothesline for everyone to see. And something told her that whatever Maia and Colton were talking about in that car, it wasn't likely to be good for Emily. But Emily didn't seem upset.

"Don't worry," Emily said, almost bragging. "I have everything covered. . . ."

Now Kate was really worried.

KATE WAITED UNTIL SHE GOT HOME before she used her cell phone to call Lee Devlin. Lee's company, District Discreet, was Kate's go-to squad for quiet investigations and unobtrusive background checks. Lee and her partner, Sierra Dudicroft, had been instrumental in helping Kate uncover Charles Talbot's unsavory past as well Emily's. They had also asked no questions when Kate asked them to bury both sets of the secrets deep.

If anyone could ferret out information about the relationship between Timothy Colton and Maia Bari, it would be Lee.

When the investigator answered the phone, laughter tipped her voice, obviously thanks to caller ID. "As I live and breathe. Do I call you Chief Rosen or Madam Secretary or what?"

"Chief will do. Emily has already claimed 'Her Highness.'"

"What can I do for you, Chief Assistant to the Honorable Her Highness?"

"The usual skulduggery. I need to put you on retainer."

"Don't you have watchdogs from the Secret Service, FBI, CIA, Homeland Security, all at your beck and call now that you're an honest-to-goodness White House insider?"

"Sure. I control all the men in black now, too, especially the ones with the helicopters and memory-flashy thingies." After they shared a laugh, Kate added, "This is more of a personal matter, Lee."

The words *personal matter* weren't a code phrase, per se, but the investigator knew that the time for jokes had vanished. Her voice changed, reflecting a much more serious attitude. "What can I do for you, Kate?" she asked quietly.

"First, there's the matter of a retainer for legal purposes."

"Hang on." After a few seconds of clicking keys on a keyboard, Lee returned. "Your retainer of $1,000 has been duly charged to your credit card on file and noted in our ledger. Client confidentiality is now evoked."

"Good. I take it you heard about the accident that happened on the night of the inaugural balls? Maia Bari and Timothy Colton?"

Lee whistled softly. "Who hasn't? Until the crash, Washington had no idea they had an updated version of Carville and Matalin—love across the party lines. How sweet. Or in this case, how tragic."

"Was it love?"

"You tell me. That's the assumption the press is making. They were together in a car. That's enough to fuel general speculation. I take it you weren't convinced?"

"We'll get to that. Speaking of press speculation, what have you heard beyond the official reports?"

"Why ask me? I thought you had your own Deep Throat for these matters."

Kate did. Through luck, perseverance, and more luck, she'd cultivated the cooperation of the pinnacle of Washington insiders, Carmen del Rio, a woman who knew everything about everybody and kept most of it to herself. No gossip went uncollected, no news tip unfiled. Given two points, Carmen could not only draw a line, but a conclusion with 99.99 percent accuracy. Washingtonians of all profile levels from mildly important to holders of the highest offices kept Carmen happy and informed for fear of what she might do if she became less than enthralled with them. Such was the height of her real power that she seldom had to act.

Dubbed the "godmother of gossip" by one brave and probably now headless soul, Carmen usually held court every afternoon in the tearoom at the Willard Hotel, but a bad cold had interrupted that tradition for several weeks. Kate knew that even her singular nonreciprocal relationship with Carmen couldn't overcome the woman's crankier demeanor when sick.

"My usual source is unavailable," Kate responded.

"Yeah. Head cold. I heard. Could be the death of an old bat like her."

"I have no idea what you're talking about," Kate lied. Talking about Carmen also fell under general fight club rules. "Back to the question at hand."

"Yes. Colton and Bari. Unlikely duo. I don't know of anyone who knew of the pairing before the accident. No gossip. No innuendos. Plenty after the fact, though."

"Can you wade past the retrospective rumors and get me some hard facts about their precrash relationship?"

"Absolutely."

Kate hesitated for a moment before she continued. She

wanted to believe with her whole heart that Nick had nothing to do with the wreck, despite George Richfield's leading questions. Her logical side whispered that the best way to be assured of Nick's innocence was to prove it with fact.

Faith and fact, she told herself. *It doesn't have to be one or the other. They can work together.*

She took a deep breath and continued. "And there's a part two that requires double-secret confidentiality." It was a phrase that Lee had coined during a more lighthearted time. Kate had requested an investigation into a fraternity house prank gone awry involving the actions of a senator's son at a kegger, and the *Animal House* references continued not only for the duration of the investigation, but long after.

"Double-secret confidentiality it is. What, or should I ask, who?"

"Nick Beaudry."

"Him again?" Lee had investigated Nick when he first reappeared in their lives after being lured to work for Charles Talbot. At that time, Kate had no idea what his agenda might be or how much damage he could cause Emily's campaign. As her ex-husband, he could have either gone for the jugular for a quick slaughter or been content to watch her slowly bleed to death. To their surprise and relief, he had done neither.

"The FBI thinks Nick might—and let me stress *might*—be a player in the curious but unfortunate saga of Colton and Bari. Can you look into his role in the Talbot campaign, specifically with respect to anything he might have had to do with Timothy Colton?"

"Sure. But what about the femme fatale? If you ask me, this Bari chick seems the more likely candidate to have gotten her hooks into him. Good-looking guy, gorgeous woman . . . you know the chances."

Kate figured it was wise to cover all her bases. "Okay, her too. But what I really want to know is if there are any whispers of discord between Colton and Beaudry, especially when both of them worked for Talbot. Were they buddies? campaign comrades? bitter enemies?"

"My money's on all three. But I'll get you everything I can find. Anything else?"

"I suspect that's enough to keep you busy. But you might see if you can find out if any of the three had their fingers in political pies I should know about."

"Will do. I'll contact you when my report is ready."

"Thanks."

Once she hung up, Kate tried to distract herself by checking her personal e-mail while eating dinner. Between her long workdays and the commute home in traffic, she'd been toying with the idea of moving closer into town. She glanced down at Buster, who barely controlled himself as he waited for a treat. The house rule was if he managed to mind his manners for the entire meal, he always got a doggy treat.

"Not yet, buddy."

Living closer to the White House would mean a Georgetown loft or maybe a high-rise apartment in Crystal City. Neither would be convenient for a dog owner. Right now Buster had a nicely landscaped yard that he could access at will thanks to the doggy door. He chose that moment to prove the worthiness of their location by clambering to his feet and heading outdoors for a brief respite.

Kate glanced around her house—little more than a bungalow. Now that she had more of a nine-to-five job—more like 5 a.m. to 9 p.m.—maybe it was time to hire someone to remodel her house. Spruce it up. Go through all those ideas she'd collected from reading too many decorating magazines and watching handyman shows on the road. Maybe it was time to make this place a home so that when she got off work, she came home to comfort and beauty.

Buster rocketed in through the door and skidded into the pantry as if to remind Kate where she kept the dog treats.

"Comfort, beauty, and Buster," she said as she reached in and retrieved a dog cookie. "What more can a girl ask for?"

Love?

★ ★ ★ ★ ★

> "Perhaps the most interesting aspect of Ms. Benton's first week in office is the manner in which she swung for the fences on the domestic forefront, all but disavowing any similarities between the former administration and her own. But with respect to foreign affairs, she was content to walk to first, defining no grand lines of demarcation between her foreign policies and President Cooper's."

Emily snorted and tossed the newspaper toward Kate. "One of these days, Ferlander is actually going to write an article without sports metaphors. Then all three of his readers are going to be lost."

Dozier Marsh, Emily's chief political adviser, waited until his breakfast was served before speaking. "Metaphors aside," he said, gesturing with his fork, "he's accurate with his assessment."

"Et tu, Brute?"

Kate spoke up. "You did exactly what you said you'd do while campaigning: placed your priority on domestic issues—" she paused to thank the waiter who served her fruit, oatmeal, and toast, all at her request—"putting your own house in better order before making new foreign policy changes."

Emily leveled her with a stern gaze. "You've never gone to a real baseball game, have you?"

"No."

Dozier laughed. "I can tell. You didn't understand the nuances of the metaphors."

Kate contemplated her meal and then closed her eyes for a quick grace. When she opened her eyes, she realized the reactions of those around her to her actions were varied—from those who followed her lead and said their own silent grace to those who showed a mild amount of distaste either for her quiet faith or her lack of baseball knowledge.

It was hard to tell.

Kate straightened in her chair, aware that every adviser at the table was watching her, albeit politely. When they were colleagues of sorts, all working toward the common goal of Emily's election, there had been a sense of camaraderie. But now, in a more official setting, formality had replaced familiarity, which meant she had to be more circumspect about her role in the administration. That included not hiding her faith and knowing how to admit ignorance of a subject.

"I know that swinging for the fences means hitting a home run, and after four balls, you walk to first base. I believe that's common in every form of the game from Little League to the majors."

"I forgot you didn't grow up living and breathing baseball." Emily leaned back in her chair and pushed slightly away from the table, her usual signal that a story was about to begin. She didn't like distractions when she got wound up to tell some bit of Benton family lore. The newer of the advisers politely stopped eating in order to savor the story. Those who had sat with Emily for meals on the campaign trail or when she was governor kept eating while they listened. They'd heard most of the old stories before, and they knew their time for a meal might get rare to the point of vanishing if they didn't eat up now.

Emily addressed the table with only a bit less enthusiasm than a revival preacher. "My dad loved baseball. We had diamond box seats at RFK and he took me to every home game for the Senators, even when I was in diapers. Dozier, I think you came a few times too, right?"

Dozier was still attacking his breakfast with gusto. "A couple. But I'm more of a football fan. You know . . ." He waved a piece of bacon. "Go, Redskins."

Emily continued with her reminiscing. "I think Dad actually went into mourning the day they announced the Senators were leaving town. He refused to take me to that last game because he knew the fans would likely get unruly. I was only seven at the time and I didn't understand. I do however remember being so very mad at him for not taking me. But sure enough, the game turned into one big, ugly scene. The fans were so mad and got so wild that they stormed the diamond, tore out the bases, ripped up the sod, and caused the game to be forfeited to the Yankees. The *Yankees*," she repeated. Everyone knew that fact added an additional level of insult to injury.

Kate threw caution to the wind. "So that makes you an expert on baseball terminology?" She dug into her bowl of oatmeal, not waiting for an answer or permission to eat.

Emily sighed with dramatic exasperation. "'Swinging for the fences' doesn't automatically mean you'll hit a home run. It means you're putting everything you have in that one big swing, and if you connect, you'll knock it into the outfield bleachers. But if you miss, your big grandstanding effort will be nothing more than a very big, very public failure. Everyone can see that you gave it all you got and you failed. Miserably."

Kate held her spoon in midair. "I stand corrected. But at least the article falls short of saying, 'A swing and a *miss*.'"

There was a moment of silence around the table, as if everyone was looking to their fearless leader to determine if the pun was worthy of her laughter. If so, then they would feel free to join in. Kate understood the sense of deference but didn't feel compelled to echo it. Emily was their president—not their queen.

She grinned at her own humor, whether anyone else did or not, and jammed her spoon back into the oatmeal.

Emily locked eyes with hers for a moment; then her face folded into a smile as she used her spoon to tap out a light three-beat rhythm on the table before clinking it against her water glass. "Rim shot."

The participants at the table dissolved into laughter. The waitstaff discretely tucked away in the corners of the room changed their postures every so slightly, obviously relieved to learn that their new president had a sense of humor. Kate joined in with the laughter, glad to see her old friend emerge from beneath the trappings of the mostly somber office.

One of Kate's duties as chief of staff would be to help the president find those occasional moments of mirth and give her a brief respite from the burden she would be carrying for the next four and perhaps eight years.

After the laughter died down, Emily took a swig of her coffee. "Oh, that reminds me, short of a worldwide disaster, I want to be able to throw out the first pitch for the Nationals." She turned to Dozier and added in a conspiratorial stage whisper, "Cooper missed doing it last year and caught flak about it from the public." She turned to everyone else at the table and even managed to address the near-invisible staff. "I realize that for most presidents, it's good PR to do the ceremonial pitch, but for me? Honestly?" She grinned. "I've dreamed about it for years. And I'm a good pitcher, aren't I, K?"

Kate nodded solemnly. "I've watched her bull's-eye a womp rat in her T-16 back home."

Dozier looked puzzled, but most of the other advisers recognized the *Star Wars* reference and smiled.

Emily's expression went from a polite grin to a smile that filled her eyes as well. Kate considered this the "true" Emily—smart, responsible, and lighthearted when the occasion called for it.

With an air of amused deference, Kate dutifully wrote in her notes. "Barring worldwide disaster, throw out first ball," she repeated. She turned to Francesca Reardon, their foreign affairs adviser. "The world disaster bit is on your shoulders."

The older woman reached up and lowered her glasses, peering over the top of them. *"Me?"*

None of their morning meetings so far had held quite this

light of a tone, a sense of bantering between the advisers. Kate wasn't sure if it was a sign that everyone had gotten more comfortable in their positions after several weeks or what.

Or what occurred shortly into their meeting.

Emily leaned back in her chair, this time pushing away from the remains of her breakfast. "It's time for us to present O:EI to the public. And trust me, not only will I be swinging for the upper deck, but the ball's going to land there."

Operation: Energy Independence was Emily's three-pronged plan to help the U.S. wean itself from its dependence on foreign oil. The first directive, nicknamed Operation: Resource, was to free up federal lands for oil and coal exploration in order to replace foreign oil with sources located within the U.S. To mitigate the possible environmental costs, the plan would require carbon offsets and also offer long-term incentives to U.S. companies to replace their fossil fuel use with that of energy derived from renewable sources such as wind, solar, geothermal, hydrokinetic, and other long-term strategies not yet invented.

The second directive, Operation: Retool, included tax incentives and rewards for those companies and manufacturers who increased the energy efficiency of their production by utilizing these new power sources as well as improving the efficiency or consumption rates of their end products.

Operation: Research, the third directive, would increase research funding and encourage development and eventual production of hydrogen fuel cell technology. If the fuel cell could eventually replace the combustion engine, the U.S. demand for oil would plummet and those federal lands could be returned to their protected state.

In order to pay for all this, Emily's proposed bill would repeal the billion-dollar tax breaks oil and gas companies had been receiving for years.

"No more tax loopholes," she declared. "We give the oil companies access to federal lands, but we don't pay them for the privilege. Simultaneously, we retool our existing technologies, making them more efficient, and we fund serious research into a clean, renewable alternative."

"It's about time," Dozier drawled. "I remember the old days when I used to fill up my Lincoln for *less* than a Lincoln. Now five bucks will get you barely enough gas to reach the next station down the block." Before anyone could comment, he raised his hands in mock defeat. "I know; I know. Get a car with better fuel efficiency." He picked up his coffee cup and growled, "Some cramped import. I remember when 'Made in Japan' wasn't considered a good thing at all. Now you have to go to Goodwill to buy something made in America."

Rather than let his nostalgia and complaints start a digression and distract the conversation, Emily stepped in. "In order to get grassroots support for Operation: EI, we should present this to the people first. The energy companies can be brought in later. We need a groundswell of support to bring this off."

"How?" The question was echoed by several of her advisers.

"Just like I did when I campaigned. Commercials. Blogs. YouTube. We use twenty-first-century tools to promote our twenty-first-century programs."

Kate sat back and watched Emily outline her plan. One of Emily's great strengths was her ability to see and understand not only the big picture, but the various components that comprised the whole. She was seldom surprised by an outcome or caught unaware by an element she'd missed in planning stages. Yet, despite her abilities, she had no problem relinquishing control of those components and putting their construction or planning in the hands of her handpicked advisers.

"Choose people to work for you who are smarter than you," Emily always said, "but make sure you understand at least 75 percent of what they're saying. Any less than that and they'll start to think they're superior to you and the lines of authority will get blurred."

Kate looked around at the others, already engaged in deep discussion, and hid her smile as she sent up a quick prayer.

We're going to do some great things together. . . .

Kate waited until Emily was between meetings before stepping into her office. Most people thought Emily, like the presidents before her, spent all her time in the Oval Office. In reality, Emily, as well as her predecessors, spent as much if not more time in the president's private study. It was a small room, less than half the size of Kate's office, decked out with pictures from Emily's personal collection, comfortable furniture, and a desk that was far less a national treasure and much more a functioning piece of furniture.

The most striking thing about the office was the pair of tall windows with curtains that stretched up to the ceiling, effectively dwarfing the room. Emily had good-naturedly complained that she had the smallest office in the West Wing until Kate pointed out that she was the only person with two offices and that oval-shaped one was pretty big and pretty nice.

Emily was hunched over her keyboard when Kate tapped on the doorframe.

"Got a minute?"

She looked up, smiled, and pushed back from the desk. "One or two. Whatcha need? I have my own plane. Helicopter. Army. Anything you need."

"The oil lobby."

"Aha. My new best friends. At a distance, of course."

"How far of a distance?"

Her sunny disposition darkened a little. "Who's asking?"

"Nick."

Emily made a face. "I'd rather not. I try to make it a point to not mix business and family."

Kate gaped at her. The Benton family had ironclad ties into all sorts of areas within the White House and Benton administration. "I can't believe you're saying that with a straight face."

Emily pursed her lips for a moment in thought. "Then try this: I try to not mix business and ex-family."

"That I understand. So you're not inclined to meet with him?"

"Not inclined. As in, declined."

"Okay, I'll tell him."

Emily continued without any prompting from Kate. "I may have helped him by recommending him, but it doesn't entitle him to any other favors."

"Understood." Kate started to walk out the door, but Emily continued.

"I mean, that's enough generosity on my part, right?"

"Sure."

"Good."

As Kate eased out the door, she took one more look at Emily, now studiously working on her computer.

The phrase "The lady doth protest too much" lingered in her mind as she headed back to her own office. There wasn't a single drop of coyness in Emily Benton's body, so where did this sudden insecurity come from?

Exactly how much of a debt did Emily owe Nick Beaudry?

SEVERAL DAYS LATER, Kate had just finished a string of three back-to-back meetings and seated herself at her desk when her cell phone rang. Facing a stack of reports to review, she debated letting the call go to voice mail until she read the caller ID: *District Discreet*.

She answered. "Lee?"

"I have that report you requested, Ms. Rosen."

The formality of Lee's voice set off a few alarms. Kate had expected to get the results by e-mail. Why the phone call?

The investigator continued. "Perhaps we can meet and I can give it to you in person."

In person? Lee never requested in-person meetings unless something was wrong or the material so sensitive that they didn't trust it to be transmitted over the phone or Internet. Kate shivered at the memory of the last bombshell Lee had delivered in person, early in the campaign. Whatever the investigation had turned up concerning Timothy Colton and Maia Bari, it had to be bad.

"The usual place?" she asked.

The last time they'd met in the parking deck at Lee's office building, then drove to Pentagon City mall—just two anonymous women in a sea of shoppers. But perhaps now, thanks to Kate's higher profile position, she'd lost some of her anonymity.

"Not this time. When are you headed home tonight?"

Kate consulted her schedule and added the requisite two hours for the unexpected tasks that seemed to pop up every evening—par for the course when working at the White House. "Nine thirty, if I'm lucky."

"You took the Metro today, right?"

Kate didn't want to know how or why Lee knew this particular piece of information. Depending on her schedule, she sometimes came into town on the train and other times used a car service. But Lee wanted her to take the Metro now, it was clear. Less chance of an audience . . . or a tail.

"Can we meet on the platform at the Vienna Metro station?"

The Vienna station was only one stop beyond the Dunn Loring station, which Kate used. Once they finished their clandestine meeting, she could simply hop on the Metrorail and head back to her station, where her car was parked.

"Sure. It'll take about a half hour for me to get there. The train usually leaves McPherson at a quarter till ten."

"Okay, then we'll meet around 10:15. When you arrive, don't say anything when you see me, but just do what I do. Text me when you leave."

Kate didn't know whether to be amused or alarmed by Lee's James Bond imitation. The woman didn't usually skew to the dramatic. She preferred more cloak than dagger. Kate agreed to the meeting and hung up. But her sense of danger intensified all out of proportion to what she'd asked Lee to look into.

At nine o'clock, after a particularly long and hard day, Kate managed to put out all the fires that always cropped up after hours. The latest had been some concern over reports detailing the first hour of trading in the Tokyo stock market. Once Emily was fully briefed and the situation seemed to have calmed down in Japan, Kate gathered her things from her office, sent Lee a text message, exited the White House, and headed to the McPherson Square station.

The one advantage of working late was that the 9:45 train held far fewer folks than it did at rush hour. The car she chose was only half-full and remained so at each stop with roughly the same number of people entering as exiting.

Once the train crossed under the Potomac, it emerged aboveground into the cold, dark night, giving Kate a view of shadowy trees and cars' headlights rushing alongside the tracks. From this point on, the number of riders dropped dramatically after each stop. Most were like her—commuters headed home after a late night at the office. She fought the automatic urge to rise from her seat when she reached her normal stop and instead stayed in place to continue on to the Vienna station, the last stop on the Orange line—or the first, depending on one's perspective or direction.

When she stepped out of the train car onto the exposed platform, a frigid wind hit her and continued to blast her as she stood there, looking for Lee. The threat of snow had faded from the forecast, but someone had forgotten to tell the wind that. It still contained the cold bite of potential snowfall.

With as much nonchalance as she could muster, she glanced down the length of the platform, spotting a woman sitting on one of the concrete benches, reading a newspaper. The wind caught the pages every now and then, and one gust moved the paper long enough for Kate to recognize Lee.

A moment later, Lee stood, folded her paper, and walked into the train that had just disgorged its passengers. Kate followed, choosing the second entrance to the train car so as not to follow totally in the investigator's footsteps.

Thanks to the sparse number of riders, no one else joined them in their railcar. Once home for the evening, few commuters headed back toward the District again. Kate and Lee sat down at opposite ends of the car, still feigning no interest in the other. It wasn't until the train started moving that Lee stood, walked down the aisle, and sat by Kate.

"Two strangers meet on a train . . . ," Lee mocked.

Kate slid over. "Whatever you have, it must be bad," she said as Lee got settled in the seat next to her.

"More like . . . sensitive. And you know my motto: 'Don't take chances you don't have to.'"

"I thought it was 'The walls have ears.'"

"That too." Lee took a file from the oversize bag slung across her shoulder and pulled out the top page.

"Here's the usual background stuff on Colton and Bari. You already knew her exotic background was nothing but a sham. But I dug a little deeper, mostly into her last days, since we'd looked into her earlier years already. I found some bombshells. On the other hand, it was harder to find early dirt on Colton."

"The information was hidden?"

"No. There just wasn't anything interesting to speak of.

Up till a couple of years ago, his life was pretty much a plain story—bright guy, good family, solid education, good work ethic."

"So . . . on the surface, he doesn't sound like someone who would order an attack on someone he considered a rival for his position."

"Not *before* he started working for Talbot about eight years ago."

"You're saying that working for Talbot changed him somehow?"

"I don't know. But if I had to guess, I'd say he didn't change as much because of his association with Talbot. Instead, his finances changed." She tapped a sheet of paper that looked like the first page of a credit report. "Six years ago, he inherited a considerable chunk of property and money—roughly equivalent to the state of Rhode Island in size and assets. Once he became stinkin' rich, he kicked his childhood sweetheart fiancée to the curb and jumped right into the fast lane. Fast cars, fast money, and the fast women to help him enjoy his wealth."

Kate had seen both sides of people coming into sudden wealth: the good stewards who used it to make life better not just for themselves but for others, and those people who allowed money to derail their better nature. "Maybe he thought Talbot was his ticket to power."

"Possibly. But I'd say that with the size of his wealth, he could manage a fair amount of power on his own."

"It takes more than money to do that on any lasting level." Although Kate had grown up in a decidedly middle-class family, her association with Emily and her old-money family and friends had taught Kate a lot about the role of wealth in the acquisition and control of power. She knew that—for better or for worse—the easiest way for a person without a moneyed background to suddenly attain the privilege, the respect, and—dare she say it?—the power that came with old money was to marry into it. She was surprised to find him in Maia's company, rather than hitting up the eligible political heiresses in town. But she could certainly see Maia looking for an opportunity to marry money.

"Maybe that's why Maia became interested in him," she pondered aloud. "Achieving a fortune had to be high on her list of life goals. The next best thing for a person like her to having money would be to marry it. But what did she bring into the equation that interested Colton, besides her obvious charms? I guess the question is: would she rely on her looks alone or would she try to sweeten the deal by—let's say—selling some sensitive information concerning Emily's campaign to her opponent before the election? Or worse, by enabling him to bring her down after it?"

"Hard to say. One thing I can tell you: she was up to something. She made all kinds of contacts the last few weeks. I'm not sure what she was trying to pull, but I know it was big. But to find out what she was up to, I'm going to have to dig deeper. I'm not sure what I'm going to find when I start turning over rocks. Meanwhile, I've got motive, opportunity, and means. Motive is easy. Hers? Get rich quick, doing whatever she can. As to opportunity, I've found at least three social situations where she and Colton might—and I stress *might*—have gotten together. But nothing definitive to suggest they were getting together on a professional or personal front. I've also got her placed at the other party's campaign committee, four senatorial offices, and the Speaker of the House's private residence. She's out of work. She might just be dropping off résumés. But it worries me, especially the connection to Talbot through Colton. I've got no pictures of the two of them in an embrace, much less dating, before the election. From what I can find, they didn't get all Carville and Matalin on us until after the election. I think what bound them together might be something designed to bring down Emily's presidency."

Kate glanced around at their unconventional surroundings as a somewhat tired voice from the speaker stated, "Next stop, Dunn Loring." The announcement was promptly followed by the train's decreased speed. This was important. She had to hear it out to the end. Kate wondered if their conversation might take the entire trip back to McPherson Square. If so, it would make for a longer day and shorter night's sleep. If Buster wasn't home, impatiently awaiting her, Kate would consider just going back to her office and crashing on the couch. She'd already stashed an overnight case and several extra sets of clothes there.

She pushed ahead, despite the train's slowdown into the next station. "Okay, so maybe Maia and Colton were up to something. It might be unusual, but not illegal. Anything they can do now would be too little too late to do us any real harm." She tensed, knowing Lee hadn't taken these precautions for their meeting without reason. "So there's got to be another reason why we are playing spy games."

"Because of this." Lee pulled out a second sheet of paper displaying a family tree. "It's his pedigree." She started at his name and traced a path up his lineage to his parents and then followed his mother's branch to her parents. "Colton's maternal grandmother was married twice. Colton's mother was the product of the first marriage. The second marriage resulted in two more children, twin girls—Angela and Diane Kasdan."

Kate breathed in sharply, failing to hide her surprise. Angela Kasdan was the young coed who had been permanently injured, thanks to the deliberate inactions of a callous young college student named Charles Talbot. She'd finally died only a handful of years ago after living nearly thirty years in a coma.

Kate and Lee both fell silent as the train stopped at the platform, the doors slid open, and two couples, obviously traveling together, stepped into the car. But they took seats at the opposite end, which would allow Kate and Lee enough privacy to continue their discussion. However, they waited until the train started moving before resuming their talk in lowered voices.

Lee continued. "When Ms. Kasdan finally passed away, after spending twenty-nine years in her—" the investigator consulted another page—"'persistent vegetative state,' her entire fortune, $50.6 million, went to the only person named in her will: her nephew, Timothy Colton."

"He inherited? I'd have thought the inheritance would've made a lateral move—to her twin sister."

"Me too. So that's why I dug a little deeper. It turns out that she and her sister were on the outs when they both had their wills drawn up. Sibling rivalries to the extreme. Daddy—he of the incredible wealth—had insisted that they have wills drawn up shortly after their twenty-first birthdays. The girls hadn't gotten along for years—despite the supposed closeness of twins. Anyway, Angie chose her half nephew, Timothy Colton, as her sole beneficiary. Of course, at that time, she had nothing to leave behind to speak of, so it was more of a *nyah, nyah, nyah* nose-thumbing gesture to her sister than anything else. Then, when Daddy died five years after Angie was injured, she became a very rich coma patient. They didn't even have to tap her principal to pay for her continued hospitalization."

Kate did some quick calculations. "In 1973, Colton must have been only a baby at the time."

"Less than a year old."

"So when she finally passed six years ago . . ."

"Her still-impressive fortune, which had been invested wisely and compounded monthly, went to him." Lee handed Kate the page marked *Financial Overview*, then leaned back in the hard plastic seat, displaying a sense of triumph. "And strangely enough, six years ago is when he seemed to have made his radical change in personality."

Kate studied the report. "Money can do that to you."

Lee grinned. "Someday, I'd like to have the opportunity to experience that for myself. Firsthand. But I think his recent behavior might be more than that. I wonder if he just found out what happened to his aunt. If so, a little revenge could be on his mind. Against Talbot for killing her. Against Emily for not letting the news leak out."

Kate ignored this. "What about his family? Anyone upset that he got Angela's share?"

"Not that I could find out. The two daughters were the only heirs. Diane, the other twin, got her portion right after their father died, and since then, she's doubled it. She might have disliked that Colton got it, but I seriously doubt she would have killed for more money when she's already rolling in it."

"What else do you have?"

The investigator reached into her oversize bag to produce another folder. "Miss Maia. We already knew she was muddying the waters by trading on her resemblance to her aunt in looks and in name and confusing the heck out of the world. Half the reports said she was twenty-five; the other half, fifty-five. With her timeless sort of looks, she could have been either age. But it's her relationship—if you can call it that—with Colton that snagged my attention. It seems . . . uneven."

"How so?"

Lee produced several more pages of report. "I can't find anything that puts them together before Christmas. I can come up with four different times they've been together since that time, but none of those occasions were what you or I would call a romantic rendezvous." She pulled out four pictures, each capturing Timothy Colton and Maia Bari in deep conversation, but with body language and facial expressions that didn't exactly scream, "We're lovers!"

Lee stabbed the first picture with her forefinger. "She looks like she's been sucking on a lemon and he looks constipated. These are not the attributes of a couple planning to slide between the silky sheets at a romantic weekend on the Eastern shore."

"True."

Laughter echoed from the other end of the car, where the two couples huddled together in conversation. They were demonstrating the very sense of personal closeness that these pictures lacked. The people at the end of the car might be friends, they might be more, but they all shared a sense of comfort that reflected in their voices and body language.

Kate turned one picture over and saw a reference number on the back. "Where did you get these?"

"Interesting story." Lee lowered her voice. "An investigator I know was following Bari around as a possible corespondent in a divorce case. The disgruntled wife thought her hubby was canoodling with our subject. As it turns out, Maia was completely in the clear. She was on assignment from her boss, Marjorie Redding, to help the man pick out some jewelry for his estranged wife. My friend proved that the mystery man Maia was hanging out with was Colton, not the accused husband. Security footage at the jewelry store showed Maia was simply advising the man when he purchased a diamond necklace, bracelet, and matching earrings. The wife was appeased by the report, especially when she received said jewelry, and *poof*! No more divorce proceedings."

Kate studied the picture of Maia and Colton some more. "They just don't look like . . . lovers, do they?"

"No. Then again, she'd be smart enough to not push him. If he got his money six years ago and still is unattached, then he's probably gotten wary of women wanting him for the size of his wallet. A piece of work like her would know how to get under a man's skin, make him think the relationship was entirely his idea. She was probably only in phase two of a multistep process to snare him."

"Lee Devlin, you're a cynic."

"No, I'm a realist. I've seen people like her before. But the pictures, to me at least, seem to disprove that. He's not looking at her like a man contemplating a beautiful woman. In any case, we're talking about two people in a car together—a wealthy young man and a very opportunistic young woman.

There are only two reasons why they'd be together: business or pleasure. Right now, I don't think it was pleasure. If it was pleasure, then I could believe the wreck that killed them was an accident. A cocky young man showing off in his fast car for his girl. But if it was business, then what were they talking about? Or should I say *who* were they talking about? I'm betting it was Emily or Talbot. And I'm betting that, knowing Maia, it wasn't exactly anything that was common knowledge. I bet it was too hot to handle. Especially if somebody killed them over it."

Kate contemplated the scenery beyond the window as it flew by. Lee was saying exactly what Kate couldn't bring herself to say aloud. Thanks to Maia's unofficial position as Emily's chief snoop, the young woman had learned all about Charles Talbot's involvement in Angela Kasdan's death.

Had she decided to leverage it?

"What will you give me to tell you about how Charles Talbot essentially murdered your aunt?"

The questions that Kate needed to find the answers for were what Maia had known, and who would be willing to kill her for it.

"What about the crash itself? Do you have any gut feelings about it in terms of sabotage versus accident?"

Lee shook her head. "The Feds are sitting on all the reports, including the one that addresses the mechanical state of the car prior to the impact. If it were nothing, they wouldn't be holding it so tight. They're also not releasing Colton's autopsy, so we still don't know if he had a high blood alcohol level or evidence of drugs in his system. You're in a far better place to get those reports than I ever will be."

However, Kate knew that undue interest from the White

House into these two deaths might trigger suppositions that Emily wouldn't want openly addressed. Then again, perhaps her office could make their interest appear to be solely in Maia's death.

Lee continued. "If it were up to me, I'd consider looking in a direction no one has really mentioned yet, if for no other reason than to rule it out."

"What direction?"

"Suicide."

The word pricked Kate's ears with all the subtlety of an ice pick. "You've got to be kidding."

"Not really. If there was nothing wrong with his car, then what he was doing was far more than simple recklessness. Losing control on a rain-slicked road and plowing into a bridge or a tree doing sixty in a fifty zone is an accident. Doing over a hundred on a dark but dry, narrow, curving road in the middle of the city is beyond stupidity. Either it's a desperate attempt to escape a follower, or his brakes had been tampered with, or it's suicide."

Kate stared at the picture of Timothy Colton that was clipped to the inside of the file folder. What reason would someone like him have to kill himself? He was handsome, healthy, wealthy, and reasonably successful, despite having worked on the losing side of a presidential bid. But then again, looks and money didn't cure all ills or solve all problems.

If he was being followed, the only question was who would be behind him that could scare him enough to drive like that. Kate didn't like the picture emerging in her imagination.

"So you think he might have killed himself on purpose."

"It's a possibility. It's certainly the answer that you and

yours should be pushing. Anything else is likely to lead them straight to Emily or Talbot."

"Are the police looking into this?"

"No one's talking. They seldom do in higher-profile cases like this. But the idea makes some sense, judging from what else I've found."

Lee pulled out another page, this one a police record. "Let's assume this is suicide. Having great gobs of money can only shield you so much. There's some trouble you just can't buy your way out of. It takes influence. Colton didn't have enough of that to charm, bribe, wheedle, or otherwise get himself out of two DUIs and three narcotics charges. And yet they disappeared quietly, evidently thanks to someone with real power and influence."

"Like Charles Talbot."

"Exactly. And because Governor Talbot pulled Colton's butt out of the fire, Colton would have to owe him big-time and do anything that Talbot needed doing. Maybe that's what preyed on his conscience. Imagine learning that the man to whom you've slavishly dedicated the last four years of your life was responsible for the death of a loved one? The very same loved one who made you into a very rich man. That's heady stuff."

"It could be—except he couldn't have possibly known his aunt. He was only a baby when she was injured. Calling her a loved one may be stretching it too far."

"Ah, but he was an adult when she died. And to many people, family is family. No matter what."

"But what about Maia? Deliberately driving his car into a wall by himself is suicide. Doing it with a passenger beside you is murder."

Lee slipped the pictures back into the file, out of sight but not out of mind. Her voice softened. "You know as well as I do that murder-suicide crimes happen all the time and often for reasons that officials, friends, and even family never quite uncover."

Kate thought about the pictures of Colton and Maia. She saw no evidence of a great love gone awry. In fact, she saw no great emotion at all. For Colton to deliberately take such a drastic step not only to kill himself but to murder Maia, there would have to be a very compelling reason combined with an overwhelming emotion—hate, love, sorrow, humiliation . . .

Or he could have been a desperate man with secrets to hide, pushed into a situation beyond his control that led to his death.

But which?

DURING THE NEXT TWO WEEKS, the Internet rumor mill kept the deaths of Timothy Colton and Maia Bari on page two—and well below the fold. Speculations flew but no real accusations, at least not ones strong enough to keep the story as a continuing front-page headline. Everyone had their theories, but nobody knew anything for sure. But the usual rabble-rousers continued with their paranoid views of the situation, suggesting that the deaths of Colton and Maia were a government cover-up to hide much more serious crimes.

Kate didn't think she was paranoid, but she couldn't shake the suspicion that was possible.

Somewhere deep inside of her, Kate agreed that there had been some sort of cover-up, but not necessarily by the government. The problem was, she wasn't sure whose crimes were being protected. In all honesty, she wasn't sure she wanted to know. Her daily prayers now included a request for God to help her to see and think clearly and to not let the mudflingers of the political world obscure her vision or her mission. The words "Lead me not into temptation" had never meant more to her than now that she worked in the heart and hearth of American democracy.

Meetings crowded her calendar, and what little private life she had dried up. To add to Kate's workload, Emily took her first out-of-the-country trip to Mexico, where she presented her Operation: Energy Independence program and, in a separate discussion, her immigration plans to President Moreno of Mexico. It was no accident that both topics came up in the same trip. They all hoped the latter would help influence the Mexican president to be amenable to the former.

Three days later, Emily and entourage traveled to Canada to speak with Prime Minister Stevens in hopes of creating a North American alliance for the energy program.

But the preparation for two back-to-back international trips had been daunting for a first-time chief of staff. Working closely with the Advance Office as well as the Travel Office, they pulled together a two-day visit to each country, coordinating everything from transportation, accommodations, and food to security logistics and protocol.

An American president didn't just show up.

There were advance teams coordinating every aspect of her trip, covering every eventuality. Even though planning such a trip was a full-time job, Kate still had her normal duties on top of that. While they were out of the country, she'd act as a conduit for White House operations so that matters of state would continue to be addressed, despite the president's absence from the Oval Office.

It was no wonder that after surviving the two back-to-back trips, Kate came down with a whopper of a cold.

Flying back on Air Force One, she commandeered a seat in the private section away from the press corps and slept fitfully. Her sinuses throbbed along with the rhythm of the engines, and in terms of her headache, the only thing worse than the takeoff was the landing.

Once home, she didn't even undress and instead, fell into bed, one arm draped across Buster, who must have sensed her fatigue and managed to temper his usual enthusiasm at her return.

The next day, she dragged herself to the office, receiving such encouraging responses as "Are you okay, ma'am?" and "Maybe you ought to go home and get some rest." And "You look hideous!"

The last remark was from Emily. Kate had met her before breakfast in the workout room, located on the third floor—the private residence. While on the trip, Emily had mentioned how she missed their friendly competition on the treadmill, so Kate had foolishly agreed to an early morning workout, not knowing that she'd come down with a world-class cold. But she showed up anyway, hoping that a good workout might burn away her ills.

Emily was already hard to work on the treadmill when Kate arrived. She even managed to deliver her scathing assessment of Kate's appearance in rhythm to her thundering steps.

Kate grimaced as she approached the second machine, setting it to her usual start-up speed. Then after a second thought, she dropped the pace to something much more sedate.

"You look like you're about to fall over."

"Give me a break," Kate complained, punctuating her statement with a sneeze. "I'm sick. That's why I look bad."

"No kidding. Oh, and by the way? If you give me that cold, I'll have you hunted down and hung at dawn."

"*Hanged.* Curtains are hung; people are hanged." Kate sneezed again. "Nice to know the powers of your exalted position aren't going to your head." She stepped onto the treadmill and started what resembled more a brisk walk than a run.

"Why don't you stop in the clinic downstairs and get some good drugs."

"Because good drugs will make me a lousy chief of staff. You know how antihistamines knock me out."

Emily punched the controls, taking her speed up a notch, an obvious ploy to demonstrate her superior conditioning. "You always were a lightweight when it comes to those things."

"I'm sick, so shoot me. Anyway, it's all your fault. You're the one who decided we need to enjoy our coffee on the balcony, overlooking the city lights of Ottawa."

"Lightweight."

"Slave driver."

"Wuss."

"Harpy."

Despite Kate's malaise, she was heartened by the bantering, seeing it as a sign that they could get back to their old friendship and leave their professional relationship beyond this one door. In all other parts of the White House, they would be the president and her chief of staff, but here, just M and K, in constant competition to be the queen of the treadmill.

They pounded together, Emily's footfalls at almost twice the speed of Kate's. For once, Emily didn't make any overt gibes about the difference in their speeds and her superior athletic condition.

After several minutes of congenial silence, Emily waited until Kate was taking a swig from her water bottle before speaking. "So, you talk to Nick lately?"

Kate almost choked, soliciting a wide grin from Emily.

"Dad always said timing is everything." She laughed at Kate's discomfort and efforts to wipe away the water that dribbled from her chin.

"You did that on purpose, didn't you?" Kate complained, mopping up her mess with the towel slung around her neck.

"It's so easy to jerk your chain. So how's the Baton Rouge boy wonder? Or is he the Louisiana loser? I can't remember."

"Ooh, the venom is running early this year. Usually you don't crank up the vitriolic sap until closer to your anniversary."

Emily upped her pace. "Of what? The date of my marriage or of my divorce? Oh yeah, they're the same day. Brightest thing I ever did—make sure our divorce was finalized on our anniversary," she quipped with a deadpan delivery. She waited a moment for the sarcasm to drip away. "So, have you talked to him recently?"

"No. You?"

"Me?" She snorted. "I want nothing to do with him."

"Then why are you asking about him? And why assume I know anything?" Sure, Kate and Nick had talked briefly by e-mail a week or so previous, but no one, especially not Emily, needed to know about that.

Her friend shrugged. "I don't know. You two seemed to . . . I won't say hit it off, but you know what I mean."

"I don't know what you mean." Kate's mind raced twice

as fast as her feet. Just the presumption that something might occur between her and Nick contained plenty of pitfalls. The last thing she needed to admit to was that she found him the least bit interesting or pleasant or—

"You're not going to start dating him, are you?"

"Date him?" Kate sputtered. "Where are you getting this stuff from? I'm the one who's probably delirious with a fever. What's your excuse?"

"I can read between the lines."

"What lines? You're imagining lines. There are no lines."

Emily's shrug was a bit more dramatic than called for. "Okay. If you say so."

Perturbed, Kate dialed up her speed, trying to work off her frustration with increased exercise. Although her sinuses ached and her lungs screamed in pain, she quickened the pace to the point where she almost matched Emily's blistering speed.

After a moment, Emily kicked her pace up a notch or two dozen and gave Kate a sly grin. "Now that's more like it."

Revelation hit Kate like a concrete block against the side of her already throbbing head. All of Emily's questions and veiled comments had been nothing more than her way of egging Kate into being a competitor on the treadmill.

Manipulation at its best. Or worst, considering your perspective.

Kate reached up, switched off her machine, stripped the towel from around her neck, and left the room without saying a word. As she stepped into the hallway, she heard Emily call out from the room behind her.

"C'mon, Kate. Don't go away. Best two out of three, okay?"

Kate stuck her head back into the room. "You don't play fair."

"You don't play anymore!"

"That's because I'm working day and night. I don't have time for play." She stifled a sneeze with the end of her towel. "I don't even have time to get sick."

Emily dialed her machine back to a sedate pace. "When's the last time you went home to see your parents? Or better yet, why don't you invite them to come visit us here?" She made a wide, sweeping gesture with her palm. "Trust me. We have enough room." Her face brightened. "Your mother would love to spend a night or two in the Lincoln Bedroom. She all but told me that the last time we talked. Find a good time and invite them up here. We'll give them the best of the dog and pony show."

"They'd love the idea," Kate said, tempering both her enthusiasm and her doubt as they mixed together in an unattractive mishmash of emotions. On one hand, Kate appreciated Emily's insight into what would honestly thrill her parents, but she wondered if it was merely another form of manipulation.

"Good. So if you're not going to continue to race me, then leave me alone so I can finish my six before breakfast."

Duly dismissed, Kate stepped into the bedroom next door that Emily had designated for Kate's occasional use and where she typically showered and changed after using the workout room.

In many ways, Emily and Kate had retooled the role of chief of staff, but the changes were more reflective of their longtime friendship along with Emily's role as a single president with no permanent family living with her in the private residence.

Luckily, Emily didn't lack for temporary company. Benton kin had been coming and going since the inauguration, depending on their assignments, both official and unofficial. As she came out of the bedroom, Kate almost ran into Maggie, who—judging by her exercise clothes—was designated as Emily's next opponent.

After exchanging pleasantries, Kate headed downstairs, then crossed over to the West Wing, where she stopped by the Navy Mess to grab some coffee. Then it was another set of stairs back up to her office. As tempting as it was to grab something to eat, she had a breakfast meeting of advisers to attend and knew she'd be well fed in twenty minutes or so.

At 7:30 a.m. sharp, Kate walked into the private dining room down from the Oval Office, where five of the seven attending officials were milling around the table. The sixth, Dozier, was already seated, awaiting his breakfast with less than his usual sense of anticipation.

Burl Bochner, the vice president, leaned over to Kate and spoke softly. "I think Dozier's a little under the weather."

Under the weather or under the table? she thought. Dozier's behavior and his health had been a bit more erratic lately, and Kate worried that he was drinking more than he should. At the moment, his eyes looked particularly bloodshot—more so than most mornings—and he didn't join in or, in his case, override the conversation as usual.

"You think he's okay?" she whispered back.

"I'm not sure. I'll keep an eye on him."

Then Emily entered the room and the conversations halted and everyone stood a bit more erect, Kate included. Emily had done a good job of cultivating a commander-in-chief bearing, despite her lack of military experience.

"It takes everything I have to not salute her," Burl whispered softly to Kate. His years in the air force showed in his bearing, his manner, and his predilection to wearing suits in varying shades of dark blue. The only concessions to his monochromatic wardrobe were his ties, each one more colorful and interesting than the next.

Emily did not immediately head for her seat at the table, indicating that some informal meet and greet would preface their working meal. As she spoke to the others, Kate craned over to take a better look at Burl's tie, which was far less ornate than usual. She had to look twice to see that the pattern was actually tiny drawings of SpongeBob SquarePants dressed as Uncle Sam.

"Great tie. My brother would love that."

His grin held a hint of bedevilment. "Can you believe it? It wasn't from one of the kids. Melissa gave it to me for Christmas."

His wife, Dr. Melissa Bonner-Bochner, had taken a sabbatical from her career as an engineering professor to move their family to D.C. and take on some of the duties usually reserved for the First Lady. Kate hadn't had a chance to spend much quality time with her but both liked and respected the woman, especially when it came to the honesty Melissa and Burl demonstrated concerning the troubles they had been having with their eldest son.

Uprooted in the middle of the school year and suddenly dropped into a new life in a new town, Kevin Bochner was having some difficulty adjusting to the changes in his life and his father's sudden prominence. The teen had already had one minor brush with the law, and both his mother and father had been adamant about him making treble reparations when most parents would have been grateful their child had received merely a slap on the hand.

"Wait until you see tomorrow's tie. Kev made it himself. It's great." With a smile of paternal pride, he added, "I may have spawned a future candidate for *Project Runway*. He's redirecting that overwhelming need to spray-paint graffiti on every available surface into much more acceptable avenues."

"Good for him. I know you're relieved."

Emily had already started her circuit around the room, greeting the staff; then she reached Dozier, still seated.

She patted him on the shoulder with obvious affection. "Didn't your momma ever tell you to stand when a lady enters the room, young man?"

He bobbed his white head. "She did indeed and she'd be rolling in her grave if she could see me now. I'm sorry, Madam President, but I'm just a little stove up this morning. If you'll forgive an old man his frailties . . ."

She gave him an indulgent smile. "Consider yourself forgiven." She stood beside his chair, her hand remaining on his shoulder and turned to address the room. "Now, if you all don't mind, let's get this meeting started."

They took their seats and the waitstaff quickly brought in breakfast, served family style. Emily had mentioned to Kate that she liked the more informal atmosphere that was generated when people were passing around heaping platters of food. It brought out hidden personality quirks—who held the platter for the next person, who took too much, who took too little, and so forth.

Burl had seated himself at the corner of the table next to Dozier, who sat at the end. When the platter slipped from the old man's hands, Burl caught it before its contents spilled.

"Are you okay, sir?"

Dozier's gaze was somewhat fixed. His face was pale and waxy-looking.

"N-no, son." He seemed to have trouble catching his breath. "I'm not feeling that good."

At that moment, Dozier slumped over to the left and would have tumbled from his chair had Burl not dropped the platter and reached for the man instead.

"Give me some help," Burl grunted as he lowered Dozier to the floor. "I think he's having a heart attack!"

THE ROOM EXPLODED IN MOVEMENT. Burl Bochner and Harold Morelli pushed back chairs to make more room on the floor for Dozier. Kate tried to get around the tangle of chairs and people in her way.

Burl loosened the old man's collar and tie and began to feel around for his pulse while Morelli bent down and listened to Dozier's chest.

"I don't hear a heartbeat."

Burl looked up with a stricken face. "I can't find a pulse."

Morelli immediately began chest compressions. An ashen-faced Francesca Reardon fumbled for her cell phone, ostensibly to dial 911, but Kate waved away her efforts. She picked up the phone next to the door in order to call in a level B code blue medical alert, which would indicate that someone other than the president required emergency medical treatment. Before she could get the words out, a Secret Service agent burst into the room, alerted by the commotion.

She grabbed his arm to stop him. "The president is fine. It's Dozier Marsh. We think he's having a heart attack. Get the doctor up here. Pronto."

Thanks to the intricate web of security, Kate knew the message would be instantly relayed directly to the doctor's office, which was only a couple hundred feet away on the ground floor of the White House residence.

A few precious moments later, Dr. Peter Crockett and two medical technicians arrived at a dead run. Between them, they carried a medical kit, a portable defibrillator, and a small tank of oxygen.

The advisers backed up and out of the room, trying to allow the doctor and his team the maximum space to maneuver. But curiosity and concern kept them close by in the corridor, where they knotted together, trying to get a glimpse of the situation without making themselves appear like vultures.

In just a matter of moments, a team of paramedics arrived with a gurney. Less than five minutes later, they loaded Dozier up.

Crockett stepped aside to allow the paramedics and the gurney to pass. The usually robust-looking Dozier looked years older, with gray, pinched features. However, he did seem somewhat aware of his location and the situation.

As he was carried past Emily, he reached out and touched her hand. She fell into step alongside the gurney, his hand in hers. Kate stayed a few steps behind. When they slowed to negotiate the first turn in the hallway, she took the opportunity to lean down and whisper, "Don't you die on me, old man. We've got too much work to do yet."

He managed a wink despite the oxygen mask.

"Ma'am?" The paramedic seemed at a loss for words. Exactly how did you inform the president of the United States that she was holding up their progress?

Kate stepped up and patted Emily and Dozier's clasped hands. Then, with the utmost care, she extricated Emily from his weak grasp.

"They're taking him to Bethesda, and you know what good care they'll give him there," she said to Emily. Well-versed in literally dozens of contingency plans, Kate even knew which of five different routes the ambulance would likely take to the Bethesda naval hospital.

Emily betrayed far more emotion than Kate expected. In any given situation, Emily was usually the picture of calmness and control, the true marks of leadership, but Dozier's serious problem obviously rattled her. She looked at the procession as it moved down the hallway, then turned to Dr. Crockett, wearing an anguished expression.

"You'll go with him, right, Pete?"

The doctor looked conflicted as if he didn't quite know what to say. Kate relieved him of that duty.

"He can't, M," she said softly. "He has to stay here. With you."

Emily bristled. "I'm not the one having a heart attack. Dozier is."

Kate exchanged glances with Dr. Crockett, wishing she could have time to explain Emily's sudden outburst. Maybe he could read between the lines and realize that Emily had a deep-rooted fear of losing yet another father figure. Even if this time it would be due to far less violent means, the loss would be just as palpable.

"Don't worry," Crockett said, his earnest expression

forged from having made many assurances to many families, presidential or otherwise. "He'll be in the best possible hands on his way there and even more so after he arrives. I'll stay on the radio with them the entire way."

"But—"

"It's their job. And they're going to do it better without me crowding their workspace."

Emily stiffened. "Then I'll go there too." She turned to the Secret Service agent hovering at her elbow. "Arrange for transportation. A motorcade, whatever."

"No." It was Kate's turn to object.

Emily whirled around, ready to exert the necessary authority to get what she wanted, now. But she stopped short when her angry but distressed gaze met Kate's.

"You'd be in the way," Kate said softly. At Emily's crestfallen expression, Kate corrected herself. "Not you, but your position. Your security needs. They'd have to spend precious time and manpower making sure you were safe. You'd be an unintentional disruption, and we both know it wouldn't be good for Dozier for their resources to be split. He needs their undivided attention."

Emily stared down the hallway, where the paramedics were disappearing around the next corner as they headed for the West Wing exit.

"At least let me see him out."

"Sure."

They started down the hallway, their procession gathering members as they followed. Fearing things would turn into a circus, Kate cut their convoy short with a silent gesture, and all but the security detail stayed behind.

Take them to the Oval Office, she mouthed to her deputy, Constance MacAvoy, who nodded and immediately headed down the hall to shoo the advisers into the office to wait. Connie was a new team member but an old friend who had worked with Emily during her years as the governor of Virginia. Connie was neither wowed nor cowed by people of authority, having learned to stand toe-to-toe with Emily and come away with all her fingers and toes intact.

Most of the time.

Assured that Connie would have everything in hand, Kate quickened her pace so she could catch up with Emily, Dozier, and the paramedics. They remained just inside the doorway as Dozier was packed into the ambulance. Kate knew her task now would be to help the president refocus, and the best way to do that was to toss her right back into the mountain of work awaiting the two of them.

As soon as the ambulance pulled away from the White House, the sirens wailing, Emily heaved a sigh and took a few steps down the corridor before stopping.

"You think he'll be okay?"

Kate nodded. "He's tough. And as far as I know, he's never had any heart trouble before. No prior damage is probably a good thing."

Emily's shoulders slumped. "That's right. You don't know. This isn't his first attack. Remember back a couple of years? when he took that cruise?"

Kate searched her memory, vaguely recalling that Dozier had been talked into taking a pleasure cruise to South America. But she didn't remember him having any trouble during his voyage.

"He never made the ship. He spent those two weeks in

a Miami hospital instead. Everybody thought he was off, enjoying a trip, so he never said anything to anybody."

"No one but you."

Emily managed a wry grin. "He knew I'd find out. I always do."

They passed by the dining room doorway and saw that, while they'd been gone, the staff had returned the furniture to their rightful positions, removed the cold food, and reset the table for breakfast again. They continued into the corridor outside of the Oval Office and into the office itself. There, they discovered Connie had made sure the remaining advisers had been served coffee and juice while waiting in anticipation of resuming their breakfast meeting.

When Emily and Kate entered the room, the advisers broke from their small clumps and turned their collective attention to Emily, asking for news of their fallen comrade.

She showed them her best fearless-leader face, now firmly set in place. "The paramedics are taking Dozier to Bethesda, and I have all the confidence in the world that the doctors there will do an excellent job in treating him. If anyone can get him back on his feet, it'll be the staff there at the naval hospital."

The responses were somewhat generically hopeful, as if none of them were terribly certain that an eighty-two-year-old man who drank and smoked too much would bounce back quite so easily.

No one wanted to contradict their president.

But Kate knew Emily's resolute statement was less a matter of trying to convince the others and more of trying to convince herself that he would recover.

Emily gestured in the direction of the dining room. "Shall we try breakfast again?"

Food was the last thing Kate wanted at the moment, but she realized the importance of returning to the status quo. As much as everyone might be tempted to slow down, if not suspend business for the sake of one man, it simply wasn't feasible. It was imperative to trigger Emily's ability to compartmentalize the situation and return her attention to the day's multitude of tasks at hand, the first of which was drafting, then vetting, a statement that Harold would deliver to the press corps concerning Dozier's medical condition. It took only moments for the statement to be drawn up and okayed. Harold excused himself and headed for the Press Briefing Room on the north side of the building.

Everyone knew that it took only a whisper to stir up the hornet's nest called the White House press corps. A rapid response from them would prevent undue speculation and short-circuit rumor. Once delivered, the statement concerning Dozier would hit the wire services and Internet news feeds in nanoseconds.

The advisers remained understandably quiet as they filed into the dining room and took their seats. Once the waitstaff delivered the platters of food to the table, Emily seemed somewhat at a loss for words. Then she said something that Kate had never heard her utter before.

"Uh . . . Kate, do you think you could say a prayer or something?" She hesitated for a second, then added, "For Dozier?"

Kate's spirits soared upward at what she considered to be a colossal moment in time—Emily asking for help and support through prayer with an air of sincerity that Kate had never seen before. This was no contrivance for propriety's sake, but a real request, reflecting a kernel of faith that Kate always hoped rested at the center of Emily's soul.

Before Kate made any response, she sent up her own quick prayer, asking for the right words to help wedge open the crack that was evidently forming in Emily's hard resolve against most things religious. Such a task required a keen hand and sharp eye and just the right tools from God.

Help me to help Emily, she prayed silently.

The advisers all bowed their heads, and a moment later, Emily did too.

The words came effortlessly to Kate, obviously given to her in answer to her request.

"Lord, we'd like to thank you for this opportunity to come together and join our voices, our energies, our thoughts, and our prayers. Please be with our friend and colleague Dozier Marsh, who has just fallen ill. Be with the doctors and nurses who are and will be seeing him. Give them wisdom in treating him and patience in caring for him. Help us to keep him in our hearts and our prayers. As for the duties that lie before us today and in the coming days, please grant us the courage to help lead this great nation to the best of our abilities. Help us to learn from those who came before us so that we can make this world better for those who come after us. We ask you to turn our sorrows into joys and our weaknesses into strengths through Jesus Christ, our Lord. Amen."

*Amen*s echoed around the room, including a clear, strong response from Emily.

A new sense of lightness filled Kate's heart. She couldn't help but feel buoyed by the hope that her efforts to become a better beacon had finally worked and Emily was starting to see the light on her own. As much as Kate had faith in God's bigger plans, she'd still worried that she failed to serve him well enough to help those plans come to fruition. She didn't want to believe it might have taken a potential calamity such as Dozier's illness to crack Emily's hardened conscience. Nonetheless, she raised her own quick prayer, thanking the Lord for finding a way to extract some potential benefit from such an unfortunate situation.

The advisers all settled down to breakfast once again, but Kate's attempts to eat failed. The earlier excitement had soured her stomach so much so that she asked for and received hot tea instead of her usual morning coffee. The only solid food she felt she could handle at the moment was toast.

The morning agenda went by quickly, as if nobody really wanted to raise any unnecessary points to keep them at the table longer than they had to. Kate suspected that the others, like her, couldn't quite shake the image of a gray-faced Dozier slumping over in his chair. She studiously avoided looking at his empty seat, which had been moved to the corner of the room and the table set for one less than before.

Even the temporary removal of his place seemed so poignant and sad. . . .

Kate shook herself mentally. Potential personal tragedies aside, the country still needed running, and its leadership still had their duties to tackle. After finishing their agenda and their meals, the advisers filed out quickly, all scattering down the corridors to their respective offices, probably ready to recount their eyewitness accounts of Dozier's attack to their office staff.

The spread of information would be a welcome replacement for idle speculation. Even in the White House, rumors had a way of amplifying, just like in any other workplace, despite the existence of official statements.

One of Kate's lesser-known responsibilities was to make sure that unfounded, unsupported rumors didn't escape into the atmosphere beyond the building. But in almost any given situation, it was like trying to stuff air back into a punctured balloon. At least Harold's press briefing would help stem the tide of misinformation with a quick statement of fact—from an eyewitness, no less.

Kate spent the rest of the morning in meetings but, like Emily, insisted on and received updates of Dozier's condition every half hour. The paramedics had stabilized him during the brief trip to the naval hospital, and Dr. Crockett had arranged for an impressive cardiac team to be already assembled by the time Dozier arrived.

As unfortunate as it had been that the immediate past president had had some heart problems, it did mean that the hospital responsible for his primary treatment had an experienced and renowned surgical team ready at the White House's beck and call.

By lunchtime, they received news that after a battery of tests, the doctors had determined that Dozier had a 75 percent blockage and would have to undergo quadruple bypass surgery. Said surgery was scheduled for early the next morning.

In dealing with his office, Kate learned that Dozier's only real family consisted of an estranged son who lived and worked in Japan. Although Dozier's longtime secretary, Dorothy, had been able to track down the son and inform him of his father's health issues, John Fitzgerald Marsh stated that he regretted he'd be unable to return to the U.S. in time for his father's surgery.

Dorothy was dabbing at her eyes when she stood at the door to Kate's office. "Do you have a minute, Ms. Rosen?"

"For you? Absolutely." Kate stood, greeted the woman with a hug, and then ushered her to a seat, closing the door behind her.

"I just can't believe that Jack won't come to be with his father," she complained, continuing to sniff into a wad of tissues. "A son should be with his father at a time like this. I don't understand what his problem is."

For as along as Kate had known Dozier, he'd never mentioned the existence of a son more than a handful of times. It'd been mostly in passing, but never with a sense of pride that a father might use when speaking of his son the successful businessman. And yes, as far as Kate knew, Jack Marsh was just that—a highly successful businessman with no overt vices nor any arrest record or other such aspect that his father might not want brought up in casual conversation.

Whatever stood between father and son, it was of an extremely personal and private nature.

On the other hand, Kate had heard dozens of stories concerning young Emily, recounted with Dozier's usual flair for storytelling. He knew stories about baby Emily, little Emily, all the way up to college-bound Emily and beyond. But not once did any of the tales, tall or otherwise, include anything about his own son, who had to be about Emily's age. How could Dozier know such elaborate stories about her without one or two of them including his own son?

What could have torn that family apart so badly that a son would refuse to have anything to do with his father, especially during a time when his father's health—if not his life—seemed to be in jeopardy?

Kate couldn't help but think about her own father. Blessed with good health, his retirement had simply meant that he took the energies he once dedicated to his career as a plant manager for Glaswell and applied them to his favorite projects at home, at church, and in the community. As to the state of his health, Kate might not know the exact times and dates of every medical appointment her mother and father had, but she always expected and, more importantly, always received an update, even if they were usually reports of good overall health.

By two o'clock, Kate had managed to shuffle her schedule so that she could leave for the hospital in order to visit Dozier. There was no way they could make all the arrangements to get Emily there until almost 7 p.m. Plus, the president's afternoon was filled with two meetings with foreign dignitaries from South America, discussing trade agreements.

By two thirty, Kate reached the hospital, passed through all the security checks, and entered Dozier's room. He was asleep, his snores almost drowning out the sounds of the monitoring equipment. Kate hadn't been there more than a minute when a nurse came into the room to adjust one of the leaders on his chest.

"How's he doing?" Kate asked.

The woman smiled and said in a soft voice, "Well enough to proposition three of the staff members." She looked at him with obvious affection. "Randy old soul . . ."

"I didn't know that last one was a fellow," Dozier whispered. "The long hair fooled me. What'd he call those things again?"

The nurse grinned. "Dreadlocks, Mr. Marsh."

"Dreadlocks. Silly name for a silly hairdo. Looked like someone made him some pigtails out of a couple dozen Brillo pads." His face softened. "But he was a nice fellow, even if his hair did look a bit silly."

Katie leaned down and touched his hand. "How are you doing, Dozier?"

He smiled around the oxygen tube perched beneath his nose. "Fair to middling, Miss Kate." He took Kate's hand in his papery one, then looked at the nurse. "You know who this is, don't you, Sadie Mae?"

The woman's name tag read *Sarah McRay*, but she didn't correct him. "No, sir, Mr. Marsh. We haven't been introduced."

"Then allow me. Sadie Mae, may I have the pleasure of introducing you to the first female White House chief of staff, the Honorable Kathryn Rosen, Esquire."

The nurse smiled. "Pleased to meet you, ma'am. It's a real honor. And I just want you to know that I voted for Ms. Benton," she said proudly.

Even after the election was long over, Kate continued to be amazed by the number of people who started every introduction with that proclamation. As much as she appreciated the validation, she sometimes wondered if they thought she would be any less gracious to someone who kept their secret vote a secret.

"Thanks." Kate learned it was the best answer in this case. She turned to Dozier. "So what do the doctors say?" She already knew their diagnosis but thought it only proper to ask him.

The old man made a face. "Too much rich food, not enough exercise." His expression turned even more sour.

"And they're giving me what-for about my cigars. They want me to cut down to only one a day," he complained in a voice a petulant child would use.

Kate replied just as the responsible adult would in this equation. "Then you'll cut down to one a day, Dozier. Simple as that."

"You listen to Ms. Rosen," the nurse said, walking toward the door. "You need to cut down, if not cut it out altogether." She patted the doorframe as she exited as if saying, *I'll be out here if you need anything.*

"So says the nonsmoker," he grumbled.

"So says the White House chief of staff. Think of it as me protecting a valuable asset. I want you well and back at your desk as soon as the doctors say it's time for you to return."

Judging by his poor color and the aged translucence of his skin, she wondered if that day would ever happen. The disadvantage of hiring someone with almost sixty years of political experience was that amount of wisdom and acumen came in an eighty-year-old package. Perhaps they'd been too hasty to make him a full adviser and should have given him fewer responsibilities.

She'd never forgive herself if she thought she'd helped work him into an early grave. She reached over, snagged a chair, and pulled it to the side of the bed so that she could be on a more even level with him. "So how are *you* feeling? Honestly?"

He drew in a shaky breath. "Better than I did, that's for sure. They've got me taking the whole pharmacy right now to help me feel better." He nodded toward the IV bag suspended overhead. "And Lord only knows what they're pumping into me from that thing."

He coughed slightly, struggling to catch his breath. "Then tomorrow, they'll crack me open like a piñata and try to figure out where my heart is hiding."

She smiled. "It's in there. Trust me."

He pushed his head back into his pillow and sighed. "I wonder." He stared at the ceiling, obviously lost in thought. "Jack's not coming. Not that I blame him." He turned toward her. "I've never told you much about my son, Jack, have I?"

"Not much."

"Apple of his mother's eye." He raised one feeble finger to wag it slightly. "Not a momma's boy, though. Named him after JFK. I knew Jack Kennedy was destined for greatness when we worked together on a couple of senatorial committees."

His expression faded for a moment, then sharpened again. "My Jack and I never got along. Either too much alike or not enough. I was never sure. Ever since his momma died, he hasn't had much time for me. An occasional card or phone call. Now I'm lucky if it's an e-mail every once in a blue moon. I wanted him to follow in the old man's footsteps—be the next Jack Kennedy—but he turned his back on politics." Harsh lines bracketed his mouth. "And on me too."

He tried to grip Kate's hand but he had no strength. "Don't forget your parents, Katie-girl. They're the reason why you're on this green earth."

Kate thought about the three e-mails she'd received before breakfast from her parents—one from her mother asking for an opinion between two dresses and two from her dad, including a forward of the latest joke he'd received from a friend.

Her parents were a daily part of her life, even though they lived almost a hundred miles away. Her parents might have been a bit confused by her choice of occupation, but never once had their love been conditional on working in a field of their choosing.

Dozier managed a grin that looked more like a grimace. "But you're a good daughter. I know that. You wouldn't let your father die without coming to see him one last time, even if you hadn't spoken to him in the last ten . . . fifteen years."

She knew exactly what the old man lying in the hospital bed wanted her to say and she gladly said it. "Dozier, you're not going to die. You're going to have the surgery, and after you recover from it, you're going to eat right, exercise daily, and cut down to one nasty cigar a day."

His chest rumbled, and at first she was concerned, but she realized a moment later the sound was laughter mixed with a few coughs.

"Yes, Chief."

"That's better. Now, what can I do for you to make you more comfortable? You need any reading material?" She looked around the room, which was decorated more like a swanky hotel room than a hospital room. Emily, of course, had insisted that he be given the presidential suite.

As much as it pained Kate to know that Dozier's own son had essentially turned his back on his father, she took some relief knowing that Emily had stepped in as a worthy replacement as Dozier's unofficial daughter. Her fondness for the old man was almost as legendary as he was.

"Emily is coming by around eight. I think official visiting hours might be over by then, but they're not going to turn away the president."

"She's a good girl, our Emily."

"Yes, sir, she is."

"I'm honored to have been in her inner circle."

She knew she had to wave off the pity party. Allowing him to wallow in his misfortune wouldn't help him in this situation. "You're still in the inner circle."

He shook his head and released a phlegmy cough that racked his entire body. "No, I have to step down. She can't afford to keep me close. Not anymore. I'm a liability now."

"What are you talking about? This—" she indicated the monitoring equipment that surrounded the bed—"is just a minor inconvenience. Once we get you healthy again, your duties await you. And don't you forget that, mister."

His reddened eyes swam in tears and he clutched Kate's hand. "No, I can't stay in the administration. I've done something. Something bad. And it's going to hurt our Emily if I don't separate myself from her and the White House. Immediately! It's a matter of life or death."

DOZIER'S GRASP TIGHTENED ON HER FINGERS, growing almost painful. "I can trust you, Kate. I know you want the best for her. And you . . . you . . ." He coughed again, his whole body shaking with the effort as he tried to sit up.

"Calm down, Dozier. Everything's all right." Kate could do little else but extricate her hand and help brace him so he could cough more easily. He was far too fragile to slap on the back to help with the coughing. After the painful barrage of explosive coughs, he slumped onto the bed again. She helped reposition his oxygen tube and other monitoring wires and leads, muttering words of assurance.

His eyes remained half-closed, as if the energy to open them was beyond him for the moment. "She's never going to forgive me. I'll have given her reason to hate me, just like I gave Jack."

"Shh . . . Emily loves you unconditionally. If you've done something, just tell her and she'll forgive you."

"No, she won't." He squeezed his eyes shut and tears spilled down either temple. "I'm going to die . . . without a single member of my family at my side. I've either outlived them or run them off. All I'll have is a couple of business acquaintances who have taken pity on an old man. I'll die and then they'll forget all about me."

Before Kate could argue otherwise, he pushed on. "And what happens after that? I have no heavenly award waiting for me. Not an evil ol' rascal like me. I've done too many bad things, hurt too many people." He turned his tear-streaked face to Kate. "I don't want to hurt Emily. Or disappoint her. But I never thought what I did would come out or matter in the long run. I guess I never expected my run to last this long. Getting old just means you've had more time to do stupid things to hurt people."

As much as Kate didn't want to learn what new scandal waited in the wings, she realized she needed to know—if not for Emily's sake, then for Dozier's pacification. She prayed that she could come up with a response that would ease his concern and help him stop suffering so much. That sort of mental turmoil couldn't be good for the upcoming operation and the recovery afterward.

Later she'd worry about how it impacted Emily.

"What can I do to help, Dozier? If I can do anything to help, to fix things, I'll certainly try."

He released a ragged sigh. "Tell Emily I'm sorry. I should have said something when she brought that girl into the campaign."

By *that girl* Kate somehow knew exactly whom he was talking about. Her pulse quickened and her breath caught in her throat. "You mean Maia?"

He nodded. "Like the apple that Eve used to tempt Adam. All shiny and pretty on the outside, but full of evil and temptation on the inside."

His analogy was a bit strained, but Kate didn't want to correct him. What she wanted to know was more about an apple called Maia. "What do you mean? What did Maia do?"

"Temptation," he said between gritted teeth. "It's been my downfall all my life, you know. My Miriam said as much on her deathbed. She said, 'Dozier, you gotta resist the temptations of the office. If you don't, your greed will bring you down someday.'" He sniffed. "I don't want my greed to bring down our Emily. I don't want to let her down like I let Jack down. I never meant to involve her."

Despite being lost at what he was talking about, Kate did her best to calm him with generic assurances. But behind the platitudes, she couldn't help but be worried. Dozier was talking life-and-death matters. Maia was already dead. What was lurking under the surface here? How could she learn more without getting him even more upset? But that wasn't a problem, she realized. The man was determined to tell her no matter what the cost.

"She was such a pretty young thing, that Maia girl. Despite what she was doing, I never wanted her dead."

A shiver went up Kate's spine.

He drew a deep breath that seemed to help him regain some control. "I want you to promise that you'll forgive me—forgive an old, selfish man who couldn't control his greed and his lust." He reached up and touched Kate's face. "I know you work hard to keep a direct pipeline to God. I've seen it in your eyes, in what you do and say every day."

His next statement caught Kate completely by surprise.

"And I've resented that fact ever since we met."

At her puzzled expression, he added, "Not resented you but resented that you could work in this business and not get caught up in its seamier side. We both know that politics can be a dirty, filthy business. But you seem to rise above it. They call you Spotless Kate behind your back, you know. Nothing bad seems to stick to you—no stains, no grime."

She tried to laugh. "Spotless? Hardly. I'm tempted by the same things that have tempted everybody else—money, power, position. Maybe the only difference is that I keep asking for help in order to resist those things I ought to resist. And when I've failed—and trust me, I fail to resist many things—I've asked for forgiveness from God."

"From God?" He almost spat the words out. "It's too late for God to forgive me."

Kate gripped his hand. "It's never too late. God's capacity to forgive is infinite."

Dozier coughed out a laugh. "He and I haven't been on speaking terms in years . . . a lot like me and Jack. I've already fallen a long way down. Too far to be forgiven." His focus wavered. "I could tell you stories . . ."

She waited, not wanting to prompt him for details but hoping he would offer them on his own. Somehow she knew it wouldn't take much to open the floodgates.

She was right.

Dozier pressed the heel of his hand to his closed eyes, scrubbing away his tears. "I never meant to hurt Jack, but I did. And I definitely don't want to hurt Emily, but I've made a big mess of things."

His breath caught in this throat. "I thought I'd been careful," he said in a low voice. "Nothing was in my name, not outright. But somehow that little vixen Maia found out."

Watching Dozier confess was like watching a train as it hurtled over a trestle that ended halfway over the river gulch. "Found out what?" she prompted.

"I couldn't help it," he said like a plaintive child. "I couldn't turn it down, not that kind of money. I've worked hard all my life and I ought to be able to profit from that hard work."

"Dozier . . ."

"It's Pembrooke."

"What about it?"

"I've accepted some . . . payments for helping put them in the right place to get some key government contracts."

"How much?"

"No cash, mind you. Just a little bit of stock and more in stock options."

The admission caught Kate short. She had expected worse—a tale like Charles Talbot's, of personal debauchery or some capital crime gone unpunished. But this was still enough to rattle her.

How had she missed it? She'd done a deep background check on Dozier when it became evident that he was going to be part of Emily's inner circle during the campaign. She performed a similar check on every person who became part of Emily's "Kitchen Cabinet." At no point had she, or later the FBI investigators, uncovered anything that even suggested he held any stock in the Pembrooke Group, one of the world's largest petroleum technology industries. Such possession would have immediately been a red flag, screaming, "Conflict of interest!"

Not only did Pembrooke have deep infiltration into almost every aspect of oil production around the world, but they also had hundreds of government contracts, many of them large military ones. Dozier must have sat on over a dozen committees that were instrumental in awarding contracts to Pembrooke.

Kate found herself lowering her voice in deference to the sensitivity of the news. "How much stock?" Her mind raced ahead. If it was a few paltry shares, then perhaps he'd simply overlooked his ownership, having lost the particulars in a sea of similar stock holdings.

"Right now, I own only a couple of shares—not that much really. But the big problem is that I have a long call stock option I was going to exercise as soon as we got her energy program off the ground. We both know Pembrooke is positioned to make a killing on the program, and because of that I stand to make a lot of profit."

"How much?" she repeated.

"Fifteen the first year."

Her heart sank. "Thousand?"

"Million."

She fought to catch her own breath. "D-does Emily know?"

"I never told her."

Even though Dozier was deathly ill, the old man still clung to his cagey ways. They both knew that not telling Emily and her not knowing were two totally different things.

Despite a part of her that whispered she should back off, considering his condition, Kate knew this might be her last chance to get any details. "So Maia found out about this?"

His face grew paler than before.

"Not quite. She found out that I got involved with

Pembrooke while I chaired the House Armed Services Committee. She'd been blackmailing me for the last two months, ever since she figured out how they've been paying me for my cooperation and influence. You can't imagine the amount of money she extorted from me. And I think she had dirt on everybody. I don't know where she got it, but I know she was trouble. She hinted she could bring down Emily—the whole government—any time she wanted to. I couldn't have that. I was so relieved when she died."

Kate couldn't help herself. "Dozier!"

He nodded. "I know. You have no idea how sorry I am that this happened. It was wrong. Unconscionably wrong. I wanted to tell you, but the scandal went a lot deeper than just a conflict of interest with an adviser. I didn't want to admit it before, but I have to now." He reached out blindly for her hand. "Kate, I'm dying. I know it. You know it. I can't go to my grave with something like this on my conscience." His lip quivered with emotion he barely kept in check. "But I don't think God will forgive me for being a greedy old so-and-so. He's going to let me burn in hell, isn't he? For all the evil things I've done?"

Kate realized she needed to push aside her worries about Emily's political liabilities and deal with the more pressing issue of Dozier's concerns about his eminent disposition. She closed her eyes and prayed for help, for guidance, for the right words.

He touched her hand. "Can you forgive me, Kate?"

She opened her eyes and found a smile. "Of course I can, Dozier. And I do. But my forgiveness isn't as important. Ask for God's forgiveness. Explain to him what you realize now. Tell him what mistakes you've made and ask him for forgiveness."

Dozier turned his head away. "It can't be that easy."

"Of course it can be. If you mean what you say and say what you mean. If you're being honest with yourself and with God. His grace is large enough for the most undeserving to come to him. All we have to do is ask him into our hearts, ask him for forgiveness, repent, and follow him."

He turned back to face her. "He'll wipe the slate clean?" His momentary look of hope faded fast. "But knowing me, if I survive this, I'll just dirty it up again."

"That's why you pray for guidance and forgiveness every day. We're all imperfect. We all fall from the path, sometimes by inches, sometimes by miles. But the difference is we can be forgiven if we truly believe in God."

"Forgiven for a lifetime of sin?"

"Yes." She nodded. "All you have to do is believe with your heart."

"My heart . . ." His laugh turned into a grunt. "It's as broken as my soul. God may be willing to fix one with forgiveness, but I seriously doubt he can fix the other. I don't know if he should even try. Seems to me it'd be better if I left this world in a hurry, before I can do anyone else any harm." His eyes clouded.

"I've done terrible things, Kate. Not just in the past but recently. I'm truly sorry about them. I just hope it doesn't come back to hurt Emily. She's the one person I've always tried to help, never wanted to hurt."

"I know, Dozier." She took his hand. "And she knows that too."

"Will you tell her I'm sorry?"

"Emily will be here to visit you in just a couple of hours. Why don't you ask her yourself?"

"I have a feeling I'm not going to be here in a couple of hours." Panic began to fill his eyes. "I'm so sorry about what I did to Maia. I never wanted the girl to die, even if it was the perfect solution to my problems. I just wanted her to stop." He tried to cough but obviously had no energy left. "And Jack. Tell Jack I forgive him and I hope he'll forgive me."

"Of course," she said, even as she wondered, *What did you do to Maia? What kind of perfect solution?* But instead of voicing the thoughts screaming in her head, she maintained her reassuring smile as best she could and kept her voice even. "Tell me about Maia, Dozier."

His eyes drifted closed. "It was too easy. . . ."

"Dozier?" *Don't go to sleep now. I need to know.*

He didn't respond. Suddenly the machinery monitoring his vitals released a loud alarm. She stared at the jagged lines on the screens, not quite sure what she was looking at.

Two nurses burst into the room. "Code blue. Get the crash cart."

Kate retreated to the far corner of the room, rocked by both the medical emergency and what appeared to be Dozier's deathbed confessions. The only thing she could do to help was pray—for Dozier's soul and, as an afterthought, for increased clarity concerning his confusing statements. And as always, she prayed for Emily's sake and safety.

After twenty minutes of valiant efforts, the medical team called the death of Dozier Marsh at 4:01 p.m.

AFTER EVERYTHING CALMED DOWN and the team dispersed, Kate took a few minutes to compose herself in the corridor and then stepped into the sitting room of the presidential suite and used her cell phone to call Emily on her private line in the Oval Office.

"It's me. I'm at the hospital."

"So how's the old reprobate? I bet he wants me to smuggle in cigars and whiskey when I come. Well, you tell the old coot that it's habits like that—"

"M, stop." Kate's heart wedged itself in her throat, threatening to choke her words. "He . . . he didn't make it."

There was a long moment of silence on the other end.

"I'm so sorry," she added, the words weak and the sentiment barely a shadow of what enormous sorrow she felt for his death as well as his self-recrimination.

After more silence, Emily spoke in a small voice that sounded nothing like the fearless leader of the free world. "He's really gone?"

"Just a few minutes ago. It was another heart attack. While I was talking to him. The doctors did everything. But . . ."

A small note of self-reproach tinged Emily's words. "I should have been there."

"There was nothing you could have done."

"I should have been there," she repeated, this time with almost an air of hostility. "He would have stayed alive for me. Stayed alive long enough to have the stupid surgery." Hostility disintegrated into open bitterness. "Dad couldn't do it—couldn't love me well enough to hang on until he got under the knife—but I thought Dozier could do it."

Kate cringed. The only other time Emily had displayed any similar resentment had been after watching a documentary on her father's life and death while imbibing the larger part of a bottle of very expensive wine.

"C'mon, M. Your father loved you. And so did Dozier. You can't blame them for . . ." What could she say? For dying?

Emily's voice grew stronger and the note of anger and resentment faded. "I know that. Logically. But it still feels like they've both left me because neither one loved me enough to want to stay."

She coughed, and Kate knew it was her friend's way of gaining control over the threat of tears. After so many years in the public eye, Emily automatically controlled her emotions in private as well as in public. "I guess Jack will have to come back now. I'll call him. I know what to say to make him come. He might not love his father as much as I did, but I know I can shame him into showing Dozier the proper respect now."

Then she added in her clearest, most powerful voice, "After all . . . I *am* the president."

* * * * *

Kate wanted to wait until the initial uproar over Dozier's death had calmed down before she talked to Emily about his deathbed confessions. However, as she waited for the right place and time to speak with Emily, she found herself concentrating less on his illegal stock holdings and worrying more about his confession about being involved somehow with Maia's death—and Maia's threats about Emily.

After returning to her office, she closed the door and fired up her computer. She needed facts, data—anything either to give an amorphous rumor a definitive size and shape. And the sort of research she needed couldn't be turned over to just anybody. She needed the truth, and then she needed time to figure out what to do with the truth. She didn't intend to hide it, but she did need time to digest it before full disclosure.

She tried to ignore her conscience that persisted in asking, *You want time to spin it?*

Maia Bari, Tim Colton, Dozier Marsh, and the Pembrooke Group.

Where did their lives intersect? What did she know? Dozier had said that he should have warned Emily *before* she brought Maia into the campaign. Did that mean he'd known Maia prior to her involvement? If so, how? When?

Only one person might know. Maia's boss, Marjorie Redding.

Kate dialed.

Marjorie answered on the fourth ring. "Redding." Her raspy voice was the product of decades of smoking. Despite her expertise in knowing what other people should look and sound like, she never seemed to take the advice herself. Over the years, her short and squatty figure had grown shorter and squattier and her hair had finally become an impossible reddish pink hue, which Kate's mother had once described as "halfway between shrimp and flamingo."

Despite the fact that Kate couldn't see her, she knew the woman's makeup had become almost clownish, surpassed only by the garish colors of her wardrobe, which tended toward purple, green, and orange.

And yet, she was the reigning expert in the image consultancy field, even despite her personal choices. But after years of working alone, she'd surprised everyone by hiring a much younger assistant, Maia. Now Kate wondered exactly how the employment opportunity was created. A bit of creative blackmail on Maia's part?

"Marjorie, it's Kate Rosen. I hope I'm not disturbing you."

"It's almost nine o'clock at night. I'm an old woman. Of course you're disturbing me." Her voice lightened as if suddenly remembering Kate's new position. "In any case, what can I do for the chief of staff of the White House?"

"I didn't know if you'd seen the news tonight."

"Dozier?"

"Yes, I wanted to make sure you knew. I know you two went way back."

"Too bad about him. There aren't many of the old-school politicians around anymore. He'll be missed."

"How well did you know Dozier?"

"What do you mean by that?" There was a long hesitation. "Oh, I guess you didn't know. Back in the old days, we were quite an item. But a lot of water has passed under that bridge."

Kate was taken aback by her response. "You mean you and . . . him?"

She barked in laughter. "Don't sound so surprised. I wasn't always the old battle-ax I am now. Back in my day, I was a svelte young thing and I could have any man I wanted," she bragged. "And now that he's gone, I guess it wouldn't hurt anyone to admit that one of those young men I particularly wanted was Dozier Marsh."

Kate struggled to overcome her speechlessness, but she couldn't manage more than an "Oh."

The woman chuckled. "Not what you wanted to know, eh?"

Kate swallowed hard. "Not really."

"Then why don't you simply tell me what you want to know. We both know you didn't call just to give me the bad news. What's really on your mind?"

In light of the open invitation, Kate decided to plunge in. "All right, then. My question is—did Maia have a chance to meet Dozier before she started working with Emily?"

"Did they *meet*? Is this one of your generation's euphemisms for having an affair? If so, yes. I know exactly what Dozier saw in her, but I'll never understand what she saw in him. Sure, Dozier was well-off, but she could have easily found a younger, more . . . appealing man with far more money. Then again, old men do have a way of dropping dead faster than young ones." After a brief second, she added, "God rest his soul. . . ."

Kate's stomach did a flip-flop. Had Maia done just that? gone from Dozier to Tim Colton, a younger and richer man? "You knew they were having an affair?"

"Oh, it didn't last long. Those things never do. Either the girl gets bored listening to the same old stories, or the old coot finally realizes that she's not after him for his good looks or personality but the color of his money. But in this case, I told Maia that if she wanted to work with Emily, she couldn't have any relationships with anyone associated with your campaign staff—advisers included. So she called it off." Marjorie's voice darkened. "I made sure of it."

"How?"

The woman's laugh was suddenly grating. "I told both of them that I'd rat them out to Emily, and we all know she'd cut them out of her circle in a heartbeat if she thought either were liabilities. Since Maia was desperate for a chance to prove herself and Dozier wouldn't knowingly do something to jeopardize Emily's campaign, the two of them broke it off. Immediately."

"Do you know anything about the man she died with? Tim Colton?"

"I know who he is, of course." Marjorie paused. "And who he worked for." She used a highly derogative term to describe Charles Talbot.

"Do you think Tim and Maia were . . . a couple?"

"Him? I doubt it. He's not her type. Her idea of 'young' is a man in his fifties. In any case, anything she did after the election was her own doing. She was no longer in my employ after November 5."

"Really? I didn't know that. Why?"

There was a moment of silence. "You'll have to talk to Emily about that."

"Oh." Had Emily taken proactive steps after their heart-to-heart talk? If so, it would have been an encouraging step in the right direction. Then again . . .

Kate leaned back in her chair, the small headache that had been haunting the back of her head suddenly moving front and center. "I appreciate your honesty."

"It's my most powerful weapon and I guard it like the dragon I am. Trust me—if I learn anything more about Maia's relationship with Tim Colton, I'll contact you. My neutrality can only be stretched so far. Sometimes you have to pull the other direction to equal things out."

"Thank you, Marjorie."

After she hung up, Kate sat at her desk, dreading the trip home. For one long moment, she debated stretching out on the leather couch in her office and spending the night there. But she knew it would be unfair to Buster to leave him alone all night, even if a quick call would alert her next-door neighbor, Darlene, who'd sworn more than once that she wouldn't mind any last-minute dog-sitting request.

Also, Kate had another reason to go home. She needed to make a series of personal calls to key members of the former campaign staff, and she'd rather be comfortable at home while doing it.

It was simply a case of proper manners to contact them about Dozier's death, even if they had already heard about it on the news. She glanced at a photo of Buster on her desk.

I'm going home.

If nothing else, Buster would be a good companion to comfort her as she shouldered that particular burden.

But four hours later, long after she'd made all the calls and was dead asleep, Emily was the one who needed comforting.

"Houston, we have a problem," Emily intoned in a deadpan voice. Then she did the near impossible.

She giggled.

Kate felt every muscle in her body tense. "Emily, are you drunk?"

"No, I'm not. Yet. But I really, really would like to drink myself into a stupor."

"No, you don't."

She sounded exasperated. "I know that, stupid. Why do you think I called you? If you can't get over here ASAP, I'm going to call Chip. He'll distract me. Boy . . . will he distract me. I've been neglecting the dear boy. It's probably time we discovered the allure of the Lincoln—"

"Don't, Emily. I don't want to know." Kate knew that since Emily had been in office, her dalliances with Chip McWilliamson had gotten few and far between . . . much to Kate's relief. Somehow she couldn't see the citizens of the United States embracing the concept of the president having an official boy toy.

"Don't be a prude. Anyways, I've sent a limo. It should be outside waiting for you, right . . . about . . . now." She giggled again, suggesting that she had already finished one bottle and flirted with a second before calling Kate. "You could just jump into the car, jammies and all. No, wait. Don't. I don't think I could stand the publicity over a White House slumber party. It's hard enough being a female leader without encouraging that sort of stupidity."

"I'm getting dressed and I'll be there shortly. Why don't you get on the treadmill and do a couple of miles while you wait for me?" Maybe she could keep Emily otherwise occupied while she threw on clothes and headed into town.

"Don't wanna run." Emily's voice brightened perceptively. "Want ice cream. I know there's ice cream downstairs. Meet me in the kitchen. Oh, and bring Buster. I haven't seen him in a dog's age. He can have ice cream too." She hung up, laughing.

"Yes, ma'am," Kate said to the dial tone.

Five minutes later, Kate was both thanking and apologizing to the driver who had been rousted out of bed to pick her up. She thanked him again when he pulled up in front of the north entrance to the residence and hopped out to open her door.

"Have a good evening, Ms. Rosen." He added, "Or morning, as the case might be."

She scurried into the building, nodding at the uniformed guard who held open the North Portico door.

"Good morning, Ms. Rosen," he said with a bright grin, despite being on the graveyard shift.

She tried to return his smile, but it turned into a yawn. "I'm not ready for morning, Frank. Not yet."

His expression broadened, perhaps at being called by name or perhaps because she had Buster in tow. "Some days, morning comes awfully early. I believe the president is downstairs in the main kitchen." He bent down a little in an effort to make himself a smaller threat to Buster, who looked somewhat wary. "Is this the infamous Buster we keep hearing about?"

"It is indeed." She tugged slightly at his lead. "Buster, sit."

Buster, still excited from the unexpected car ride, sat reluctantly. When Frank offered the back of his hand for Buster to sniff, her dog took one whiff and decided the man was definitely friend rather than foe. A second later, Buster had forgotten any suspicions he had and pulled against the lead in hopes of better reaching the man to offer undying affection.

Frank scrubbed Buster on the head. "Ferocious guard dog you got there, ma'am."

"You know what they say—kill them with kindness."

"Yes, ma'am. Then he's definitely a killer." He straightened, evidently deciding that he had to return to his protective duties. "Have a good day, Chief. You too, Buster." He held open the door for her, giving her a nod as she passed by him.

They entered the building, immediately turned to the right to take the back staircase leading one floor down to the ground level. Buster's toenails made a clicking echo on the marble stairs as they descended.

Once on the ground level, Kate allowed Buster to follow his nose, and he headed straight for the savory aroma coming from the kitchen.

When they stepped into the kitchen from the dim corridor, Kate had to shade her eyes against the glare. Fluorescent lights reflected from a thousand stainless steel surfaces—the counters, the appliances, not to mention the hundreds of shiny pots and pans hanging from overhead racks.

Emily stood beside an industrial-size mixer, glaring with open hostility at it and the noises it was making. She looked ready to kick the appliance.

And she looked drunk.

"THERE YOU TWO ARE. I was starting to get worried." Emily waved her hand around the large kitchen. "You know the trouble with cooking here is that there are no small pans," she said, reaching for her wineglass and downing a healthy slug. "I think I'm making enough chocolate chip cookies to feed the entire army."

Kate had arranged for the kitchen to always keep a supply of the necessary ingredients for Emily's cookie-baking fetish, knowing that at some point, she would need to resort to cooking to work through a particularly tough issue.

But somehow, Kate hadn't anticipated that Dozier's death would have been the triggering event for a session of baking therapy. She spotted a half-empty bottle of wine sitting precariously close to the edge of the counter and took some small relief that, at the least, Emily wasn't hitting the cooking sherry. The White House chef might consider that a major violation of his domain.

Emily clutched the counter's edge for support as she bent down to Buster's level, not realizing that she'd brushed against the wine bottle. Kate stretched over the counter and caught the bottle as it wobbled, shifting it toward the center of the counter.

"Here's my favorite puppy!" Emily said, as if talking to a baby. "C'mere, Buster."

The dog happily abandoned Kate and ran toward Emily, bathing her in kisses and taking inordinate interest in her hands, which probably tasted of flour, sugar, and vanilla. After he had given her a very detailed once-over, his attention was drawn to the ingredients spilled across the counter closest to the mixer. He stood up and danced on his back feet, trying to see better.

"Uh-uh. No chocolate for you, buddy. But I'm making a batch with no chips so you can enjoy too."

Kate reached into his travel bag and pulled out a towel that would serve as his temporary bed. "Come, Buster." After a moment's hesitation, he abandoned all the more interesting smells on the counter and obediently trotted to her. After circling the towel three times, he curled into a boneless heap on it.

Kate patted him on the head. "Good boy." She turned to Emily. "I can't let you spoil him too much."

M's grin was just a tiny bit sloppier than usual, a testament to how well she could hold her liquor. "Too late. It's my privilege as his auntie to spoil him rotten. He's the closest thing I'll ever have to a nephew." She giggled as she took another sip of wine. "You know, it's a good thing neither of us ever had children. You would've retired completely from politics to play mommy, and I would have shipped mine off to military school at the age of six months." She bent down and allowed Buster to lick her face. "But instead, we're both at the top of our games, and Buster here may be spoiled, but he's still the best doggy in the world. Aren't you, Buster?"

He roused up long enough to wag his tail.

"So let's make more cookies. I'd been dying to use all these spiffy big appliances, but I've learned they're more trouble than they're worth." Emily stared at the mixer, made a face, and turned the machine off. "I'd rather stir it by hand anyway." She grabbed the huge mixer bowl and transferred its contents to a smaller metal bowl, better sized for the task.

"Sit," she commanded, nodding toward a stool hiding under the steel counter. Like a good dog, Kate retrieved the seat and perched on it.

"You know . . . Jack went to military school," Emily said as she began to stir the ingredients.

Kate struggled to keep up with the sudden change in topic. Booze tended to loosen Emily's brain and make her skip over certain conversational niceties, like transitions between subjects. "Jack . . . Marsh?"

"Yep. I think it was good for him. Dozier would have made a pretty lousy everyday dad, but he was a great holiday and summer break dad. He could keep up the Ward Cleaver stuff for a couple of weeks if he really, really had to."

Her face darkened. "Now that I think about it, I think Jack was always jealous of the relationship I had with my dad." She scratched her chin, depositing a smudge of flour. "Then again, if my mother had had her way, I would have been shipped off to some freakin' boarding school, probably deep in the Alps." Her face brightened. "But Dad refused to let her send me away." She laughed. "That's why we lived where we did—so I could be a day student at the best private school on the Eastern seaboard."

Kate knew the basics about Emily's early education years, even the bit about Claire Rousseau Benton's less than maternal attitudes, then and now. Kate had seen the woman in action and tried to avoid confrontations with her at all costs. Whenever she spent any time in Claire's company, Kate always went home with a much stronger appreciation for her own mother.

Emily glared at the mixture in the bowl, studied the ingredients on the counter, and then tossed another handful of flour into the dough and continued stirring.

"Dozier tried to send him to my school, but Jack just didn't fit in. He actually pleaded to go back to military school, and Dozier finally relented and let him return. I never understood that."

"Some people need more discipline and regimentation in their lives."

"Yeah, and most of them graduate and become little tin soldiers. But not my Jack."

Your Jack?

A timer dinged, and Emily walked over to the wall of gleaming steel industrial ovens, opened one, and pulled out a tray of perfect cookies.

The aroma hit Kate, a tidal wave of chocolaty goodness. Buster stirred, but Emily quickly pacified him with a chipless cookie.

"Hush, puppy . . ." She giggled. She turned to Kate. "Here. Catch!"

Kate found herself juggling a fiery-hot cookie with both

hands, trying to cool it off enough not to burn her tongue on the gooey chips. Although she wasn't hungry, the cookie was tempting nonetheless.

Emily reached into the refrigerator and pulled out a small carton of milk, which she also tossed toward Kate. "Heads up!"

Kate dropped the cookie in time to intercept the carton that hurtled toward her. "Watch out!"

"You gotta keep on your toes around me, girl."

Kate opened the milk and drank directly from the waxy cardboard spout. "Tell me about it. I'm wondering if Mom kept my old toe shoes from my very brief career as a ballerina. I might need them again."

"I've seen you dance. They won't help."

Kate stuck out her tongue at the president of the United States.

"Hey, don't complain. Look at the perks. Fresh homemade chocolate chip cookies at—" she squinted at the large clock that hung above the wall of sinks—"3:37 a.m."

"Don't gloss over the fact that this benefit is definitely offset by being woken up out of a sound sleep at three o'clock in the morning to take a twenty-minute ride into work in order to get said cookies."

"It's the price you pay." Emily picked up a cookie, stared at her wineglass, shrugged, then dunked it in the wine and ate it. The look on her face suggested that it hadn't been such a good idea.

"Where are the glasses?" Kate looked around, scanning the area, and then pointed to the milk carton. "I'll share." It was the perfect opportunity to distract Emily from drinking any more alcohol. In Kate's opinion, milk, cookies, and solace made for a much more suitable combination for Emily's physical and mental health.

But Emily foiled her plans. She shook her head. "Nope. It's whine and wine and chocolate. It's the only way." She dropped to a second stool and sighed. "I don't want Dozier to be gone. I need him."

Now they were getting to the real topic. "I'm going to miss him too," Kate responded, hoping she was turning the correct release valve in hopes of bleeding off some of Emily's turmoil.

"No, you're not," she said too quickly. "You always thought I was being overly sentimental, having him on board." Although Emily managed to say the words with a smile, there was still an accusatory bite to her words that compelled Kate to defend herself.

"That's not true. I just didn't want to put him in such a key adviser role. He brings . . . brought a great sense of political history with him, and that was invaluable, but I think there were other people out there with equally good grasps of history but with much more modern points of view."

"But that's why it was important to have him involved. I was raised by an old-fashioned politician. I know that world of politics as well as I know this one we live in now. Dozier helped me keep everything in perspective. I didn't always do what he wanted or support the concepts he wanted, but sometimes I made my decisions based on the differences between then and now. Sometimes knowing the old-school agenda meant I knew I had to do the polar opposite because I knew full well how the old ways had failed miserably."

Kate bit into the cookie, now sufficiently cooled. "I just had some problems with his ideas. For example, he wasn't too fond of me. He merely tolerated me for your sake. You always seemed exempt from the limitations he wanted to put on others."

"You mean other women."

"Among other things, yeah."

"That's because I was essentially his surrogate child. He knew what I was capable of, but he was never convinced any other woman—any other person—had had the same upbringing, the same experiences, the same chances for office as me. And he knew for certain no other woman had a political heritage anywhere close to mine. Every time I proposed putting a woman in my own inner circle, I had to prove her credentials to him. You included." She grinned. "And if Dozier could accept my reasoning and my choices, then I knew all of America would take them on face value. He was my toughest critic."

Her face fell. "And he's gone." A fat tear trickled down her cheek, and she picked up a cookie, shoving it into her mouth whole. After a few seconds, she washed it down with the remains of her wine and poured herself another glass.

They remained silent for over a minute until Kate couldn't stand it anymore. "Is his son coming to the funeral?"

Emily nodded. "I had to play a couple of trump cards, but he's coming. I saw to that."

Kate wondered if she should even ask the nature of those trump cards. With Emily, it could be anything from emotional blackmail to . . . to something she didn't even want to consider.

But Kate was concerned less with Jack Marsh than she was with his father's dying words. She knew Emily might be the only one who could unravel their meaning, but Kate feared the revelation would lead her into asking other questions with even more unsavory answers.

She stared at her friend, her boss, her president. Emily's eyes had become a bit glassy and her hand trembled slightly. The wine had already loosened Emily's tongue a bit. Was this the right time to inquire? Of course, catching Emily off guard was always an adventure and, on rare occasions, an expedition into the unabashed truth.

"M, I have a question."

"Shoot, K." She began to stack the cookies, turning them into a single tower that wavered and finally toppled over. "Oops. Broke a couple. Cook's privilege to eat the broken ones."

She played with the broken pieces, trying to match them up together again like a crumbly puzzle. She started to toss one to Buster but pulled back, admonishing herself. She reached for a chipless cookie, broke it in two, and tossed Buster the smaller piece, eating the other part herself.

Kate drew a deep breath and plunged in. "It's about the last conversation I had with Dozier—before he . . . passed on. . . ."

"What about it?"

"He made a sort of admission to me that I think you need to know about."

"What? He confessed to something?" Emily leaned forward on the counter, resting on her elbows. "Do tell. Was it sex, drugs, or rock and roll?" She began to laugh.

"Stop," Kate commanded, surprised to see Emily respond instantly. She squeezed her eyes shut for a moment. "He said that he'd done something to . . . to Maia. I think he might have had something to do with her death."

At first, Emily looked puzzled; then the confusion slid from her face. "Why that old goat! That randy old goat. He didn't kill her. That's ridiculous. Isn't it obvious?" She began to laugh. "They had an affair. I had no idea the child was that cutthroat. She actually tried to sleep her way into the inner circle?" She continued laughing as she put her head down on the counter, toppling over the newest cookie tower.

Buster stirred at the sound, but a curt gesture from Kate made him grumble softly, close his eyes, and return to his cookie-less dreams.

Kate reached out and touched Emily's arm. "That's not what he meant."

Emily raised her head, revealing her eyes red from laughing and from too much imbibing. "Then I don't understand."

"He asked . . . forgiveness for something he did to Maia. And to Tim Colton. That could only mean one thing."

Alcohol had dulled Emily's wits and reflexes. It took her a moment to realize the implication of what Kate was saying and to realize her cookie structure had fallen. She pretended to be more concerned with the tower than the question. "Oh . . . so you think he had something to do with their accident," she said in her best offhand manner.

Kate nodded. "That's what it sounded like to me."

"So what is he supposed to have done?" Emily began a third tower to rival the first two. "Crawled under Colton's car and cut the brake lines himself?"

"I don't know. He didn't exactly say."

Emily's blurred expression suddenly sharpened. "Exactly what *did* he say?"

Kate searched her memory for the precise words. "At first, he said to tell you he was sorry and that he should have said something when you brought 'that girl into the campaign.'"

Emily's brow furrowed. "So does that mean Maia had been working with Dozier . . . or maybe against him . . . before Marjorie sent her?"

Before Kate could answer, Emily made a dismissive gesture. "He'd probably run into her before and realized she wanted to get involved high up in my campaign. You didn't have to be around her more than a moment to understand that was her ultimate goal."

"I don't think that's it." Kate hesitated, trying to find the right approach. Dozier's most damaging confession, if not handled right, could blow Emily's administration out of the water.

When she shifted Emily's wineglass beyond her friend's reach, Emily tensed visibly. "What is it, K? Don't hedge. Just say it."

"I don't know how we missed it. We did an in-depth financial review of every potential person around you. It should have shown up."

"What should have shown up?"

Kate drew a fortifying breath. "Dozier holds . . . held a substantial interest in the Pembrooke Group—for years. Evidently Maia found out and had been blackmailing him over it." Kate waited for Emily's explosive reaction, but instead of ranting and raving, the president simply rose from her seat and began to pace around the counter at which Kate sat.

"How much?"

The simple question surprised Kate. "I don't know yet, but from what he said, he held a smaller amount of stock when he was on the Armed Services Committee. But the bigger problem is—he held an extremely large stock option. Maybe as a deferred payment. I'm not sure. In any case, it looks bad. For him and for you."

Emily responded with an expletive between gritted teeth.

Kate continued. "He said he stood to gain at least fifteen million when O:EI rolled out."

Emily stopped pacing and leaned against the counter, drumming it nervously. "That wasn't bright. Not bright at all."

The metallic rhythm grated on Kate's nerves, and Buster whimpered, wakened by the noise. She stooped down and comforted him, then turned to Emily. "We have to do something."

"Like what? 'Oops, we didn't know Dozier failed to disclose his connection with the very company that is likely to make a killing when our pet project is put into play'? Trust me, the press will eat that up and not believe a single word. But they won't stop with Dozier being the appetizer." She stopped making the irritating drumming but instead slammed her fist against the counter, an obvious expression of her building frustration. "They'll make me the main course, roasting on the spit of public appeal."

"But we can't hide it, M."

Emily continued to pace, her face screwed up in concentration. Kate watched in dread and fascination as her friend's expression revealed her inner workings. She'd come up with an idea, work through its ramifications in her head, then either improve upon it or discard it.

It was a process that Kate had learned long ago to not disturb. The consequences of interrupting the process were far less appetizing than the solution or resolution she ultimately divined.

Finally Emily held up two fingers. "As I see it, we have two choices. Choice number one: We go scorched-earth and eradicate all the records that connect Dozier with Pembrooke."

Now it was Kate's turn to weigh in as a devil's advocate, pointing out all the flaws to the solution, whether she approved of it or not. In this particular case, she definitely didn't approve.

"That would be impossible. There's no way you can guarantee you'd access all the records, especially if he used any offshore companies." Kate studiously avoided the use of the word *we* and put the onus on Emily herself. This was a solution Kate wanted no part of, whether it would be effective or not. It was unethical.

Emily nodded. "True. We'd also need to be wary of the scorched trail back to the White House. I think you'll like choice number two much better." She offered a terse smile. "We do nothing."

"What do you mean?"

"Just that. Nothing. We can't hide the truth because we're not actually sure what the truth is. Dozier was a sick man. Who knows what he was raving about on his deathbed." She pushed into Kate's face. "Who else can confirm what he said to you?"

"No one. I was there alone."

Emily failed to hide the gleam of triumph in her eyes. "Maia's dead and no one overheard his confession to you. No witnesses."

Kate closed her eyes. *But I'm a witness. . . .*

"Tell me you haven't started any investigations into his financial records or reviewed his financial disclosures?"

"Not yet. I wanted to tell you about it first."

"Excellent. Then we'll choose door number two. And your job is to not look."

The order took her by surprise. "What do you mean?"

Emily dropped to the stool. "Just that. Don't look. Don't investigate. Don't ask, don't tell. Forget what he told you. He was a confused old man who was raving as he was dying. He had no idea what he was saying."

"Emily—"

"If we start digging into his finances now, we could be accused of trying to start a cover-up, even if all we're actually trying to do is uncover the truth."

"But—"

"But nothing. If we actively look for the information, then we open ourselves up for accusations of wanting to whitewash his memory or, worse, covering our own rosy red rear ends. If someone else finds it, all we do is haul out all our extensive reports that showed him clean and clear. After all, the FBI looked into his finances and they didn't find anything, right? If someone discovers he was a principal owner of a bunch of bogus holding companies—which is how I assume he hid it all this time—then we put the blame solely where it should be placed—on Dozier himself for hiding the truth from us."

"How can you suggest that we do nothing?"

"Because it's the answer that contains the maximum amount of truth."

"Except for the fact we learned about this yesterday."

"Then forget what you heard. Discount it. Lose it in the

emotions of the day." At Kate's expression of dismay, Emily added, "Don't look so shocked, K. The old man would have given me this advice himself if the tables had been turned. But the beauty of it is that it's mostly all true. We had no idea Dozier had positioned himself to illegally profit from O:EI. However, there's no real difference between learning about it now or learning about it three months from now. No one's going to profit from it now that he's dead."

"What about his family? They'll inherit."

Emily's lips curled into a glacial smile that the American public had never seen, but Kate had, too many times to count. "There's no one but Jack, and don't worry about him. Considering the bad blood between them, I sincerely doubt he's even in the will. And if he is, I can take care of him. So—" she laced her fingers together and stretched her arms out as if to signal the end of the discussion—"are we clear?"

A battle warred inside Kate, part of her wanting to argue with her friend, the other realizing that the president's mind had been made up.

"Yes, ma'am."

IT WAS TOO CLOSE TO MORNING for Kate to bother going home again, so she spent the next couple of hours in her office, stretched out on the leather couch with Buster curled around her feet. Indecision wouldn't allow her to sleep for more than a few fitful minutes at a time.

By dawn, she'd mapped out what she thought was the best strategy to work in the background and clean up behind her president. Despite Emily's edict that their best plan of action was no action at all, Kate knew full well that overt inaction was counter to Emily's natural programming. Her need to be proactive would lure her into activating either the scorched-earth method or at least a modified version of it.

Kate's plan was to preserve the original evidence, which she believed would prove—even to a doubtful America and beyond—that Dozier had lied to everyone about his holdings.

If Emily was determined to scorch the earth, Kate would resow it with the same crop, essentially making sure she could replace the missing files with the untouched originals. It was ambitious at best, but no more so than Emily's plan.

But the key to success was getting there first. And to do that, Kate had to find a way to reopen Dozier's financial records without tipping off Emily or a scandal-hungry press. That meant Kate had to find a way to get the information that didn't utilize her usual manpower so that absolutely no trail led back to the White House.

Luckily she had an idea or two how to make that happen.

The second step in her plan would be to learn more about Dozier's will. If his son, Jack, was in line to inherit his father's properties, Emily would have to convince him to forfeit potential millions. How likely was that? Then again, Jack and Emily had known each other for years. What Jack Marsh might not be willing to do for his estranged father, maybe he'd do for Emily's sake or at her request.

Until she learned more about Jack Marsh, he would remain an unknown variable in her calculations.

Usually such uncertainties left a bad taste in Kate's mouth and a rock in her stomach. The only thing that kept her going was the bottom line—that neither of them had realized or had prior knowledge of Dozier's involvement in Pembrooke. No one did, including a team of trained, independent financial investigators who had failed to uncover any inkling of his involvement.

But would a jaded American public believe their protestations?

She doubted it.

Much too soon, Kate began to hear occasional muffled voices from the hallway outside her office, signifying that the West Wing was starting its day. She rose from her makeshift bed and freshened herself, changing into the spare suit she kept hidden in the armoire. Buster began to sniff the furniture, a sure sign that he needed to relieve himself.

"Not in my office, you don't," she warned him. Once he was leashed, they headed outside together, where he examined and rejected every column of the pergola that sat outside her office, forcing her to take him toward the more spacious Rose Garden. After sniffing and subsequently ignoring what seemed to be every bush, he finally picked his target.

While he was busy, Kate heard a tap on the window and saw Emily, framed in one of the Oval Office windows. She crooked her finger and Kate's stomach began to churn.

Once he'd completed his task, Kate led Buster to the door leading from the garden to the Oval Office, telling herself she was shivering only because it was a chilly morning.

They had hardly stepped into the room before Emily pulled her over to the fireplace, where small flames licked the ceramic logs. "You must be freezing. Here, warm up."

While Kate rubbed life and feeling back into her hands, Emily squatted down to pat Buster, who responded with his usual declaration of undying love.

"You two need to let me apologize for calling you out last night." When she glanced up at Kate, a rare look of sadness filled Emily's eyes.

Or was it simply the lingering signs of her hangover?

"I never felt as alone in my life as I did last night in this big old house. I didn't think Dozier's death would have hit me that hard. I really needed the company." Her sigh was somewhat ragged. "But I sure didn't need that much wine."

I tried to distract you from drinking is what Kate wanted to say. But instead, she took the accommodating coward's way out. "That's okay." After a second, she added, "Buster enjoyed getting out of the house."

That made Emily smile. "Did you like your cookies, buddy?" She rubbed his ears. "We have more." She rose, walked over to the side table closest to the fireplace, and retrieved a white pastry box tied with a red ribbon. "Here." She handed it to Kate but addressed her comment to Buster. "In case you get hungry today, little man."

She turned and faced Kate, the brief flare of amusement fading from her eyes. "Although I was more than a little tipsy last night, I do remember everything we talked about. I've spent most of the morning reexamining our conversation. I think I was wrong."

Kate tried not to betray her inner thoughts.

"We can't take the chance that no one will look into Dozier's finances now that he's dead. We need to find out the truth for ourselves, immediately, then present it to the public."

Emily's suggested course of new action caught Kate by surprise. A sudden flare of guilt fired up inside of her, one that condemned her for failing to believe her friend could make the right and moral decision. But another part of Kate whispered in warning that Emily was merely saying what she thought Kate wanted to hear.

Unaware of Kate's turmoil, Emily blithely continued. "I called Jack a little while ago, and he's flying in for the funeral. We'll have a chance to talk to him and figure out how to present our findings." She paused and pierced Kate with her sharpest eye contact. "Don't worry. This will work out. I promise. But I need to ask you this—don't do anything yet. Don't start delving into Dozier's records; don't start investigating how he hid this from us. Let me talk to Jack first. He deserves to know what's happening before we start digging up Dozier's sins. I promise we'll do the right thing."

She reached for Kate's hand and squeezed it.

"Promise."

⋆ ⋆ ⋆ ⋆ ⋆

Four days later, when Kate was introduced to Jack Marsh after the funeral, she'd expected to meet either an irate man, angry to have been pressured into attending his estranged father's funeral, or a relieved man, glad to embrace the fact that the strained relationship had finally ended.

Instead, he was quiet, polite, and far more forthcoming and circumspect about the family discord than Kate expected. After the service and interment at Arlington, they returned to the White House, where Emily ushered Jack into the Blue Room and offered him one of the chairs nearest the fireplace. Although the sun had shone during the graveside service, the cold air held the usual bite of the last days of February. While plenty of people had attended the services, only a handful had been invited back to the White House. Burl and his wife had been pressed into service, making nice with a trio of Dozier's remaining contemporaries on the opposite side of the room.

After Emily, Kate, and Jack all got settled in the chairs, Kate tried to hide her surprise when Emily reached forward and grasped the handle of the ornate silver coffeepot sitting on the low table between them. She poured a cup of coffee, offering it to Jack Marsh. The action was uncharacteristically domestic, meaning Emily either was extremely distracted or was working an agenda she'd failed to mention to Kate.

Kate knew she could make book on the latter.

"Where has the time gone?" Emily pondered aloud as she poured a cup for herself and, in the most surprising move of all, a third cup, ostensibly for Kate. However, Kate knew that Emily's largesse was probably stretched past its limit and that she would be responsible for retrieving the cup herself.

Emily acknowledged Kate's murmur of thanks with a quick nod and the hint of a wink.

The hidden message?

Don't get used to this.

Then Emily turned to Jack. "The last time we saw each other was when? Wasn't it Christmas? Far too many years ago."

He took a sip, then cradled the cup in both palms as if to warm himself. "I remember that. I'd just finished working a big job in Ecuador the week before." He colored slightly. "I never did thank you for letting me crash your family's holiday celebrations."

She waved away his belated concern. "No thanks necessary, Jack. The way I figure it, you're practically a Benton."

He took a bracing sip of coffee. "It certainly seemed like it sometimes." He graced her with a smile that didn't quite reach his eyes. "How's your mother? I got a nice note from her last month telling me that you'd won the election." He chuckled. "As if I hadn't heard . . ."

"She's fine." Emily added an artful sigh. "You know Mother . . . she still lives in the Dark Ages. She thinks people living in Japan might not have access to the news in America. I've tried to explain to her the intricacies of the Internet, satellite news organizations, and such, but it's simply over her head. Technology is *so* not her strong suit." Her laughter had a hollow ring to it. "She's fried the last three cell phones I've given her. In fact, the third one lasted only a week before she completely destroyed it."

Emily was on a real roll, her mother being her favorite subject of amused ridicule.

"And yet she lives most of her time in France and seems able to have no trouble keeping up with my life here even when she's over there. Go figure."

Jack laughed. "Ah, but that's European elitism for you. She probably thinks Japan is still a quaint little country with odd-looking people making transistor radios."

Emily took a sip of her coffee and nodded. "Probably so. In any case, she's definitely stuck in the sixties." She paused, then added almost wistfully, "I think Mother always resented that I grew up."

Kate said nothing, but having gotten to know Claire Benton over the years, she thought the assessment was dead-on.

Evidently Jack did too. "I guess it's hard to consider yourself eternally young when your children are no longer children but have become adults."

Emily released an almost brittle laugh. "Exactly." She leaned forward with a gleam of conspiracy in her eyes. "One time—when she was halfway to being totally blitzed—Mother actually admitted that her sense of self-identity took its hardest blow when Hepburn died." Emily raised a wagging finger and added, "Audrey, not Katharine.

"Mother always used to preen shamelessly when folks said she looked like a young Audrey Hepburn. But now, half the journalists who interview her don't even know who Audrey Hepburn was."

A hint of a real grin crossed Jack's face. "And the other half are probably thinking, 'An *old* Audrey Hepburn.'"

"Ouch! Be nice to me or I'll tell her you said that." She all but punched him in his arm.

This time, his grin expanded to something much more genuine, reflecting in his eyes. "You always were a rotten little kid."

Emily brushed off his statement by rolling her eyes and turning to Kate. "Don't believe him. Jack always was and always *will* be a big bully."

"That reminds me." He turned to Kate, as if suddenly remembering she was there. "I just want to say how much I appreciated all you did for my father. The hospital visit, the funeral arrangements . . . everything."

"It's the least we could do," she said. "Dozier was a great friend, a formidable politician, and an invaluable mentor." It was no exaggeration when she added, "Dozier was . . . family." Maybe not her favorite "uncle," but one nonetheless.

To her surprise, Jack blinked, evidently battling a tear or two as some emotion swelled inside him. He avoided any response or explanation by taking another sip of his coffee and simply nodding.

Emily busied herself by pouring another cup of coffee. Her telltale cough meant she was choking back some emotion of her own. "The old man was the last of his kind, you know. There's no one left of his generation now."

Jack glanced beyond Emily's shoulder at the two old

men who were ranting at Burl and Melissa, evidently taking advantage of the opportunity to impart their own particular brand of wisdom to the younger and therefore ignorant generation. The third gentleman had fallen asleep and was starting to snore. Burl still looked accommodating and interested while Melissa was starting to glaze over.

Jack leaned closer. "I can think of one or two that are still kicking around. I'm not too sure about number three."

Emily gave the trio a dismissive nod. "I'm not talking about deaf and deafer over there. As soon as this is over, we wheel the ancient mariners back to the nursing home and reward them with pudding. But your dad—now he was different. He was an asset to my campaign, not to mention my administration, up to the day he died. Sharp as a tack but lethal like a sword."

"That's because you kept him young. You made him feel wanted and valuable." Jack's face darkened for a moment. "You were a far better surrogate daughter than I ever was his natural son."

Kate watched as Emily struggled for the right response. The polite thing would be to decry his statement, but that might be hard to do if Emily actually agreed with him.

Luckily the ancient mariners began to rise from their chairs and wander in their direction, giving Emily an excuse not to respond as their conversation group expanded. To Kate's relief, the topics lightened somewhat in tone as the informal reception turned more into an impromptu wake with the group recalling some of the lighthearted moments in Dozier's life.

The mariners, all of whom were Dozier's old navy buddies, told stories of his very brief military career on the sea—spending much more time telling tales of Dozier at port than of Dozier at war. Evidently one of the old men had known Dozier when he met Jack's mother, and the topic changed to Dozier's life as a husband and father.

But as the older generation told their stories, Kate watched Jack Marsh's reactions. He remained polite, making the appropriate responses when called for, but his laughter was restrained as if he didn't quite find his father's younger antics as amusing as everyone else did.

From the conversation, Kate gleaned the fact that Emily and Jack Marsh had spent a considerable portion of their childhood together. Although Emily's early years had been lived primarily in the limelight, thanks to her family's public service, somehow Jack Marsh's role had escaped the notice of the press or the historians.

Kate knew this for a fact because she'd researched Emily's life from a journalistic point of view in order to anticipate what a nosy reporter might find if he looked hard and dug deep. And at no time had Jack Marsh ever come up in any excavation into the life and times of Emily Benton other than as a person in passing.

Nevertheless, the two of them had a discernible history. Emily told stories and Jack added minor details that betrayed a close friendship that seemed to suddenly end shortly after her high school graduation. Neither of them alluded to either a problem or a person that came between them, but Kate had a feeling by the way they danced around the topic that it had something to do with Dozier himself.

Whatever it was, Jack Marsh had evidently left his home and family shortly after high school to seek his own fortune in places where his last name didn't come with any appreciable political baggage.

She figured this out not because of the impromptu wake but because she'd researched him thoroughly after realizing that he might be a key player in their problems concerning Dozier's financial legacy.

Kate decided that Jack had deliberately led his life in polar opposition to Emily, seeking to escape his family's professional birthright rather than embrace it as she did as the next generation of the Benton dynasty.

While they all talked, Kate stayed in the background as an audience member rather than a participant. That allowed her to watch Emily, a master at work.

Emily danced with certain subjects, deftly avoiding several potholes as she steered them away from Dozier in his role as a father figure and, instead, kept the topics in far safer areas. She didn't exercise control over the conversation solely because she was president; such ownership came to her naturally, and Jack easily kowtowed to her control as if quite used to it.

Kate wondered if that meant he'd be a more willing informant when it came to the irregularities they needed to uncover and perhaps cover up again.

After the requisite amount of reminiscing, one of Emily's aides arrived right on prearranged cue to "remind" her of an unavoidable and pressing appointment. Emily rose and apologized for having to return to her duties. "The country isn't going to run itself, you know."

Polite laughter ensued. She made the obligatory salutations to the ancient mariners, showed Jack a surprising amount of affection, and then excused herself, heading back to the Oval Office.

Kate, along with Burl and Melissa, walked their tottering guests slowly through the Cross Hall and into the Entrance Hall, flanking them like border collies leading an easily distracted herd. Once the three guests were bundled up in their vehicle to be driven back to the old mariner's home, she was left to make a somewhat awkward farewell to Jack Marsh.

Before he stepped into his car, he paused, one hand on the door. "According to the doctors, you were with my father when he died."

She nodded. "We'd been talking and then he had the second attack. I stayed in the room until they decided he was . . ." *How do I say this gently?* "Until they realized he couldn't be resuscitated."

Jack held out his hand. "Then let me offer you a special thank-you. I should have been there, but since I wasn't, I'm glad he had someone like you. Someone he actually liked and trusted."

Kate tried to ignore the implication that Dozier neither liked nor trusted his son and, instead, tried to accept the compliment on its surface merits.

"You're welcome." She thought about Dozier's confession, the unanswered questions about his actions. Added to that, there were his occasional misogynistic comments, how he sometimes clung to old ways and outdated language that tended to grate against the nerves of those more politically correct people who worked with him. But for all his flaws—and he had many—Kate still mourned the loss of the man for his own sake.

She glanced up into Jack's eyes, finding only the barest physical resemblance between father and son. "I really am going to miss Dozier."

After a beat, Jack released a sigh. "So am I."

"Are you going to stay in town for a while or are you headed back to Japan immediately?"

His expression suddenly became very reminiscent of his father's. "No, I'm going to go about thirty feet down the driveway, stop, and back up as if I remembered I left my scarf on the chair. Then you're taking me to the Oval Office, where you, Emily, and I are having a closed-door meeting to try to figure out how to fix this mess my father created with his finances."

He paused. "Didn't you get the memo?"

JACK MIGHT NOT HAVE PURSUED a career in politics, but Kate realized immediately he had the necessary skill set to survive, if not thrive, in the profession had he chosen to work in that arena.

Emily wasted no time sitting him down and telling him exactly what problems his father had caused by failing to disclose that he held a large stock option in Pembrooke. When she mentioned how the company was in the prime position to make a sizable amount of money when Operation: Energy Independence was put into action, he sat up straight.

Once she was finished, he leaned forward and asked quietly, "What are you going to do?"

Emily shrugged. "What can we do? Kate and I agree that we have to tell the American public what we learned."

He remained quiet as if pondering her words; then he shook his head. "No one would ever believe you."

Kate wasn't sure if Emily's reaction of shock was real or not.

"What?"

"C'mon, Emily. No one would ever believe you didn't have a hand—both hands—in this. Our families go back too far for anyone to believe Dad could even sneeze without you knowing about it." He sat back on the couch and draped his arm across its cushions. "They'll simply believe that you're trying to minimize your role in what could amount to a huge scandal. One that could result in removal from office."

He made a theatrical effort of glancing at his watch. "Congratulations. I think you'll be setting a record. Your administration lasted almost six weeks before the first talks of impeachment."

Emily glanced at Kate as if to say, *Sorry, but it looks like we have to scrap our plans.* "Then what do you suggest we do?"

His smile wasn't a particularly pleasant one. "I can think of one or two options."

"Such as?"

"First, I'd just as soon not see my father's name smeared posthumously."

Emily's gaze sharpened as if she had suddenly made a leap in logic. She dropped down to the couch next to him. "So, do I assume you are his heir? you get everything?"

His expression grew less predatory. "I get most of it. He had a few charitable requests, but I get everything else. To my utter surprise, may I add."

"You shouldn't be all that surprised. You two might have had some bad blood, but it was family blood nonetheless."

He looked as if he was contemplating her words. "True. But I'm willing to show there's a difference between father and son, especially when it comes to the concept of greed. And I think that might help you."

Emily managed to infuse several meanings into a single word. "Explain."

"Sure. What you have to first understand is that I didn't expect to inherit anything, so I'm ahead of the game. I don't have to be so greedy that I take everything. Is there a way we can retroactively redirect his stock option—maybe make it appear the future money was earmarked for some higher purpose?"

Kate took an involuntary step forward, ready to insert an "Absolutely not," until she saw how Emily's grin lit her face, softening her sharp features.

"Exactly! That's why I've always loved you. You think just as fast on your feet as your old man, but you're actually nowhere as corrupt as that old shark."

Kate couldn't remain quiet any longer. "You're willing to give up what amounts to a substantial inheritance, just to preserve your father's name?"

Emily tried to interrupt her. "Kate—"

"No. Jack needs to know exactly how much money we're talking about." She turned to the man sitting on the couch. "Your father said he was expecting a $15 million return in the first year alone." She expected Jack to be either amazed or disgusted by the amount, but what she didn't expect was the reaction she did elicit from him.

"So?"

Jack turned toward Kate. "Let me repeat. I'm not a greedy man. I guess you don't hear this often in Washington, but let me say this again. I don't need the money. I'm doing quite well on my own." A thoughtful look dropped over his face. "I'd much rather see the control of the stock option go somewhere worthy to offset his avarice. It seems almost . . . tainted to me."

Kate realized this was a prime example of someone doing the wrong thing for all the right reasons.

Emily ignored his more altruistic reasoning and concentrated on the execution of their solution. "Since he appears to have hidden his ownership through the use of several offshore holding companies, it might be simply a matter of making some retroactive changes to the last company in the chain—once we figure out who holds what. The real difficulty will be unraveling all this quietly."

Kate watched numbly, not quite believing what she was hearing.

Jack stroked his chin in obvious contemplation. "I'm thinking that maybe it ought to go to some charity."

Emily nodded eagerly. "That way, if anyone gets nosy and starts to follow the trail, it'll show that Dozier was involved, but only as a conduit to the final destination, some tree-hugger, green charity that'll make even the most hardened journalist go 'Aww. . . .'"

Jack continued to stroke his chin. "That'd work. But . . . it has to be a charity I don't currently work with and something Dad might have chosen. After the fact, I can come onto the board as a sort of legacy to my father's posthumous involvement."

Emily leaned over and bussed him on the cheek. "I knew you'd find a solution. I have always been able to rely on you."

He adopted his first genuinely warm smile, betraying a current sense of closeness with Emily rather than a nostalgic one. "Are you going to make this happen, or am I?"

Kate had remained quiet to this point but knew she had to insert herself into the conversation. "I want to go on the record to state that I'm against this idea. I think it would be far better to put your cards on the table and simply explain to the world that Dozier kept this vital piece of information a secret, even from us. After all, it's the truth. All this under-the-table paperwork could backfire on you if someone catches on."

Emily stood, taking advantage of her position to tower over Kate, who had remained seated. "Trust me. They won't catch on."

"You can't be sure."

Emily glanced at Jack. "Yeah. I can be sure. The man's a miracle maker."

* * * * *

Kate waited until she got back into her office before she allowed her sense of concern to turn into open panic. Discounting the eventual funding of some yet unnamed charity, what Emily was doing was still wrong on all levels. As much as Kate understood the need to protect self, lying to the American public—even with good intentions—was rife with problems, not to mention a dozen or so large pits filled with alligators.

Her head throbbed as her imagination began to work overtime to spell out exactly what sort of mess Dozier had put them in and how much messier it might get once Emily and Jack started their "renovation" plans.

"Lord, what do I do?" she prayed aloud, frightened by the amount of panic she heard in her own voice. "We didn't know about Dozier. Given how many scandals have torn apart the White House in the past, I hate to admit Jack's right—no one will believe we had no knowledge of this. But what Emily's planning to do—to hide the truth—that's not right, either. What should I do?"

The answer didn't come in the guise of a burning bush, a clap of thunder, or any other overt symbolism. She simply looked up.

Hanging above her desk was a photograph of her and Emily on graduation day, both decked out in cap, gown, and colors. They'd been standing on the steps of the library, and in taking the snapshot, her father, their intrepid photographer, had also gotten the inscription over the library's entrance.

Cognoscetis Veritatem et Veritas Liberabit Vos.

"You will know the truth and the truth will make you free."

If Jack was going to make widespread changes to organizational records through whatever manner—bribery, break-in, or such—what Kate needed was a pristine copy of those records before they were altered. She needed a snapshot of the real world before Emily's revisionist handiwork gave it a makeover.

She picked up the phone to call District Discreet, then hung up after the first ring. Call it paranoia, call it being overly cautious, but since she'd already made her objections known, Emily might predict what her next actions would be and easily guess what company Kate might use to ferret out the unfindable.

Kate needed to use a different route than her usual one, and that meant trusting somebody other than Lee and Sierra to dig up the truth.

But who? The more people who knew the truth, the less security they had.

Who did Kate trust enough to reveal this less-than-flattering side of Dozier Marsh, revelations of Maia the blackmailer, and Emily's efforts to sanitize the past?

One person.

Nick.

She used her cell phone to call him, and it rang four times before he picked up.

"Beaudry."

"It's me. Kate. I saw you at the funeral," she said, realizing only after she spoke that she sounded slightly accusatory.

"Yeah, I felt like I needed to go."

"It was a nice gesture. But I'm not sure why."

"I guess I got to know Dozier pretty well when M and I were together."

"As I recall, you never really liked him." She was beating around the non–burning bush, but she needed time to formulate her plans, then find her courage to implement them.

"I didn't like Dozier butting into my marriage, but I guess he felt like he was protecting her like a father protects his daughter. I didn't . . . dislike the man. For an old-time politician used to twisting the truth when it was convenient for him, once we made peace, he was always pretty straight with me."

Nick offered a rosier view of the past than she'd anticipated, but his description of Dozier twisting the truth was all too accurate.

"Can we talk?"

He cleared his throat. "Aren't we doing that now?"

"I mean—" she searched for the right words—"privately."

"Sure. When? Where?"

She'd already come up with the answer. "There's a diplomatic reception here this evening for the new ambassador from Ecuador. I can put you on the guest list."

"At this late date?"

"Hello? Chief of staff here."

He paused as if contemplating the idea. "Can you get me a little face time with the ambassador? Nothing antagonistic or long. Strictly business."

She bristled a bit. "Is it a conditional yes, then?"

He backpedaled quickly. "No, nothing like that. I was just wondering if I could kill two birds with one White House visit. I'm still willing to come whether you can get M to let me talk to him or not."

There was a moment of silence, and then he spoke again, his words holding a hint of confusion mixed with mild regret. "I don't play those kinds of games, Kate. I thought you knew that."

"Well, I was hoping that was the case." She splayed her hand across her forehead, her headache reminding her that she really needed to take some meds or risk it turning into a migraine. "I'm sorry. It's been a long day already, what with the funeral and everything."

Emphasis on everything.

"I wasn't trying to be accusatory." She searched for the right phrase of apology and settled on a legal one: "*Absit iniuria verbis.*" *Let injury by words be absent.*

He made a choking noise, then laughed. "I know it's been a hard day if you're resorting to law school Latin."

You don't know the half of it, she thought.

"Rest assured, no offense taken." His voice remained lighter. "I've had days like that too. When you're the person at the top, you get used to the idea that without exception, everybody wants something. Or so I've been told. I'm still a very small cog in a great big lobbying machine."

She heard a tapping sound at her door. "Hang on," she said to him. She covered the mouthpiece and then called out, "Come in."

An aide cracked open the door, realized she was on the phone, and made the universal expression for *Oops! Sorry. I can wait until you're off the phone.*

She held the aide at bay with a raised forefinger and turned back to the phone, trying to sound light and carefree. "If it's any consolation, sir, this job has its coglike attributes too. But apparently, this cog is being paged. I have to go. See you tonight?"

"Someone walked in?"

"Yes."

"Got it. See you tonight."

That evening, Kate knew the minute that Nick walked into the room simply by the look on Emily's face. Others might not have recognized the very brief flash of irritation across her face, but Kate knew it all too well.

The commander in chief was not happy, and she wasted no time in complaining to Kate.

"What's he doing here?" she said in a terse whisper.

Kate lied. "I don't know. But I'll get rid of him."

"You do that," Emily said while nodding and greeting

the people in the reception line. "I've already given him as much slack as I can stomach."

Kate caught Nick's eye and gestured toward the door where he'd just entered. She followed him as he wheeled about and stepped into the hallway.

He crooked a smile only after he was out of Emily's view. "Her Majesty is not pleased."

"Of course not. Her Majesty will never be pleased. You know that."

To her surprise, Nick chided her. "Hey, give her a break. She went to a funeral today for a very close friend. She's allowed to be in a bad mood."

Kate hated to admit that not only was he right, but he was being much more solicitous than she was at the moment. "Point taken." She looked around to make sure no one could overhear them. "By the way, I'm out here reading you the riot act for showing up."

He looked confused. "But you invited me."

"I did. But Emily doesn't know that and never needs to know that."

"Why?"

She grabbed his sleeve and tugged him, forcing him to follow her. "Because I have a very big problem, and you're the only person I can trust."

"Me? Wow. I mean, don't you have all sorts of people who are supposed to do what you say? The FBI, CIA, NSA?"

"Not this time." She continued walking. "Just look irritated as we talk so anyone passing us thinks I'm getting you out of Emily's eyesight and giving you what for."

He stumbled along with her, keeping up the act. "So, I

guess this means I have no chance of getting a little face time with the ambassador tonight?"

She offered a plastic smile and nod of greeting to a couple coming their direction. After they passed, she whispered, "No, but I promise I'll make it up to you another time."

As they continued along the hallway, they passed by several more guests and a couple of aides. Kate knew the aides would be instrumental in providing the rumor mill with this particular bit of gristle—the chief of staff intercepting the president's ex-husband and hustling him out of the White House. The gossipmongers and pundits would delight in the news.

Time to add a bit to the drama. "I don't care how you got on the invitation list," she said a bit louder than she normally would. "We both know this isn't a good idea."

Nick gave her a questioning look but played along nonetheless. "Don't blame me. I got the invitation, I responded, and I came. How was I to know Emily knew nothing about it?"

She led him past the Map Room and had the key to the medical clinic already in her hand, so it took only a moment to unlock the door and guide him in.

"I'm not sick," he joked once they were safely inside, the door locked behind them and the lights switched on.

She released the breath she'd been holding. "I am. Sick with worry." At his reaction to the room, she shook her head. "It's okay. No one will interrupt us here. I made sure of it."

Kate had planned carefully, trying to find a location that was both close to the reception and would offer them complete privacy. Being the White House chief of staff meant she could get the keys to specific offices without too many questions, and the White House physician's on-site clinic filled the bill nicely.

She'd arranged for the entire on call medical staff to be treated to a movie premiere in the White House theater as a personal thank-you for their speedy reaction to Dozier's collapse. They'd still be only steps away from the president should any medical emergencies arise.

Nick settled himself on the couch. "Okay, Kate. Why all the skulduggery?"

Kate contemplated sitting on the arm of the couch but knew she wouldn't be able to sit still. So instead, she began to pace the small office, spilling her guts and telling him everything that had transpired—Dozier's deathbed confession, Jack Marsh's involvement, and Emily's plans.

As she explained, Nick's posture shifted from a carefree "Tell me a story" pose until, as she finished, he was perched on the edge of the couch, elbows planted on his knees and his head cradled in his palms as if the details were making his head ache.

After she finished her recitation, he sighed noisily into his hands, then looked up at her. "You honestly think Dozier had something to do with the crash?"

Now that her nervous energy had been given an outlet and she'd been able to actually voice the story, fatigue set in, and she dropped somewhat ungracefully to the couch and sat next to him. "I'm not sure," she said, stifling a sudden yawn. "All he said was that it was his fault and that he didn't mean for her to die. But he was pretty straightforward about the blackmail part."

"Oh, man . . ." He shook his head, then spoke again, his voice low. "So what can I do to help?"

An unexpected sense of relief coursed through her. She hadn't been sure whether his sympathy for her plight might be overwhelmed by his glee in Emily's predicament. "Emily has asked Jack to do the 'dirty work' so no one can say that the White House had a hand in it. All I want you to do is get to the files before he does."

He glanced up again, this time shock etched in his features. "You mean you want me to steal them?"

Her stomach clinched at the thought. "Absolutely not! I don't want you to do anything but get a copy of them before any changes are made."

His gaze narrowed. "How is an archive copy going to help?"

"I'm not sure, but if any of this is made public and people learn that changes were made, then without a basis of comparison, they can make it out for much worse than it actually was."

"So if anyone catches wind of this and starts to scream scandal, you can pull out a copy of the original and show that the changes weren't as invasive as they could have been."

"Exactly. And a copy dated . . . let's say, tomorrow, would show that any changes were done posthumously, helping to substantiate that we didn't know anything about it until after Dozier's death."

Nick remained quiet for almost a minute, and Kate wasn't sure whether his silence meant he wasn't going to help after all.

A split second before she reached her breaking point, he looked up. "Are you *sure* Emily didn't know anything about this beforehand?"

"About Dozier's finances?"

He nodded. "It sounds like something she would have

cooked up with him on the sly. I was never privy to all of their secrets."

She thought back to Emily's genuine expression of shock. After the last year of the campaign, Kate had decided she'd become an expert at reading the truth—no matter how bitter or poignant—in Emily's face.

"No," she said, hoping she sounded as resolute as she felt. "The news took both of us by complete and total surprise."

He wore his doubt as plainly as his displeasure. "I know it surprised you, but can you really be so sure about Emily? Neither you nor I had any inkling about the toll road debacle. She hid that from everyone with a straight face."

Kate searched her memory and her heart for the answer. After two hard years working on the campaign, she felt as if her sense of naiveté had been chipped away to the point that she couldn't help but view almost everything—Emily included—with a jaded eye. But this time, she knew the answer wasn't built on her hope or faith in her friend, but in raw facts and experience.

"I'd stake my life on it."

She watched his expression go from doubtful to resolute.

"Good enough for me. That settles it, then. I'm in." Nick stood. "But one more question. Why me?"

Why him indeed? Kate had already asked herself that, and the answer was twofold. "Because I trusted you before with sensitive information about Emily, and you didn't abuse that trust. Plus, you're the last person Emily expects to get involved in this. She's counting on me to follow my usual operating procedure. As far as that goes, she knows exactly which investigators I always trust when I'm facing covert issues. So I know she's keeping an eye on them."

Confusion filled his face. "I thought you said Emily thinks you're completely on board with her plans."

"She's 98 percent sure I'm in agreement with her, but the 2 percent of doubt will make her wary. She'll watch me and the people I trust like a hawk."

He gave her a critical once-over that made her feel as if he could see right through her protective shell and view all of her discomfort, her fears, her worries, and her sense of guilt for essentially working against her president. "You've changed. You're more . . . skeptical, less trusting than you used to be."

"Once burned . . ." She shrugged. "And maybe, just maybe, I've been a bit too trusting when it comes to Emily. She's no less susceptible to temptation than anyone else."

"Maybe more so. You know what they say about what absolute power brings."

"Yeah. And all I want to do is make sure she's not erasing something that doesn't need to be erased." Kate stood, reached into her evening bag, and pulled out a folded sheet of paper on which she'd scribbled a grocery list. Embedded in the list were the names of the three holding companies that she'd spent most of the late afternoon and early evening tracking down.

She handed him the paper. "Here's where to start."

He examined the list, raising an eyebrow over her unusual precaution, then slipped the paper into his inner jacket pocket.

"I'm afraid time may be of the essence. I just hope we're not too late."

"I'll do my best." He paused and took her hands in his. "You know I'm not doing this for Emily." He waited a moment; then his face grew a little red as he quirked a brief smile. "Okay, so part of it's for Emily. I consider this part of the reparation that I need to make to her for the years I spent more time in the bottle than I did with her. But I'm also doing this because I consider you a good friend."

When he made eye contact with her, his momentary flush faded, and she found herself caught up in the seriousness and sincerity of his expression.

Kate wasn't sure why she reacted like she did. She wasn't an impetuous woman, but she did understand the value of taking proper advantage of a situation. Maybe that's why she stood on her toes, reached up, and kissed him.

THE KISS WAS SHORT, furtive, and the instant she pulled away, a thousand accusations flooded her mind, making her feel as confident as some idiot schoolgirl acting on her first crush.

"I'm sorry," she said, secretly thrilled she hadn't stuttered through her schoolgirl's apology.

In a perfect world, he would have said, "You have nothing to apologize for," and then planted a kiss worthy of the movies on her. But this was the real White House, not an episode of *The West Wing*.

Nick looked thoroughly uncomfortable.

Rather than repeat her apology, she scanned the clinic's reception area, spotted a shelf of everyday first aid supplies, and grabbed an adhesive bandage.

"Here," she said, handing it to him. "Put this on and it'll explain why we were in here."

Nick opened the package, pulled out the bandage, then hesitated. He held it out to her. "You do it." He pointed to his head, then bent at the knees so she could better reach his forehead.

After the fact, Kate realized that sometimes the unsuspecting actors in an unscripted drama do hit their cues right.

Her hand remained steady as she peeled off the backing from the small bandage and then placed it near his hairline, covering the scar he sported from the attack months ago.

She felt his breath on her face as she inspected her handiwork. Then she felt his lips touch hers.

Although her mind swirled with thoughts, they only served to provide a pastel backdrop to the emotions that created broad strokes of color in her mind. Reason and logic didn't disappear completely, but the thrill of the moment certainly pushed them to the back of her thoughts.

After several seconds, he pulled away.

"Where did that come from?" he whispered.

"I don't know."

He leaned his head against hers. "I didn't expect to feel anything. I even told myself I couldn't feel anything. You're Kate. You're my ex-wife's best friend."

"I know what you mean. You're my best friend's ex-husband. It violates the BFF code."

"BFF?"

"Best friends forever."

He nodded, instantly understanding the implications. "Yeah, I can't imagine that Emily would approve."

The words came instantly and with a sense of candor that astonished Kate, even as she spoke. "I don't need her permission or her approval."

He kissed her again, this time longer and with an

increased sense of urgency. When he pulled back, he drew in a long breath. "This is definitely not what I expected to happen tonight."

"What did you expect?"

"Decent hors d'oeuvres, a glass of tonic water, schmoozing with as many people as I could, twenty seconds or so with the ambassador, and Emily glaring at me all evening long." He cupped Kate's face in his hand. "Instead, I get a James Bond assignment and a make-out session in a closet."

She pretended to take offense at his assessment. "We did not make out. And this isn't a closet."

He gave the room a sweeping glance. "Okay, but it would have sounded much worse if I said we had a make-out session in a doctor's office."

"True."

He reached for her hand and squeezed it. "Let me live my fantasy. You've given me my assignment. Let me go prove that I'm worthy of your trust."

And love? She was glad she only thought the words rather than said them because it was far too early to even begin to think along those lines. *It was just a simple kiss,* she thought as he started toward the door.

Three kisses, she corrected herself.

★ ★ ★ ★ ★

When Kate returned to the Diplomatic Reception Room, Emily caught her attention immediately, those arching eyebrows communicating, *Well?* with little effort.

Kate negotiated the crowded room, sidestepping clusters of people deep in conversation. She plastered an artificial smile on her face, hoping it masked the real smile that still lingered.

"Well?"

"Our guest left without any problem. However, he had been officially invited."

"By whom?"

Kate lifted her hands. "I assume by the same person who invited him to the inaugural ball."

"Then you'd assume wrong. The ball, yes. This? No."

Kate hadn't come unprepared. She leaned closer and whispered, "I didn't want to say anything, but I think Dozier might have engineered the invitation. And since I doubt it was for any altruistic reasons, he must have had something planned to embarrass Nick or something like that."

The explanation seemed to satisfy Emily. "Yeah, or something like that."

The rest of the reception went off as planned. Emily made her farewell at 9:00. At 9:01, White House aides began to circulate in the room and insert themselves politely in the various conversation clusters and congenially say, "The president thanks you for spending the evening with us. We hope you have a safe trip back home." It was their gentle way of saying, "Now it's time for you to leave. So leave, already." It worked with most of the partygoers who were well aware that the White House had a schedule that only major disasters or declarations of war would interrupt.

Those attendees who didn't get the initial message were reminded two minutes later by Secret Service agents who were no less polite, but whose presence was much harder to ignore.

By 9:05 the room had been cleared of all guests, food, and dirty dishes.

Kate went back to her office, gathered her things, and headed home, where she remained awake almost all night, fretting about the "mission" she'd sent Nick on. She kept reminding herself that her motives were pure—to protect Emily from herself. Kate had no intention of whipping out the copy of the original documents in order to point an accusing finger. But in case Emily's carefully made plans exploded in her face—as Kate feared they might—she wanted to be able to clarify exactly what had been changed.

But despite reassuring herself, Kate's heart and her conscience warred to see which one felt heavier. Every now and then, she whispered a quick prayer.

"Tell me I'm doing the right thing, Lord."

When neither her heart nor her conscience felt the burden lift, she couldn't help but worry that she'd chosen the wrong path for the right reasons.

Just as she had finally decided to rethink the situation in the morning and given herself permission to sleep, the phone rang.

Buster woke from his deep sleep with a confused howl. Kate automatically reached with one hand to pat him and reassure him that the mean old phone meant him no harm while using her other hand to find the mean old phone on her bed stand.

"Kate? It's Nick Beaudry."

She heard something in his voice she didn't like. "What's wrong?"

"I need a lawyer."

Every muscle in her body tightened. What had she gotten him into?

"Why? Are you in trouble?"

"No." He paused, then repeated, "No. Not trouble. But I have two agents here who want to ask me a lot of questions, and I've declined to answer them until I have my lawyer present. They seem insistent on asking them right now."

"In the middle of the night?"

"Interesting timing, don't you think?"

"I'll be right there. Tell me where 'there' is."

He gave her directions to his apartment, which he described as "almost in Crystal City." Since time was obviously of the essence, Kate merely threw on jeans and a sweatshirt and pulled her hair back into a ponytail. As much as she might want to look like a lawyer in a sharp suit and perfect makeup, she would have to contend with only sounding and acting like one.

A heavy rain had been falling since midnight, and as a result, water flowed fast in the gutters and congregated in the low spots on the side of the road. But despite the more treacherous road conditions, she managed to dress, drive, and arrive in less than twenty minutes.

To her surprise, she learned that Nick didn't live in one of the glass and steel high-rise buildings, but a very mundane, squatty brick apartment house that, from the outside, looked as if it hadn't been renovated since it was built in the early fifties.

Evidently his position as a lobbyist with Better Energy Alliance didn't include a paycheck large enough for fancy digs. When she knocked on the door, someone other than Nick answered. For one moment, she worried that she'd mixed up the directions and knocked on the wrong door. But she took a closer look at the man standing in the doorway and pegged him immediately as FBI.

"You the attorney?" he said in a gruff voice.

"Yes. And you?"

He dipped into his pocket and pulled out a leather wallet and showed her his photo ID that proved he was with the Bureau. Special Agent R.T. Stoffler.

"What's the R.T. stand for?"

"It doesn't. It's just R.T."

"Good to know. Where's my client?"

"In the kitchen." He stepped back to allow her to enter the apartment. She shrugged off her wet coat, looked around, and found a peg rack conveniently placed next to the front door. After depositing her coat there, she turned to take in the view.

Although the living room was sparse, its furniture all matched in a sort of cheap, nondescript, nonpersonalized way. It was obviously a furnished apartment. A dozen or so boxes—about half of which had been opened, the other half still sealed—had been piled in the corner.

The agent led her to the kitchen, where Nick and a second agent stood at the counter. She'd expected to see Nick being grilled, not drinking coffee and talking sports.

When he spotted her, he stopped in midsentence and developed a guarded smile. "Oh, good, you're here. Thanks for coming out."

She didn't hide her displeasure. "In the rain," she reminded him.

"Especially in the rain," he repeated. "We've been just shooting the breeze until you got here. Special Agent Deakins has been working heavy on the good cop routine in hopes that he'll disarm me with his congeniality and rip some sort of confession or something out of me. I'm not quite sure yet."

Kate thought the second agent was going to choke on his coffee, his motives having been so plainly interpreted.

But Nick wasn't finished. He reached into his pocket, pulled out a dollar, and handed it to Kate. "Your retainer, ma'am." He then turned to the two men. "Special Agents Stoffler and Deakins, may I present my attorney, Kathryn Rosen." He waited for the slightest pause before adding, "The White House chief of staff."

The two men stared at her, trying to look past her über-casual clothes, her utilitarian hairdo, and her makeup-less face. Recognition dawned.

"Ma'am?" Agent Deakins nodded toward the kitchen table and pulled out a chair. "We apologize for not recognizing you immediately."

She decided to give the man a break. "I doubt my own mother would recognize me like this." She accepted the seat. "Now what questions do you want to ask my client and about what topic?"

"His whereabouts prior to the crash that killed a woman named Maia Bari and a man named Timothy Colton."

Kate didn't have to fake an air of exasperation. "What questions do you have that I haven't already answered for your superior?"

All three men looked somewhat puzzled, Nick included. Deakins was the brave one to speak. "Someone in our organization has already spoken with you?"

"Yes." She leaned across the table, her palms outstretched. "Do you not compare notes or check with your superiors before showing up on a man's doorstep in the wee hours?"

Deakins dropped into the seat across from her. "We weren't aware you'd been involved in the investigation."

"I happen to have been with Mr. Beaudry the night that the accident occurred."

Stoffler tried this time. "So you spoke with our field supervisor?" He named a name.

"No. Higher than that." She was now playing a game and waiting for them to catch on.

He mentioned another name, evidently higher up in the food chain.

"Higher." At their continued confusions, Kate decided to play her trump card. "A few days after the unfortunate incident, I spoke with Director Richfield, who asked me questions in the privacy of the Oval Office so as to spare the president any undue discomfort or embarrassment of any publicity concerning the fact that her chief of staff offered an alibi for the whereabouts of the president's ex-husband on the night of question."

At their stunned silence, she added, "Evidently you didn't get the memo."

Deakins stood quietly, guiding the cheap kitchen chair back under the table as if it were a Chippendale original of unfathomable worth. "No, ma'am, we didn't get the memo. However, please be assured that we're anxious to determine why that key piece of information was not adequately relayed to us." He turned to Nick. "Sir, please accept my personal apology for disturbing you in the middle of the night." Deakins then turned to Kate. "And, ma'am, I highly regret that you had to come out here on what turned out to be—because of us—a fool's errand."

Moments later, the two agents were gone, the door closing with only the quietest noise behind them.

Nick stared in the direction of their departure. "If I hadn't heard it with my own ears, I wouldn't have believed it." He turned to Kate. "Was that the truth? The director of the FBI actually questioned you?"

She nodded. "I was mortified. Sitting there in the Oval Office—Emily looking on. It was like being called into the ultimate principal's office."

"I can imagine. And he asked questions about me?"

She nodded. "Had you arranged to meet me, why were you there, when did I first see you, what condition were you in . . . Things like that."

"I bet Emily was having a blast."

"I don't know about that. She admitted to being the one who saw to it that you had a ticket to the Constitution Ball."

"Really? She actually admitted to it?"

Kate nodded. "Surprised me, too."

He shook his head. "Will wonders never cease?" He looked up, then colored slightly. "I really appreciate that you were willing to come out here in the middle of the night and act as my lawyer."

"I'm glad you called. I doubt anyone else could have found the right answers to make them hightail it out of here."

"You had the right ammunition, for sure."

An awkward silence muffled their conversation like a heavy blanket of wet snow. But instead of snowing, the rains outside had subsided from roaring storm to gentle mist.

Despite her better efforts to stifle a yawn, it escaped nonetheless. "I . . . I better head home and try to get some more sleep before I have to go into the office."

He stood and offered a hand to help her up. "You don't know how much I appreciate this, Kate. Having a friend I can call on . . ."

"Even in the middle of the night," she supplied with a grin. "I didn't mind helping, Nick. Not at all."

He led her to the apartment door, helping her with her raincoat. "Drive carefully." He pushed back the curtains that covered the living room window. "I think this is only a momentary lull. The weather forecast for tomorrow is more of the same."

"At least if it starts up again, I won't have to contend with much traffic."

"True. Good night, then. Or good morning, as the case might be." He opened the door and cold air seeped into the living room.

"Good night."

"Drive carefully."

"I will."

Nick put a merciful end to their awkward good-bye by giving her a hug that felt as confusingly pleasant as had the kisses they'd shared earlier that evening. He complicated matters even more by tightening his arms and saying, "I really do appreciate everything, Kate."

She liked the brief sense of security of his arms. For a passing moment, she could simply enjoy having someone else be protective of her and give her a break from being her own primary protector, defender, and all the other roles she played as a single female in a position of high authority within the White House.

He then leaned down, his lips brushing her ear, and in a husky whisper, said, "As to our little problem? I pulled some strings and should be getting a copy of the original filing documents for the last shell corporation that links you know who with the stock options. He hid everything as a Panamanian foundation, not a corporation."

The moment of intimacy dissipated and the reminder of the duties of her immediate world flooded back. He pulled away a little and offered her a grin of triumph. "That's why you had a hard time finding it."

"How did you ever pull that off?"

"My father had twelve brothers and sisters and my mother had seven. I have first cousins almost everywhere in the world, including one who's an expat living in Panama. He runs an employment company and specializes in providing a wide variety of services to law firms, everything from shredding services to the night janitorial staff. He was able to get a copy of the original dated application and all the requests for changes. It'll show a clear picture of the foundation's origins and when certain changes were made."

"I assume it's just as illegal in Panama as it would be here, right?"

"Knowing Donnie? Absolutely. He's never been one who played well within government restrictions. It's the reason he doesn't live in the U.S. anymore." Nick sighed. "My family runs the gamut of everything from working stiffs down to what my mother always called 'guttersnipes.' I'd like to think I skew more toward the working stiff side of the family tree."

Kate suddenly realized she was still within the circle of his arms. She pushed back, their business conversation not matching the more personal nature of their position.

"When are you supposed to receive the files?"

"They're coming by courier tomorrow. Or I guess that would be today—this afternoon."

"Then you need to find a place to stash the proof." She looked at his apartment. "Not here."

"Of course not." He concentrated for a moment. "What about my storage unit? When I left the city to move back to Louisiana last time, I gave up my apartment, so I had to get a friend to pack up and store my stuff in one of those month-by-month storage units." He thumbed back over his shoulder. "When I returned, *this* was the only place I could find on short notice. And since it was furnished, I just left the other furniture and stuff in storage."

"If they get a warrant for your apartment, they'd probably also include any satellite storage units. They can track stuff like that down through bank records, credit card files, or such."

He winked. "They can't if there's no paper trail. The buddy who packed everything up? He *owns* the moving and storage company. He's not charging me, so there's no way anybody can track it down."

"So you'll hide the papers there?"

"Seems like the best solution. I can get you a key to the place as well to make sure you have access to it." Lightning split the sky and thunder rumbled several seconds behind the light.

The rain began to fall again. "I . . . I better start home before it gets worse."

"Good night, then." He reached for her hand. Then after a moment's hesitation, he pulled her closer to him for one long and thrilling kiss that sent a bolt of electricity clear down to her toes.

When they finally broke apart, he kept his grasp on her hand and drew in a breath that was almost shaky. "Oh, boy."

She held on to his hand as much for balance as anything else. "My sentiments exactly."

"This . . . still confuses me."

Kate felt her face redden. "Me too."

"So what are we going to do about it?"

"Go slow?"

He nodded, giving her a much more chaste kiss on the forehead. "Agreed." He gave her hand one last squeeze. "But it's not going to be easy."

KATE DRAGGED HERSELF to her office a few hours later, coming to the conclusion that she'd finally lost the boundless energies of her youth—the vigor that allowed her to easily overcome any interruption of her normal sleep pattern. Evidently, when the pendulum had swung back after their two hard years of campaigning where sleep was a luxury rather than a necessity, she'd gone from surviving effortlessly on a couple hours of shut-eye to needing as much as possible in order to function the next day.

When had forty-five become ancient?

And when did a couple of kisses keep her from falling back to sleep, especially when she was exhausted? Once Kate had arrived home, she'd stayed awake for another half hour or so, suffering from a persistent, non-erasable memory loop where she relived the kiss and tried to interpret what it might mean to her and to Nick.

But now that she was at work, her attention was drawn

fifteen or so different directions simultaneously. One of those directions was the weather.

Winter had been alternating between "colder than usual" and "warmer than usual," bypassing "usual" as quickly as possible when fluctuating from bitter to dreary to mild and back to bitter again. Although the White House had been monitoring severe weather around the U.S. and dealing with the aftermath of heavy snowfalls in the upper Midwest, record rainfalls in California, and wildfires in the Rockies, it was the building storms in the Atlantic that threatened to affect the White House on two different levels. Question one: What sort of economic impact would potentially dangerous weather have on the East Coast? And question two, the more highly personal: What happens if it hits Washington as hard as they're predicting?

I don't have time to worry about the weather, Kate told herself as she hurried to the first of six back-to-back morning meetings. Nevertheless, she instructed her aides to give her weather updates between each meeting. As the chief of staff, she would have to adapt the president's schedule to accommodate the foul weather, perhaps postponing a trip on Marine One to Andrews, where Emily was scheduled to welcome back returning troops. Then again, chances were equally good that the troops would be either delayed or rerouted due to the weather.

By eleven o'clock, the decision was made to reroute the incoming flight to McGuire Air Force Base in New Jersey, thus relieving Emily of that particular duty.

In the midst of her next meeting, Kate felt her phone vibrate twice, signifying an incoming text message. Surreptitiously she opened it to read the not-too-cryptic message:

The eagle has landed—N

Although Kate didn't really expect any burden to lift from her shoulders, somehow she felt slightly more encouraged when she got Nick's news. But that feeling dissipated once Emily got her behind closed doors between meetings four and five.

"Congratulate me. I got rid of one more complication in the ongoing saga of Dozier Marsh."

Kate tried to hide the fact that her heart had jumped straight up into her throat. "What complication?"

"Something you, Jack, and I failed to consider when we were talking about correcting our problem. We skipped right over that part."

"*What* complication?" she repeated.

"Maia was blackmailing Dozier, right? But we never asked ourselves how. What actual evidence or proof or such did she hold over his head?"

This time Kate failed to hide her reaction.

Emily watched her carefully. Too carefully? "See? It could have been a critical error—a loose end that could have tripped us up. But luckily we found it."

"We?" Kate found her voice and knew a certain amount of opposition would be expected. "Do you have some plumbers I don't know about?"

Emily raised one eyebrow. "Very funny. Don't ask questions if you don't want to know the answers."

"Emily . . ."

The president dropped to the couch and made a show of propping her feet on the coffee table, a position that no one in their right mind would attempt in the Oval Office but her.

The message?

Her office. Her rules.

"At my insistence, our investigators—well, actually your investigators; good ones too, may I add—found the proof in, of all places, Maia's cell phone. She had one that could record video and audio, and turns out she'd made a recording of Dozier bragging about how much he stood to earn when he exercised his option. She even had him explaining all about long call stock options and the intricacies of hiding assets in offshore accounts." She shook her head. "Poor old fool."

Kate's head felt as if it would explode with the possible implications. "What makes you think she didn't send a copy of the video to somebody else? a hundred somebodies, at that?"

Emily's smile bordered on predatory and she rose and walked toward Kate. "You told me you selected the company because they were thorough but discreet. And they were both. They said they checked her phone as well as her phone records. She never sent any files to anyone because she didn't have the capacity on that unit, and that would have been the only way to upload it elsewhere." She clapped Kate on the shoulder as if to congratulate her on their joint triumph.

Kate's skin stung at the site of the contact.

Emily continued, unaware of anything but her own sense of accomplishment. "I just thought you might like to know that there will be no loose ends. Jack is taking care of our paperwork problem. He got out before the storm and is flying to Panama City even as we speak."

Kate feigned ignorance. "Florida?"

"No, the other one in Central America. That's where Dozier evidently did all his offshore banking." At Kate's look of confusion, Emily shook her head. "Don't worry about it. He did a decent job of hiding his assets in a dummy corporation, owned by a dummy foundation. We'll just clean everything up a bit. Jack's going to arrange for a couple of save-the-whatever charities to be the beneficiaries of the foundation. Dozier's name will never be financially connected to Pembrooke again."

She lowered her voice as if worried anyone could hear beyond the soundproof walls. "Nothing is going to stop Operation: Energy Independence. Nothing."

By this point, Kate had made the transition from being simply scared by her friend to being practically overpowered by panic on an almost absurd level.

"Good." She tried to appear relieved but was afraid she wasn't pulling off the look. Her voice was too high, her hands threatening to shake. "Anything else?" she added with as much of a casual air as she could conjure, clutching the file folder in her arms for dear life.

Emily shook her head. "Nope. I just wanted to keep you up to speed."

"Thanks." Kate headed for the door and was only a few steps away from uncertain freedom when Emily spoke again.

"Oh, but there is one more thing."

Kate turned slowly, waiting for an anvil to drop on her head or a red dot to center itself on her chest, right over her heart.

"The investigators think they found the connection between Maia and Tim Colton. Evidently she used that same favorite cell phone to record a conversation she had with him when he was very, very drunk. He was comparing our campaign with Charles Talbot's and how they dealt differently with 'disloyal' members of their staff. In her recording, he bragged about how he and two buddies—" she used finger quotes—"'took care' of Nick." She shook her head in mock sympathy. "I didn't realize he'd been knocked around that hard. At one point, they were even afraid they'd killed him."

Emily released a theatrical sigh. "Oh, well. Better luck next time."

This is not happening. This is not happening, Kate repeated to herself like a mantra. She did everything she could to maintain her facial expression while she searched for an appropriate response. Finally she settled on "Good to know" as being flippant enough to appeal to Emily's sense of inappropriate whimsy and few enough words for her to utter without breaking into a scream.

Once outside the Oval Office, its solid curved door closed behind her, Kate leaned against the wall of the corridor, trying to catch her breath and calm her heart and do both without attracting undue attention from the Secret Service agent who guarded the door.

Headache, she mouthed, massaging her temple. The agent gave her a terse but sympathetic smile.

Kate headed for her office with such determination that staffers automatically stepped out of her way, very much like they did when Emily stalked through the halls. *White House Handbook Rule #5: Never stand in the way of or try to stop and talk with a president on the move.*

Once back in the relative safety of her office, Kate groped blindly in her desk drawer, finding her bottle of aspirin and taking three. She chased them down with half a bottle of lukewarm water she'd opened early that morning but not touched after that. But aspirin alone wouldn't be enough to calm her pounding head, much less provide her the instant wisdom or courage that she so desperately needed.

There was only one way to address both. She dropped into her chair, planted her elbows on her desk, held her throbbing head, and prayed.

I don't know what to do, Lord. Is there really such a thing as doing the wrong things for the right reasons? Emily had nothing to do with Dozier's greed, and I can understand why she wants to preserve his dignity and reputation, even after death. She loved him like a father.

On the other hand, I honestly believe that Operation: Energy Independence is a very important program, and I don't want the greed of one man to stop the program from being put into place.

All I want to do is protect Emily from herself. But now I'm having to lie to her—or at least sidestep the truth—and I don't like doing it. I need your help, Lord. Please help me preserve the truth without creating new lies. Guide me, please. In Jesus Christ's name, amen.

She picked up her briefing and headed to meeting number five. They had barely started when a Secret Service agent stepped into the room.

"Ladies and gentlemen, I must ask you to relocate. We're under a tornado warning. They just spotted a funnel cloud on radar near West Springfield, headed this direction. They think this storm is likely to spin off a couple more tornadoes."

Kate rose from her seat, knowing that her composure would be instrumental for a calm evacuation. Soon after they started working there, the staff had participated in several emergency preparedness drills—covering natural and man-made threats to the White House and its occupants. Thanks to their training, everyone knew what to do and where to go. Her position was with Emily in the PEOC, the presidential emergency operations center located under the East Wing. The PEOC was the designated shelter for natural and man-made disasters due to its reinforced walls and ceiling, which made it a securable, self-powered capsule within the building.

One of its greater advantages was that, despite threatening weather, the president could continue business as usual, thanks to the room's vast array of communication equipment. It was essentially the president's technologically equipped on-site underground bunker.

When Kate was cleared into the room, Emily had already been hustled there by her Secret Service detail and was being settled into the private conference room with a cup of coffee.

"Lovely weather we're having here," she quipped.

They sat around the inner conference table, facing a polished wood panel at the end of the room that had been pulled back to expose a large flat-screen television, which featured the up-to-date eye on the weather, including live shots of flooded streets and one intrepid cameraman showing a funnel cloud as it touched down near George Mason University.

Any ideas of conducting the nation's business faded as they all played spectator to nature's fury on the big screen. According to the reporters, the path of this particular storm was tracking from Fairfax toward Alexandria and seemed to be headed for their general area.

Fifteen short minutes later, the storm hit. Thanks to their

internal, protected location, they couldn't hear the fierce roar of wind or the rain pelting the bulletproof windows of the aboveground floors. The lights dimmed twice but never quite went out.

"The generators just kicked in," Kate said, not quite sure why she was whispering.

After a few more minutes, they stepped out of the executive briefing room and into the larger portion of the center, where the staff was already functioning as an information clearinghouse, collecting and assessing damage reports.

"Early reports say that the tornado touched down on the Virginia side of the Potomac, went up, and passed over most of the District without touching down. We have reports of trees uprooted and some downed power lines but no real damage here. But looks like parts of Fairfax County were hit hard."

Kate spoke before Emily could. "Where in Fairfax?"

The briefer pulled up a map on the largest screen, where a traveling cursor was depositing red stars to mark confirmed locations of damage. Kate realized her own home was directly in the path between stars.

Emily recognized the problem as well. "Buster's home alone, isn't he?"

Kate nodded, feeling too numb to accept or discount any particular possibilities. But it was Emily who reflected the emotion that Kate wanted to release.

Concern creased her friend's features. "We've got to find out if he's okay, if your house is okay." She turned to the briefer controlling the screen. "I want someone to contact the chief of police in Annandale or someone from the Fairfax sheriff's department—whoever you can reach. I want a report about Kate's house ASAP."

Although Kate appreciated Emily's concerns, in her mind, there was something fundamentally wrong with redirecting manpower to serve one person when there might be hundreds, if not thousands, who needed more help.

When Kate tried to say this, Emily cut her off. "It's my prerogative as president and I'm going to use it. All they have to do is drive by your house. If the place is intact, then that's all we need to know."

Kate shook her head. "Before you call out the troops, let me try my neighbors first." She punched in the number, and after several clicks and a few extra noises, the phone rang on the other end.

"Hello?"

"Darlene? It's Kate. So is everything okay there?"

"I was hoping you'd call! We were worried. Yes, everything's fine here. The big tree at the corner fell down and landed on the Fortenberrys' car, but that's the only big-ticket damage. You may be missing a few shingles, but your roof is okay. I hope you don't mind, but when we heard the warning, Carl went right over and got Buster and brought him over here. We didn't want him in there by himself."

Kate felt the tension fade from her body. "You don't know how much I appreciate that."

Emily tugged at her arm. "Is everything okay? How's Buster?"

Darlene's voice grew hushed. "Is that . . . the president?"

"Yes, it is. Darlene, I just want to thank you and Carl so much for taking care of Buster. I wasn't as much worried about the house as I was about him."

"Your neighbors got Buster?" Emily released a relieved sigh. "Thank heavens." She reached for the phone. "Let me talk to them."

Kate knew that there was no option but to hand Emily the cell phone. Emily covered the mouthpiece and said, "What're their names again?"

"Purcell. Darlene and Carl."

"Mrs. Purcell? This is Emily Benton. Do I understand you've got Buster safe with you? You don't know how much we appreciate hearing that. Kate would probably deny it, but he's a pretty important person around here, maybe even more important than her."

Polite laughter ensued. Kate reached for the phone but Emily swatted her hand away.

"Was there any damage to your place?" Emily listened and made the appropriate clucking sounds of sympathy. "Well, we just wanted to check and to say thank you so very much. Oops . . . Kate has another call coming in. Yes, well again, thanks."

Kate reached for the phone again, but Emily grinned and turned away as if playing a particularly annoying game of keep-away, answering the next call herself. For one panicked moment, Kate worried that the call might be from Nick. That coincidence could set off a chain of events that could end in explosions of the worst kind.

Emily's smile broadened. "Hey, Miz R. No, she's here. We were just checking on Buster and her place. Both are fine. Did you have the same bad weather down there? Really? How's Mr. R.? Always good to hear. Wait, here she is."

Emily held out the phone and Kate snatched it from her hand. "Mom? Are you and Dad okay?"

She learned that the storm cell that had spun off funnel clouds in northern Virginia had done much of the same in central Virginia. Although her parents' home had been spared any damage, her father's workshop thirty yards away had lost its roof and one wall, and they had been without electricity for over an hour.

In the grand scheme of things, they'd been spared from the worst, and for that, Kate sent up a prayer of thanks. But she'd just as soon see them for herself to be assured that they weren't playing their "We won't tell her how bad it really is" game. Maybe she could juggle her schedule so that she could take the time to drive down to check on them the next morning. After all, the next day was Saturday, and she had only two meetings scheduled for the morning, and Emily had a quiet weekend planned.

Emily easily read her mind. "Take off the weekend," she said with her usual autocratic manner. "After all, you've probably not had more than a few hours to yourself since the inauguration. You deserve some time off."

"But—"

"We're talking about one lousy weekend, Kate. You have two deputy chiefs who can cover your responsibilities for two days. Plus I know you're going to check your e-mail every hour on the hour, anyway. You don't have any meetings that can't be rescheduled."

Kate raised her hands in mock surrender. "Okay, okay. I'll head down to see Mom and Dad tomorrow."

Emily made a brushing motion with her hand as if saying, *So, get out of here already.*

Kate wasted no time in heading back to her office, where she put her escape plan into motion. Rescheduling wasn't as difficult as she'd anticipated, and with two deputies to call upon, her duties would be well covered for forty-eight hours or so.

However, getting home that night was an adventure thanks to the flooding that had closed several streets and even a few underpasses. Even though the threat of tornadoes was long gone, rain continued to fall, which exacerbated the flooding situation. Kate had driven to work that morning, which meant she had to drive home on a gridlocked interstate. As she headed home, Kate saw the end results of the high winds and heavy rains—billboards ripped to shreds, tree branches scattered across sidewalks and driveways, trash heaped wherever the torrential rain flowed and receded. More than a few traffic lights swung at awkward angles, having been knocked askew by the winds. Her efforts to avoid the traffic turned into a series of waterlogged detours that meant she didn't reach her home until almost seven o'clock, despite the fact she'd left the White House far earlier than usual.

When she finally reached her neighborhood, she saw evidence that the usual roving bands of Good Samaritans who lived there had been busy, cleaning up behind the storm. Her neighbors were one of the main reasons she didn't want to move closer to the city. Years ago, she'd lucked into an older part of Annandale—just a couple of streets actually—where somehow, old-fashioned traditions had curiously survived. It was a place where neighbors watched out and even took care of each other.

Some kind soul had already cleared away a heavy branch that had fallen near or perhaps even across her own driveway. She now had a neat pile of firewood stacked beside her garage thanks to someone's thoughtfulness.

When she knocked on the Purcells' door, she heard Buster and their border collie, Barkley, both howling with delight. After again expressing her undying thanks to Darlene and Carl, she presented them with a box of cookies baked by the president herself along with Emily's handwritten note of thanks.

She thought Darlene was going to hyperventilate.

After thanking them once more, Kate tucked Buster under her coat to protect him from the rain that had picked up again. Once inside, she made a quick circuit around the house, making sure there had indeed been no leaks in the roof, no windows broken by flying debris.

It appeared that the electricity had been off at some point during the storm, but the house was still intact. Relieved, Kate nuked a frozen dinner and sat at the kitchen table, watching the local news coverage of the death and devastation that had swept up the East Coast from South Carolina to New York.

She glanced at the *0* on her answering machine, staunchly saying there had been no new messages. She'd learned the hard way the last time the electricity had gone out that an interruption in the power would reset the counter, even if there were new messages. She pushed away from the table and crossed to where the machine sat and pushed the Play button.

"You have six messages. Message one—today at 2:26 p.m."

The call was a hang-up, as were the second and third calls.

"Message four—today at 4:09 p.m."

"Kate, it's Nick. I sent a text message but I'm not sure you got it. I got that information we were waiting for. Give me a call and we'll talk."

"Message five—today at 5:14 p.m."

"It's Nick again. I tried your cell, but the weather is playing havoc with the coverage. When you get this, give me a call."

"Message six—today at 6:58 p.m."

She looked at her watch and decided the message must have been left while she was picking up Buster. There was static in the background of the call, so much so that she had to listen intently to make out Nick's words.

"It's me. I'm okay. I'm headed over to the place I mentioned to stash stuff there. I'll—"

The call ended abruptly and she listened to the silence, waiting for the next message, but heard only "End of messages."

Kate scrambled through her purse and pulled out her cell phone, confirming she'd missed several calls. She hit Redial on the last missed call and waited, tapping her fingers between unanswered rings.

"Kate?"

"Yeah, it's me. Are you okay? Did your apartment get damaged?"

"I'm okay. The apartment got messed up a bit. The high winds took out a window and some of the roof. So there was some water damage. Nothing major, just annoying. I just grabbed my clothes and I'll be staying in a hotel in Crystal City until I can find a better place."

"I'm so glad you're safe," she said, making no effort to disguise her relief. She told herself she was only displaying simple human compassion, but it was hard to ignore the dramatic decrease in her heart rate at the same exact moment she heard his news.

"I've got the file with me and . . . well . . ." There was a catch in his voice. "You need to see it."

Her momentary sense of relief faded. "Why?"

"I don't want to try to explain it on the phone. Can we meet somewhere? There's a twenty-four-hour coffee shop here at the hotel. I want to get your take on things so we can figure out what to do next."

The question begged to be asked. "Is it worse than we thought?"

"Oh yeah. Far worse."

Kate had a sinking feeling his assessment meant only one thing. Emily wasn't covering up for Dozier's sake.

She was trying to hide her own involvement.

INSTEAD OF VISITING HER PARENTS, Kate decided to stick around home. Surrendering to her growing sense of unease, she called them and explained that she was working on a very sensitive project.

"Of course, we understand, honey. We totally understand. When it comes to the position you're in? Your duty isn't just to Emily, but to God *and* your country."

Even though they had no idea of the complexity of her problems, that one simple reminder of her scope of responsibilities helped to solidify her plans. Even though she hated to ask them to lie, she did, and they agreed without complaint or question to maintain the illusion that she was home, visiting them for that weekend.

The subterfuge would give her two days to work with Nick and unravel whatever new knots the Panamanian paperwork might have revealed. Plus she needed to tell him what she'd learned from Emily about how he'd been an involuntary part of Maia's extortion efforts.

When she arrived at the hotel, the look on his face confirmed her fears that the files contained something really bad. Her news could wait.

She slid into the booth across from him. "Break it to me gently."

Silently he pushed several pages across the table to her. "I've already stashed the originals, but I made copies for you and for me. But for the most part, Dozier did a good job of covering his paper trail. That was the whole purpose of setting everything up in Panama. Their official records don't include pesky things like the names of the owners."

Her sinking feeling reached new depths. "So we won't be able to prove that Dozier owned the corporation?"

"No, but we can prove that he's the investment manager of the Panamanian foundation that owns the corporation."

"I guess that's a good start."

Nick nodded. "I understand now why Donnie lives there. He's smart, but he's as crooked as they come. He's probably knee-deep in this whole business. Turns out Panama is one of the more popular places to hide assets by starting an offshore corporation—in this case, Green World Energy JED Inc." He pointed to the top page.

"So Dozier owns the corporation?"

"No. The corporation is owned in part by a Panamanian foundation named D-JED Energy Foundation. Since foundations don't have owners, the official paperwork only lists some Panamanian lawyer—a stand-in name used during formation to keep it anonymous. Then the lawyer steps aside and reassigns the position to the applicant. The country doesn't require that these changes be recorded in any official national database."

"So Dozier becomes the founder without leaving any paper trail behind."

"That's it in a nutshell. Pembrooke set up their stock option deal in the name of Green World Energy JED Inc., which is owned jointly by three Panamanian foundations—D-JED, J-JED, and E-JED foundations."

She stared at the paperwork, trying to wrap her brain around an impossible concept.

Nick pressed on. "What helps us is that Donnie got a copy of the original application that Dozier made for the foundation and the corporation." He sorted through the pages and pulled out one from the middle of the stack. "So we have proof that shows who the *D* was in JED. Do you want to hazard a guess who the *J* and *E* might be?"

Jack and Emily . . .

"Maybe she didn't know anything about it," Kate said, trying desperately to convince herself of her friend's innocence. "Maybe Dozier did all this without her knowledge or consent."

"Do you really believe that?" he asked quietly.

"I want to." Kate closed her eyes and rested her aching head on her hands. "But I don't. And I can't believe that's all Maia had on the old man. What now?"

"We work several directions. First, I sic Donnie on finding the foundation applications for J-JED and E-JED. Chances are they were started at the same time and probably with the same law firm handling the paperwork. Next, as we found out with the toll road fiasco, if there's one Benton in the woodpile, there are apt to be others. We both need to take a very close look at O:EI and try to figure out what other companies are likely to benefit big-time from the profit it's going to make in one, two, even three years from now. Then see if we can find any Bentons or Benton cronies at the heart of those companies. Finally we work on what Maia was up to the last few weeks of her life."

It was a daunting task, something better attempted by a whole platoon of federal investigators, not just the two of them. "Do you know how long it's going to take to try to track this stuff down? You do know how many Bentons there are roaming the world, right? And Lee tells me Maia was pretty busy."

He adopted a brittle smile. "The way I see it, we have two days. That's approximately two hundred cousins a day and four little visits to Washington power brokers."

She and Nick began their list-making task at the hotel coffee shop, but it didn't take long before they suspected every innocent bystander of trying to listen to their private conversation or attempting to look at the data on their laptops.

"We're being ridiculous," Kate said as they changed topics to the totally mundane for the sixth time until a passing couple walked out of hearing range.

"Are we? If this goes where I think it's going, we both might find ourselves in the firing line."

"You can't believe that."

"I sure can. This whole thing stinks."

He rubbed at the small scar at his hairline, an inadvertent reminder to Kate that she had news she'd meant to tell him earlier.

"Um . . . that reminds me." She stalled by taking a long draw of her coffee, which had become tepid and tasteless. "This morning M called me into her office and told me that when it came to the blackmail situation, we'd all overlooked one important factor."

"What factor?"

"We never tried to figure out, much less locate, what sort of proof Maia used to hold over Dozier's head."

Nick's eyebrows knitted in concentration. "I'd just assumed he'd said the wrong thing at the wrong time."

"If so, then it might have been nothing more than her word against his. Something like that might have made for bad press, but I don't think Dozier would have paid her untold sums of money without some sort of evidence."

"True. He was the practical sort. I'm sure he insisted on seeing concrete proof before he paid a dime. So M has been looking for the actual evidence?"

"Not only looking for it, but found it. It seems that Maia used her cell phone to capture a video of Dozier bragging about how much money he had made and would make from Pembrooke. It looks like Emily had her thoroughly investigated. Emily's on edge over her. One thing Maia had on her phone was something she'd been using to blackmail Tim Colton too. It might explain why they were in the car together."

"Really? What was it?"

Kate looked down, surprised to see she'd been shredding her napkin. She pushed the small bits of paper to the side. "When M's investigators recovered Maia's phone, they found a sound file with Tim explaining how he and two other guys jumped you because they'd thought you'd been disloyal to Talbot."

"That part I never quite understood. I even vaguely remember someone using the word when they switched from fists to a baseball bat. *Disloyal.* How?"

"Talbot convinced them you'd leaked the information about his involvement in Angela Kasdan's death to us."

The revelation made Nick sit up straighter. "But I only knew about it because I was there when you were telling him over the phone. . . ." He paused. "Oh. I get it. What a slimeball. He knew I overheard it, so the beating was his best solution to making sure I wouldn't mention it."

Nick remained quiet for a moment, then slammed his hand on the table, making his coffee cup rattle in its saucer. "You know what this means, don't you?"

Kate stared at him. "No. What?"

"Maybe I should be glad you don't think like a criminal lawyer. Until now, we could only guess that maybe Tim had something to do with the attack on me. Nobody had any proof. But if his confession exists, then that really does make me a prime suspect in his death. If I know M, she'll make sure the police play connect the dots so that the blame points to me."

"Connect the dots?"

He lowered his head and his voice. "Sure. Leaps in logic. What if Maia told me Tim was behind the beating? What if I decided to kill him in retribution? And what if I decided it made sense to take out her too so that no one ever learned of my real motive?"

"Too many what-ifs. You're not a killer."

"Emily would desperately like to believe the worst of me. That's what acrimonious divorces are all about." He sighed and closed his laptop. "Sometimes it doesn't seem worth the time and effort to fight her." He crossed his arms on top of the computer and rested his head on them. "Do you know how badly I want a drink right now?"

"Don't give up." Kate punched him lightly in the arm to get his attention.

He recoiled, sitting up and rubbing the point of contact. "Ouch."

"Don't forget Dozier's deathbed confession. He said he was—and I quote—'so sorry' about what he did to Maia. If that's not a confession of something terrible, I don't know what is. He was frantic to be forgiven for everything he'd done, including whatever it was he did to Maia." Her mind raced ahead. "If you think about it, the fact that Maia was blackmailing Tim means that it's still a good argument for it being a case of murder-suicide."

Nick shook his head. "No one believes that Tim drove into a wall and risked killing himself simply to stop her from blackmailing him."

"What if she had plans that would bring down Emily's government and destroy Talbot's reputation forever? She had the goods. She could have done it. It would have destroyed people's trust in the presidency for a long time. Tim Colton might have given his life to stop her, if that was the case."

Their gazes locked across the table, and after a moment, he drew a deep breath and placed his hand on his laptop as if to open it again. "I'd like to believe that of him. But, remembering the feel of his fists on my skin, it doesn't seem likely. . . . And there's something else. . . ." He hesitated.

"What now?" Kate asked.

"M doesn't like the idea of a stalemate, and I think that's about the best we're going to be able to do chasing this info down. Maybe she doesn't even like having us know about it. If she's willing to lie, cheat, and steal to maintain the status quo, I don't want to even *think* about what she's willing to do to get ahead. And if we're chasing something she wants kept secret, she's going to do everything in her power to stop it."

"She won't do anything to hurt me." Kate wanted to sound resolute and firm, but the words and the sentiment behind them were unavoidably hollow.

"You *hope* she's not going to hurt you. But you can't be sure."

"I have nothing to hide. I've done nothing wrong."

"You're talking to me right now. That alone is tantamount to treachery." His features softened slightly. "And what about last night?" He reached across the table as if he was going to touch her hand.

Okay, so we kissed. But that's all. She pulled her hand back and hid it beneath the table in her lap. "Nothing happened last night."

After a beat, he diverted his gesture by reaching for a packet of sugar. "I know that. You know that. But it might not have looked like that to someone else on the outside looking in." He tore open the packet and poured it into his cold coffee, stirring with more vigor than necessary. "Imagine an investigator with a camera sitting outside my door. You come out in the wee hours of the morning, looking much less put together than you usually are. We kiss and he gets everything on film."

The mental image robbed Kate of breath for two diametrically opposed reasons. She sagged against the wall of the booth. "But there was no camera. Was there?"

"No, but there *were* two FBI agents there, sent on a fool's errand in the middle of the night." He took a sip of his coffee and tried not to make a face. "How hard would it be for M to have had them sent? Or anticipate that, when confronted, I'd call you for help? Or that you'd respond in the middle of the night? Or that you'd be able to stop their questions by mentioning your discussion with their boss? A discussion that M witnessed, maybe even engineered in the first place?"

What had initially appeared to be an unfortunate situation just grew much more ominous, and the consequences more threatening.

Nick templed his fingers over his laptop. "I hate to say it, but when M's involved, we have to be suspicious of everybody and everything." He began to straighten the papers, tapping them into neat piles and inserting them into the folders. "I'm not sure we should be seen together right now. For your sake."

She resisted the urge to swivel around and survey the increased traffic in the coffee shop. "So what do we do?"

"We separate but stay in communication online as we search the records from different locations. A bunch of different locations."

"You mean like move around physically?"

He nodded. "Call it paranoia, but yeah, I don't need to stay in one place." He leaned forward, tapping the laptop. "Someone kept pinging my computer every time I got online at home. The firewall has stopped any efforts to hack in, but it's made me think twice. Could be nothing. Could be something. If I move around, it'll be harder to track me down. And right now? I don't want to be where M or anybody in her employ can find me—in the real world or the virtual one."

If it were anyone other than Nick, Kate would have readily agreed it was just rampant paranoia talking. But given the circumstances over the last forty-eight hours, her ability to distinguish between fact and speculation had taken a real beating.

She looked around, finding exactly what she needed to help him with his quest. "Stay here for a minute," she commanded.

Although clearly confused by her order, he remained seated in the booth while Kate walked over to a newspaper rack filled with the usual assortment of free tabloid newspapers. She selected one she used to read when her mornings started in a similar coffee shop near the campaign headquarters in Old Town Alexandria.

Kate carried the paper back to the table and laid it out, opening it to the classified section in back. "See this ad I'm pointing to?"

"'Unending Fantasies Escort Service,'" he read aloud with more than a bit of distaste.

"I'm going to continue to point to it, but instead, look at the other page, at the bottom."

"What am I looking for?"

"The box at the bottom of the second column that shows the URLs for all of the free Wi-Fi networks in the area—Arlington, Alexandria, and the District. You can stay on the move, even stay in your car, but continue working online." To add emphasis, she pulled out a pen and circled the gaudy ad filled with impossibly built women as if it were the true the topic of their tête-à-tête.

"Interesting juxtaposition," he said under his breath. Then he added in a slightly louder voice, "If you say so," as he stood and stowed his laptop into a black briefcase.

He leaned closer. "I'm going to buy a prepaid cell phone

and call Donnie to see if he can wring a little more out of the law firm's records—mainly the applications for J-JED and E-JED. And I'm going to see what our little Maia was up to."

"We may be too late. Emily said Jack got out before the storm and was headed there. And Maia's dead, with all her secrets."

He tucked the file into his briefcase. "Then this may be our only real proof."

He tore a corner from the newspaper and scribbled something on it, handing it to her. "Here. This is the e-mail address I'll set up as soon as I get to the next Internet location."

He looked up, his eyes smudged with lack of sleep. "They may or may not be trying to monitor your computer, but I wouldn't take any unnecessary chances if I were you." He paused as if he wanted to kiss her but feared being seen. Instead, he managed a weak smile. "Talk to you soon."

When a young couple rose and walked out only moments after Nick departed, Kate wondered if her sudden feeling of fear was a product created solely by the intersection of her imagination and his paranoia.

She looked down at the e-mail address he'd scribbled.

We.Are.Not.Paranoid@gmail.com

BY MIDNIGHT, KATE WAS EXHAUSTED. She'd moved every hour from hot spot to hot spot, and the constant interruptions only served to slow her down in her efforts to uncover more information about the various holding companies and try to find the Benton cronies in the midst.

When she finally took a break, she sat back to assess what she'd uncovered. Basically diddly-squat. Not only was there no smoking gun, there was no hint of smoke at all. But the bigger question she had to ask herself was what would she do with such information if she found it?

What if Emily's family turned out to have their fingers deep in the pie of O:EI? What next? If she threatened to expose them unless they pulled out, would she be any better than Maia Bari? Sure Kate's motives would be different and it wouldn't be a matter of wanting anything in return, but the similarities in their methods would likely haunt Kate to her last day.

Where did loyalty end and duty to a higher cause begin? What if Emily knew nothing about her family's involvement? Should she be forced to shoulder the responsibilities for their misjudgments?

Kate prayed for guidance several times during the night but hadn't yet felt the hand of God pushing, pulling, or nudging her in a specific direction. It didn't mean that no answer was forthcoming. Perhaps she'd already been told what to do and was too resistant to listen or understand. Or maybe she was being too impatient in wanting an answer.

Right now.

She shivered as the wind buffeted her car, making it rock back and forth even though she was parked on a side street in Old Town. The rain had picked up over the last hour, so she switched on the radio, hoping to find a weather report. She didn't have to search hard. The Emergency Broadcast System was in the midst of issuing a tornado watch.

"That tears it," she said aloud. "I'm going home." Bad weather aside, both she and her laptop were running out of power. But before she closed up shop for the night, she brought up the instant messenger screen that she and Nick had used to stay in contact.

WHERE ARE YOU? she typed.

MARRIOTT IN BETHESDA. ONLY 24-HOUR ON-SITE OFFICE I KNEW IN THE AREA. NEEDED TO PRINT OUT SOME STUFF DONNIE SENT.

BAD?

WHAT WE FEARED.

WHAT NEXT?

WEATHER'S GETTING BAD.

TORNADO WATCH HERE, A T-WARNING SOUTHWEST OF US.

YOU SHOULD HEAD HOME.

MY PLANS.

AFTER I PRINT, WILL GO TO THE STORAGE UNIT—NOT FAR FROM HERE—AND STASH NEW PAPERS THERE.

THEN?

BACK TO HOTEL TO WAIT OUT THE STORM.

BE CAREFUL.

U2. NIGHT.

NIGHT.

Kate saved her files and shut down the computer. Once she stashed it in her briefcase, she started the engine and headed home. As she drove through the waterlogged streets, Kate kept the radio on as much for the news as for the company. Her long, hard day had gotten far longer and harder than she'd ever expected, and her yawns were distracting her with their frequency.

When she finally pulled off the main road into her neighborhood, the radio blared its latest warning, upgrading the tornado watch to a warning.

As she negotiated the wet street, she saw lights flare in several of the houses, the occupants evidently alerted by weather radios. As she pulled into her driveway, she looked over and saw Darlene standing in the Purcells' kitchen window, looking toward her house. They waved a mutual greeting, and then Kate dashed toward the front door.

Buster was still waking up from a deep sleep when she scooped him under one arm and headed straight for the basement. She'd sidestepped misfortune once today; she wasn't going to take any more chances. They snuggled in what the prior owner of the house had used as a playroom—a brightly decorated room in the basement that Kate had never gotten around to repainting in a bit more sedate color scheme. She'd at least stocked it with all the bad weather essentials in addition to using it as a storage area for seasonal items.

Whether it was the incoming weather or the fact that they were closed up in a room, Buster couldn't get comfortable. He kept whining and pawing at the door in hopes Kate would set him free. She resorted to bribery, breaking into a package of saltines and running him through his tricks—sit, lie down, beg, shake. She kept him distracted until the electricity went out. Plunged into darkness, he immediately pushed close to her with a whimper. She cradled him in her arms, and they sat together on the pallet on the floor, where Buster trembled and occasionally released a growl as if warning away hidden dangers in the dark.

Up to that point, the basement walls had shielded them from most of the sounds outside, but now she could hear the wind picking up, the sounds of something—lots of somethings—striking the house. A deep rumble filled the air, and she clutched Buster more tightly, and he responded by burrowing his head under her arm. The house shuddered twice as if the raging winds were battering it with gleeful malice.

"Lord, please protect those in the path of this storm," she prayed aloud, repeating the phrase over and over again as the wind roared outside like a freight train crashing through the neighborhood.

Although the sounds seemed to go on for a lifetime, she knew the assault had actually lasted less than thirty seconds. But that didn't mean things were safe upstairs. She'd seen things go very wrong in thirty seconds.

Houses obliterated.

Lives taken.

Worlds changed forever.

Surviving a possible tornado in a reinforced bunker in the White House surrounded by professionals trained in all manners of survival was one thing.

Surviving one by yourself in the basement of your house was far more frightening.

She waited another fifteen minutes for a second wave of bad weather to hit, but it never materialized. She grabbed her flashlight, cranked up her emergency radio, and listened. Not all clear, but better. When she finally stood, Buster didn't want to leave her lap and relented only when she reached into a box of Christmas decorations and found a plush snowman. She handed it over and it appeased Buster's need to cuddle. She tucked him and the snowman in the corner of the room and ventured upstairs to survey the damage.

When she emerged from the basement stairs, she expected to see nothing but rubble. But instead, she walked into her kitchen, which looked just as it had when she took refuge downstairs.

Her purse still sat on the table. She looked around for her laptop and belatedly realized she'd grabbed it along with Buster to take to safety. At least she had her priorities right.

When she stepped out to the porch, that's when she learned about the truly capricious nature of tornadoes. The house across the street was gone. Only a pile of rubble remained where it had sat just a half hour earlier. She sagged to the wet porch step and stared blankly at the carnage. Here she lived—on a street full of houses, those houses filled with people, all probably just like her, huddling for safety in basements or closets or bathrooms.

And what did the tornado destroy?

The only empty house on the street.

"Can you believe it?" Carl Purcell called out. He and Darlene had emerged from their own unscathed house with an industrial-size flashlight and were picking a pathway between the broken hedges toward her. They all took shelter on Kate's porch to stare at the house across the street.

Carl pointed his light at the For Sale sign that had miraculously survived the same onslaught that had literally blown the house away. "It's like some big cosmic joke. Of all the houses on this street . . ."

Darlene nodded. "It's like the tornado chose to hit the one house that could be blown away without hurting anyone."

Kate stared numbly at the sign. "There but by the grace of God . . ." She paused, then closed her eyes. "Thank you, Lord. Thank you for sparing us. Please be with all of those who have been affected by this."

A siren, then two sirens, shattered the unearthly silence.

"From your mouth to God's ear," Darlene whispered.

Carl, the unofficial neighborhood captain who usually rallied everyone to participate in group picnics, multifamily garage sales, or holiday decorating contests, took charge as usual. He ducked back into the house, grabbed his emergency kit, and the three of them began to canvas the street, making sure that everyone was okay, surveying any incidental damage, and preparing to administer first aid if necessary. Carl's background included a stint as a medic in the army, and his manner was both caring and efficient.

However, there was no need for his medical skills. Not a single person had been injured. *Another miracle,* Kate thought, sending up another wave of thanks.

After they'd finished contacting everyone, Carl dragged a piece of plywood out of his workshop and spray-painted *1 House—Empty. 0 injuries. No gas.*

"This way, the rescue crews won't waste any time stopping and can go on to the next area that might need help."

Two other neighbors helped him drag the sign out to the main road. Darlene excused herself to go inside. "We have a phone tree we activate at times like these. I just never expected to have to use it twice in twenty-four hours. I hope my cell works."

They hugged and Kate stepped inside in time to hear a mournful "You forgot about me" howl from Buster in the basement. She went downstairs to discover that the snowman had been chewed up to the point that it looked as if it had actually snowed in the playroom. But she couldn't bring herself to admonish him for it. Instead, she curled up next to him on the makeshift bed, intending only to comfort him for a minute or two.

She awoke six hours later, stiff, sore, and hungry. When she and Buster went upstairs, she learned the power had been restored at some point during the wee hours.

In the bright light of day, the destruction outside looked even worse than it had in the wet darkness. Although little damage had occurred to the other houses, the winds had deposited debris in their yards from other neighborhoods that had not been as lucky. Twisted metal and pieces of siding dotted the yards, and asphalt roof shingles were scattered everywhere like confetti.

Kate switched on the local television stations that had live coverage of the affected areas. One weatherman described the wave of tornadoes that hit during the day on Friday as "only a brief taste of the widespread destruction that was to strike again hours later."

After wreaking havoc in northern Virginia and, this time, the nearby Maryland suburbs, the storms had followed the I-95 corridor and struck Baltimore with a ferocity never felt before in the area. The Inner Harbor had taken the worst of the hit, with the National Aquarium suffering appreciable structural damage, especially to its tropical rainforest exhibit on the roof. The USS *Constellation*, permanently moored in the harbor, had lost a mast, and two banks of lights had fallen at Camden Yards, crushing parts of the left field upper deck.

But the biggest problem was that the flooding in Baltimore threatened to close down both harbor tunnels and force emergency workers to use alternate roadways in their efforts to reach affected areas.

The news anchors were already calling it the worst natural disaster to hit a major city on the East Coast.

And here I am, hiding in my house.

Kate picked up her landline and discovered she had no dial tone. Turning to her cell phone, she called her parents' number but got a fast busy signal meaning busy circuits. Her fallback position was to try her brother's number. Luckily the call went through.

"Thank God, Kate. Mom and Dad are frantic. They've been trying your house, your cell. They would have tried to get Emily except they knew you were hiding out from her."

"I'm not hiding out. Can you call them and tell them I'm fine? I don't know why I can't get a call through to them."

"No problem."

"Did the weather hit them again like it did here?"

"No, they only had more rain and some high winds, but nothing like before. We're the lucky ones. It missed us twice."

After a few more reassurances, she promised to call him back later when things calmed down and get an update on the family. But now she had other concerns that needed her more immediate attention.

She dialed Nick's prepaid cell but got no answer, and that just made her concern turn into worry. Did he get back to the hotel? Or had he tried to brave the elements to keep up his online investigation?

Kate managed to get through to the hotel and rang his room, but no one answered. Now she was getting really worried. The last time they'd spoken, he'd been in Bethesda, and he'd said the storage unit wasn't far away.

But where exactly?

She grabbed the phone book and started searching for storage units near the Bethesda area, but after finding ten without reaching the second page of listings, she knew it was useless to think she could guess where his might be.

Before Kate could formulate a plan, someone knocked on her door. Buster decided it was his cue to start barking. She closed him in the kitchen so she could answer the door without his help.

She didn't look through the peephole, expecting her visitor to be either Darlene or Carl or one of her other neighbors. But when she opened the door, to her surprise, she found Nick standing on her porch.

"Nick?"

He gave her a blank look; then his gaze sharpened as

if he just realized where he was. His usually immaculate clothes were rumpled and stained with dirt and . . .

Is that blood?

She opened the door wider. "Are you okay?"

"Um . . . yeah." He hesitated for a moment. "Maybe not so much."

She stepped out to the porch and grabbed his elbow. "Come in."

He still looked a little bit befuddled. "Okay." He moved with deliberation as if unsure exactly how to propel his body from the door to the living room. When he dropped onto the couch, Kate knew something was seriously wrong.

She moved close to him, perching on the edge of the chair next to the couch so that they were eye to eye. "What's going on?"

He dropped his head and buried his face in his hands, saying something Kate couldn't quite catch.

"What?"

He lifted his face. "It's gone. Everything's gone."

"What do you mean?"

"The storage unit. The proof. Everything. It's all gone."

She drew an involuntary breath. "The tornado?"

He nodded, then winced. When he leaned down again, Kate spotted an ugly red welt on the back of his head, just behind his ear. Without hesitation, she pulled down the collar of his leather jacket, exposing the injury and the trickle of blood that had soaked the neckline of his shirt.

"You're bleeding." She shifted his collar to examine for more injuries. "Were you at the storage unit when the tornado hit?"

He had to think about his answer. "Yeah. It hit me and then

it hit the unit." He gingerly probed his head. "You got some ice or something I can put on this? And maybe some aspirin?"

"Wait here. I'll be right back." Kate headed straight for the kitchen, but rather than get him ice, she was going to get him medical help. She picked up the phone out of habit more than anything and learned that service had been restored.

She was about to call 911 when Nick stepped into the kitchen and put his hand on the phone.

"Don't."

"Why not? You're injured."

"It's not that bad."

"It might be. I'm calling the paramedics."

"If you do, Emily will know I'm here. It'll leave a paper trail."

"That's better than a blood trail."

He managed a small grin. "Don't make me laugh. I think my head will fall off if I laugh."

"Okay. I'm calling a friend." She dialed, but instead of 911, she called the Purcells.

"I'm sorry to bother you, Darlene, but can Carl come over for a moment? With his medical kit? A friend's showed up, and I think he needs to have Carl take a look at him."

"He'll be right over."

By the time Kate put together an ice bag and helped Nick get back to the couch, Carl had entered the house without knocking and immediately went into EMT mode.

Although Nick protested that he didn't need a doctor, Kate very sweetly told him to shut up. Unhampered, Carl poked, prodded, and finally gave his pronouncement.

"As far as concussions go, I've seen worse. I don't think there're any fractures, just some healthy bruising. In cases like this, we like to see swelling. And that's going to be a real goose egg. Have you had a tetanus shot recently? in the last couple of years?"

Nick nodded, then grimaced at the motion. "In the last couple of months."

Carl applied an antibacterial ointment and then covered the bruise with a loose bandage. "Keep it clean and dry, and if the swelling doesn't go down some over the next forty-eight hours, you need to see your physician."

He turned to Kate. "And you'll need to help him watch out for infection. You know the signs. And it'd be smart to keep him awake for the next twelve hours or so."

As he rose, Carl motioned for Kate to follow him into the kitchen. She expected more instructions, but he stopped by the kitchen door and leaned closer, lowering his voice. "I'm not stupid. I know exactly who that is—President Benton's ex-husband. What in the world is he doing here?"

Kate searched for a plausible answer, deciding that the truth—at least a portion of the truth—was the best response. "I've known Nick for years. I'm not sure why he came here, but he probably knew it would be a safe haven and he could get help. He knew I wouldn't turn him down just because he and Emily don't get along."

That seemed to satisfy Carl. "Just making sure. If you need anything, you give us a call. Oh, one more thing? Keep him hydrated. I didn't smell any booze on him, but—"

She held up her hand to stop him in midsentence. "He doesn't drink anymore. He's been a member of AA for a while now. But thanks."

"I only want to know that you're safe with him around."

"I promise. I will be. And, Carl? I'd just as soon no one

knows that Nick's here." She shrugged. "You know how the press can be. . . ."

He nodded and tapped his lips with his forefinger. "Mum's the word." Then he pointed toward his own house. "I won't even mention it to the mouth of the South over there."

As soon as Carl departed, Kate returned to the living room with a glass of water and a bottle of Tylenol. She handed Nick the water and opened the pill bottle for him, shaking out three tablets in his hand. "Tell me everything that happened."

He downed medicine and half the water, grimacing as Kate insisted he stretch out and get more comfortable. "I hung around the Marriott longer than I'd expected to, mainly because of the weather. Finally it looked like it was letting up, and I wanted to stash the stuff Donnie sent me in the storage unit before I drove back into Virginia."

He ran his hand across his chin as if suddenly realizing he hadn't shaved in a while. "It was a small outside unit on the end of the building with a roll-up door. I was trying to get the key out of my pocket when the wind came up and something hit me in the back of the head. When I woke up, I realized the tornado had struck my unit and the two next to it."

"Oh, Nick . . ."

The hollowness in his dark eyes made him appear almost shell-shocked. "It looked like a bomb had exploded. Debris everywhere. Broken furniture, boxes scattered everywhere."

"The papers?"

"Gone. I thought I'd hidden them well by sticking them in the mattress box. But the only thing left of the mattress was the cotton batting in the trees across the street." He cradled his head in his hands. "Everything we had . . . all the proof is gone. They took it."

A shiver of fear coursed up Kate's arms, not as much for the missing evidence, but for his sudden irrational statement. She gave him her best soothing smile, meant for a man who might be suffering a concussion and, with that, some memory loss. "No one took it," she said gently. "It was just bad luck. Bad weather."

He looked up, fire in his eyes. "No, that's what I was supposed to think. But when I woke up, I found this on the ground." He reached into the pocket of his leather coat and pulled out a padlock.

Its hasp had been neatly sawed in two.

"IT HAD TO BE SOMEONE WORKING for Emily. She must know everything," Nick said in a leaden voice. "Everything we've been doing to uncover the truth."

"How could she?" Kate whispered.

"How else? She's the president. She's got resources at her command that no one else in the world has."

"But I'm her chief of staff. Any of her actions go through me first."

"That's what she's always wanted you to think. But we know it's not true. You knew nothing about her toll road debacle. Or when she sicced Maia on you to steal the info you had on Talbot."

Or how she used my investigators to find Maia's cell phone.

A look of bitterness crept across his face. "I bet you didn't even know much about her relationship with Jack Marsh."

Kate had already made herself search back through the many years of conversations she'd held with Emily—all the silly stories, gripe sessions, deep secrets, and such. But her friend had barely ever mentioned Jack. "She never told me much about him, so I thought they might have gotten together as kids and then something split them up."

"Not only as kids. But as adults—" his face darkened perceptibly—"while she and I were married. We'd had one of our worst fights, and that's when she told me exactly why she'd married me—strictly to get back at Jack Marsh."

Kate gaped at him, unable to say anything.

Nick spat out the words with an air of pent-up frustration that had evidently been building for years.

"Jack was the man she really wanted, but he refused to move back to the U.S. for her. But you know Emily—never let love get in the way of ambition. After all, she'd have no hope of becoming president if her prospective husband refused to live in the good ol' US of A. It's simply not patriotic. Evidently I was the runner-up and won her hand by default."

Kate began to see the bigger picture that she'd tried hard to ignore for the past three months. "And then you ran away."

He nodded. "I certainly did. I was trying to save my own life. I know Emily didn't pour the booze down my throat. I take responsibility for that. But she didn't like that I left her. I was just supposed to shut up and take whatever she dished out." He reached into his coat pocket and pulled out some soggy sheets of paper. "This is what Donnie sent me that I was printing out last night. It's further proof that she holds a grudge longer than anyone in the world." He straightened the first sheet against his knee and then placed it on the coffee table.

It was the application for one of the three bogus foundations, now listing Nicholas Beaudry as the investment manager.

"She's going for the jugular. But I'm not surprised. I've always been her favorite whipping boy. But this one . . ." His voice ground to a halt and he had to cough to speak again. "I'm sorry, Kate. I never saw this one coming." He handed her a second sheet.

She examined the sheet, trying to make out the faded print. It was a copy of the application for the D-JED foundation, but now, instead of Dozier's name and address, someone had typed in her father's name and address.

Shock robbed her of breath. Finally she stuttered, "Why D-Dad?"

"I guess because Emily believes the best defense is a good offense. If you try to blow the whistle on her now, she'll pull this out of her sleeve and—"

The blood rushing in her ears blotted out everything else Nick said. How could Emily do something like this . . . to Kate's own father? Even Emily had called him one of the finest men she'd ever known. Kate had always marveled over the consideration, respect, and—dare she say it—love that Emily had always showed for the Rosen family.

Had it all been a lie?

Nick reached over and touched Kate's hand, evidently reading her turmoil easily. "Emily loves when it's convenient to love. The trouble is you've never fully stood in her way before. But if you don't step aside on your own volition, she's ready with the type of ammunition that will either move you or remove you."

There was nothing Kate could say that wouldn't make her seem naive or foolish.

Nick continued, trying to smile but failing. "If it's any consolation, I doubt she expects to ever make this application public. It's there for one reason and one reason only—to stop us from exposing her. When push comes to shove, she's apt to use a shovel on me, but maybe she'd rather nudge you out of the way instead."

Kate stabbed at the paper with her finger, tearing it slightly. "No one in their right mind would believe my father is the sort of man who needs to hide assets in an offshore account." She stuttered to a halt. "I don't mean to imply that they would believe you'd do something like this."

"No offense taken. I'm more concerned about your father than myself. I've got experience surviving Emily's attacks." He touched his bandage. "Recently, even."

"But why Dad? He's not some high muckety-muck in the government who can peddle influence. He worked his entire life in a fiberglass plant, and it took almost thirty years for him to rise to plant manager. It's ludicrous to think he might have this sort of money he needed to squirrel away. That fact alone should make it plain to anyone with half a brain that this piece of so-called evidence is obviously faked."

"True again, but it doesn't really matter in the long run. If you try to take Emily down . . ."

Kate supplied the unfathomable, unthinkable answer. "She'll take my father down with her."

Nick nodded. "She's counting on that being her ace in the hole. That had to be the reason she didn't have Jack change the foundation into your name. You might have been willing to sacrifice yourself to support your principles. But she's sure you won't knowingly destroy your own father."

Kate stared blankly at the paper; then her thoughts centered on her parents. They'd lived a moderate lifestyle based on hard work, clean living, and a strong relationship with God. They'd brought up both Kate and her brother with the same ideals. They'd never really suffered for the lack of money, living comfortably within their means. Her father didn't deserve to have his good name and hard-earned reputation smeared falsely just to protect someone else's greed.

Kate wrapped her arms around herself to combat the sudden chill, as if something had encased her heart in ice. How many years had she devoted to Emily's political ambitions and advancement? How many times had they sat back and made grand plans to make the world better, stronger, cleaner, greater? How many joys and triumphs had they shared? How many moments of anguish and disappointment?

It wasn't supposed to be like this. Emily was supposed to do great things as president. Bring honor and glory, peace and prosperity.

They were going to do great things. Together.

When did you change, Emily? And how did I fail to see it?

Kate stood, unable to sit still any longer. She paced around the living room, a hundred thoughts swirling through her mind at one time. However, one thought kept surfacing to the top.

"I need to call Wes Kingsbury."

Nick, who had been holding his head, looked up. "Why him?"

"I . . . I've used him as my sounding board for a long time. I trust his instincts. Even better, he's a man of real faith. He knows Emily better than anybody else I know, and because of that, I've told him a lot about the problems we had with the campaign."

"He knows about Talbot?"

"Yes, and about Emily and the toll road too."

"And you're going to tell him about all this?"

"Why shouldn't I?"

Nick stroked his chin in contemplation, his brow furrowed. "It's not a matter of not trusting him. But if you tell him everything, you might be putting him in a compromising position."

"He's the last person in the world that Emily would deliberately . . ." She couldn't bring herself to say *hurt*, but her mind whispered that it was a possibility, however remote.

Nick reached over and touched her hand. "Couldn't we say that about you? Aren't you the last person in the world we thought Emily might try to hurt?"

He picked up the lock he'd placed on the coffee table and ran his finger over the jagged edges of metal. "You realize I wasn't conveniently slammed in the head by debris from the wind, don't you? I'm pretty sure a person was on the other end of the two-by-four that hit me. A person following Emily's instructions."

Kate squeezed her eyes shut, trying to remove the image that his description had placed in her head. As much as she would like Wes's counsel on this, the last thing she wanted to do was bring him onto Emily's active radar screen.

"Okay, you're right. I can't bring Wes into this. But I can't just sit here and pretend that nothing has happened."

"You could," he said softly.

"No. No, I can't. It wouldn't be—"

Her cell phone rang, slicing the conversation as effectively as a knife. She picked it up and looked at the caller ID.

"Who is it?"

She stared blankly at the readout, wondering if this was nothing less than the hand of God reaching out and lighting the bush afire in front of her very eyes.

"It's Wes."

AFTER SHOOTING Nick an apologetic smile, Kate answered the phone, wishing her hands weren't shaking quite so much.

"Kate, are you okay?"

"Yes, no damage here. What about you and your family?"

Wes released a heavy breath. "We made it through fairly unscathed, but we're one of the few lucky ones. Our area got hit. Bad." Tension filled his voice. "Not just our area but lots of neighborhoods, towns. From the reports I've received, the tornadoes ran right up between the Parkway and I-85. There's massive destruction from the Beltway to Baltimore." He paused. "Kate . . . we need your help."

"Anything, you know that. Just tell me what I can do to help you."

"It's not just for us, but for everyone else who has been affected. We've already set up several churches as shelters, but we're going to need a lot more in the way of disaster relief because there are so many different communities that have been hit. Two of the major area hospitals have taken heavy damage, so they can take only the most critically injured patients." He lowered his voice. "I know I'm circumventing a system that will eventually start to function, but we need help now, Kate. And if I have a direct pipeline into the White House . . ."

"You need to use it," she said, finishing his statement. "I understand completely. I'll do everything I can, and I'll start right now by calling Emily. And then I'll head your direction immediately. If I'm on-site, I can relay enough information to persuade her to declare it a disaster area and cut out any bureaucratic delays."

"We're working out of the church on Grant Avenue. We went there once together, remember? To talk to the minister about the restaurant donation program? It'll be easy to find. It was spared when everything around it was literally flattened."

She listened intently as he gave her directions. "I'll get there as soon as possible, Wes. And I'll get the cavalry there, one way or the other."

As soon as she hung up, Kate turned to answer the questions she knew Nick must have but, instead, saw him pick up his coat.

He struggled to push his arm through the sleeve. "Where are we headed to?"

She motioned for him to sit down. "You're in no shape to go anywhere."

He wore a look of strained but unwavering determination. "I repeat. Where are *we* headed to?"

Somehow she knew he wouldn't back down, and she

secretly appreciated his sense of resolve. "Wes says that the tornadoes did massive damage up in his area." A sudden flash of revelation made her wrap her arms around herself. *It so easily could have been here. . . .*

She pushed past the overwhelming thought and continued. "There's nothing much we can do about our own problems right now. So maybe changing gears and thinking about someone else is the better thing to do."

He nodded. "I'm game. I'd like to forget . . . a lot of things—if only for a little while."

She motioned for Nick to follow her into the kitchen, where she dug out more emergency supplies—a couple of flashlights, extra batteries, and the box of the latex gloves she'd gotten for her last painting project. "If I can get Emily to declare it a disaster area, we can probably get federal aid into the area faster than the individual communities can."

He took the bag of supplies from her. "Nice to know we learned something from Katrina. I'd never seen a bigger boondoggle down there. It was . . . unbelievable."

She reached into the hall closet and pulled out a hooded jacket, and he helped her put it on. "You were in Katrina?"

"I didn't ride it out there but returned just as soon as I could afterward to help the family." His face darkened. "I hope to never see anything like that again."

"This may be bad too."

"Couldn't be any worse." He shuddered as if the memory was too much to handle. "Nothing could have been worse than what I saw down in N'Orleans."

"Maybe we'll have a chance to do better this time," she said, fishing her keys from her purse.

"Maybe . . ."

☆ ☆ ☆ ☆ ☆

They ended up taking Nick's truck rather than Kate's car. Because the truck rode higher than a sedan, they could negotiate flooded streets without stalling and pick their way along debris-strewn roads with more clearance.

Once they reached the relative safety of the interstate, Kate called the president's private line.

Emily answered the phone herself. "Kate, thank God! I've been trying to get you. Are you okay?"

"Fine."

"Your mom and dad?"

"They're fine too. But I talked to Wes and he says his area is a complete disaster."

"We have reports coming in. Looks like from here to Baltimore caught the worst of it. Virginia dodged most of the bullets, but Maryland didn't."

"That's what Wes said. I don't have to see the area to realize we need to declare the area a disaster and get federal help in here as soon as possible."

"I've already spoken to FEMA and Homeland. They have teams headed that way. Once I get their reports—"

"You know bureaucratic red tape. I'm headed there myself. Let me take a look and call you back with the recommendation. We can get a jump on things—get help to them faster. You trust my assessment, don't you?"

To Emily's credit, she didn't hesitate at all. "Do you even have to ask? Of course. You give the word and I'll move every bit of aid we have into the area. What's the good of being president if you can't jump a turnstile or two in order to help folks?"

It was the sort of sentiment she'd expect to hear from the old Emily and hadn't heard much from the new one. It renewed her faith that there might still be a shred of her old friend buried within and all Kate had to do was fan that flicker back into a flame to heat up a colder heart.

"Thanks, M." Kate closed her phone. "She'll make the recommendation on my report."

Nick's expression didn't change as he steered around a large tree branch that blocked the right lane. "It's not going to be easy."

"What? Being persuasive?"

"No. That's the easy part. I'm talking about it not being easy to give up the right-hand seat—sitting next to Emily as she steers America." His face softened. "I realize the power has to be . . . intoxicating sometimes."

She thought about Emily's quick and seemingly heartfelt promise to act on the strength of Kate's assessment. "Who says I'm giving it up?"

"I just thought . . ." He clamped his mouth shut.

"I know." She sighed. "After everything she's done. But that call I just made? That's an example of what can be done for all the right reasons. If I stay, I'll still be in a position to influence her into doing the right things."

"Operative word: *if*. But think about it. Can you watch her all the time? make sure she's always doing the right thing? stop her when she's veering from the path?"

They were questions she had asked and would continue to ask herself. "That's the hard part," Kate admitted. "And I don't know those answers." She paused, mulling over his original question. "Not yet, at least. But as to the power being intoxicating? It can be sometimes."

"The trouble with intoxicating is that it can so easily turn to addiction. I know that all too well." After a moment, he added, "I've always admired you for your ability to resist the allure of power. Hang on," he said without pause.

She braced herself as he pulled onto the shoulder of the interstate to avoid a twisted piece of sheet metal stretching across all lanes. "Did I? Resist, that is?"

"As far as I know." He quirked a small smile, not turning his gaze from the challenges of driving.

"From my experience, I've seen how power can blind you into presuming you know best. So what about this situation? Aren't I doing the same by attempting to go over the heads of several highly trained teams of government investigators who do disaster assessment for a living? That I think I'm just as capable—no, more capable—than they are to make the call? That's pretty presumptuous and power mad of me, don't you think?"

He tilted his head as if conceding there was a sense of accuracy in her assessment. "True."

She waited for him to explain why her planned actions were actually warranted. He said nothing.

"You were supposed to say, 'No, Kate, you're not power mad.' So you think I'm making a mistake?"

"Not at all."

"Then what?"

"Then nothing. I think you're doing the right thing for the right reasons and using the power of the office to make it so. You're in a position to help, maybe better than anyone else, maybe not. But what I do know is that any decision you make, you're not doing it for fame, for fortune, for position, or for praise." He offered her a smile that spoke of something more than just friendship, of something beyond. "That's the difference between you and M. With her, you always have to look out and look deep for the hidden agenda. I'm here because I trust you and your instincts. Implicitly."

They rode in silence as the hazards of driving dominated their attention. Between impassable roadways and detours, Kate realized their half-hour trip was going to take well over an hour, if not two. They were stopped a half-dozen times by authorities but were allowed to pass thanks to Kate's credentials and their reconnaissance mission, mandated by the president.

Driving became even more hazardous as they reached the affected area. They had to be careful to dodge the flotsam and jetsam left behind by the twisters, including the downed power lines. Finally they found a partially open route to the church and ended up parking a couple blocks shy of the building in a lot that had evidently once held a child-care facility.

However, the tornado had swept the place clean. Nothing remained of the building but the playground equipment, its bright colors muted by debris.

A large crowd of people were already working in the church, which thankfully still had electricity. Kate found Wes in the center of a knot of men and women, poring over a map. When Wes saw her, his face brightened perceptibly. He motioned for her to join them and gave her a small hug when she arrived. He pointedly ignored Nick, who faded into the background with a quick nod.

"Guys, this is Kate. She's here to help." Wes didn't mention her position or how she could help, but the men seemed to accept her worth solely on his word.

He turned to her like a major briefing a general. "We've been canvassing the area, getting reports from other church groups who run disaster teams. We formed a network after Katrina, hoping to pool our resources, our volunteers, and our information. Because of that, we've got a pretty accurate picture of the devastation." He pointed to the map, which had been heavily marked up.

"The red Xs mark the homes that have substantial damage. The blue Xs mark damage to schools, hospitals, and medical offices; orange marks the more critical retailers like grocery stores, drugstores, etc."

Kate studied the map, noticing the cluster of Xs, obviously areas hit hard, but also noted isolated blue Xs in places where no other damage had been reported. "Some of these aren't clumped with the others, but standing off by themselves. Are you still waiting for information in those areas?"

"No, those are cases of isolated damage." His expression darkened. "Diane, you tell her."

A small Asian woman spoke as she pointed to each of the blue Xs. "North Higgins, Liberty Tree, Copeland . . . they're schools," she said quietly. "Elementary schools, actually, and all of them are less than three years old."

"Just elementary schools."

Another man standing in the circle stepped forward. "Cal Grant, ma'am. The area's been growing fast, so the four counties have been popping up elementary schools in the new neighborhoods."

"But other businesses and homes near the schools weren't damaged, right?"

"There are only reports of minor damage in the houses and other buildings near the schools." The man stiffened.

"It's shoddy workmanship, if you ask me." He turned to Wes. "Tell her about Frances Latham."

The name was familiar, but Kate couldn't quite remember the person. "Who's she?"

Wes released a ragged sigh. "Not a who in this case, but a what. Frances Latham Elementary—one of the newest schools in Montgomery County. It's only eight months old. Their fifth- and sixth-grade classes were holding an all-night readathon when the building collapsed on them. They huddled in the hallways for safety, but . . ."

Another man stepped forward, obviously trying to control his anger. "Hallways that were supposed to be fortified against just this sort of problem. In a brand-new building . . ." He bit off his next comment as if censoring himself. "Two dozen kids were injured, three seriously."

Kate felt as if someone had reached into her chest and wrapped a hand around her heart and begun to squeeze. "That's unconscionable."

Nick took that moment to break his self-imposed silence and nonparticipation to step into the circle of people. "It's graft. I've seen it before."

Wes remained silent, his arms folded tightly across his chest. Kate couldn't tell if his dubious look was meant for the message or the messenger.

Nick continued despite Wes's censuring posture. "I bet you'll discover that only one or two construction companies had the contract to build all these schools. When you have to pay kickbacks, the money has to come from somewhere. Using substandard materials is the easiest way to make up the shortfall."

Kate studied the map.

Nick pointed to three of the blue Xs isolated on the map from the other clusters. "Schools just don't collapse in areas where no other damage had been reported."

Kate felt a shiver course up her spine. When Emily had talked about her family's involvement in the Virginia toll road debacle, she had bragged that, because of her family's construction companies, the roadway had been built well, under budget, and on time. Her sense of pride for a job very well done had eclipsed the pesky notion of the illegality of nepotistic contracts.

But this was different.

A voice spoke up. "It wasn't just here." One of the men who had hovered just beyond the circle stepped closer. "When that first wave of storms hit earlier—Friday morning—my son-in-law in North Carolina told me they lost three schools in their area. Luckily not the one my grandkids attend." He lowered his voice. "School was in session at the time."

Kate immediately thought about her own nieces. Amy, the oldest, was in first grade.

People began to add their stories and locations of damage. Although most of the evidence was hearsay and unsubstantiated, an unsavory picture was forming. It wasn't just one school district in Maryland but something on a larger scale, involving schools in multiple states.

Kate knew without hesitation that President Emily Benton would see to it that a full investigation would be instigated in order to guarantee that the proper heads rolled for taking illegal building shortcuts that endangered children.

She pulled out her cell phone and hit speed dial.

"Who's she calling?" one man whispered.

"You'll see," she heard Wes answer. "I promised we'd get help. And she's getting it for us."

Kate stepped out of the circle, but not far enough to keep her conversation completely private. She wanted the people there to know that real help was coming and who was sending it.

Emily picked up on the third ring.

"Madam President? It's Kate Rosen."

"Oh, boy . . . with this much formality? It's not good, is it?"

"It's worse than we thought."

"Break it to me gently."

"Not only is there widespread destruction—entire communities completely torn apart—but there's a disturbing pattern of destruction in the new elementary schools in the area. Practically every new grade school in a—" she turned back to Wes, who mouthed, *Thirty*—"thirty-mile radius has been literally blown apart whether any other structure in the immediate area was affected or not. On top of the widespread tornado destruction, I think we've stumbled into a serious problem with construction irregularities. I'm hearing unofficial reports of similar problems in other states."

Emily uttered an expletive. "This is not what I wanted to hear. Okay, I'm calling the Maryland governor, and he and I will make the declaration immediately. Tell them to hang on and I'll get help there as soon as possible."

"I'll tell Wes."

"He's there? Let me talk to him."

Kate motioned for Wes and held out the phone. "The president would like to talk to you."

He managed a small smile as he held the phone to his ear.

"Madam President?" He listened intently, his formal answers dissolving from a staunch "Yes, ma'am" to "Yes" to "Sure" and ending up with a soft "You got it, M," indicating that he'd stopped talking to the president and, instead, was getting assurances from a good friend. He even laughed once.

"I'll tell her. Thanks, Emily."

He handed Kate the phone back. "She's going to do it now."

Kate pocketed her phone with a nod, then turned to the assembled crowd, which had grown larger during the call. "Ladies and gentlemen, the president is prepared to declare this a disaster area. Federal aid will be mobilized immediately. And I'll see to it personally that an investigation is started into the problems you've identified with school construction here and the other locations you've mentioned, as well as any other reports of damage that come up."

After her little grandstand play—Kate couldn't describe it as anything else—she and Nick pitched in, two more sets of hands to help settle the newly homeless, get names, and offer sympathy, a cup of coffee, and an ear.

At one point, she lost track of Nick and finally found him sitting on the floor, surrounded by a group of small children whom he was keeping enrapt with some wild tale, judging by his grand hand gestures and their wide-eyed stares.

"Quite a transformation."

Kate turned and realized Wes had stepped up next to her.

"I remember meeting him some time ago. He's not the same man that Emily married. And divorced," he added pointedly.

"No, he's not."

He gave Nick a critical once-over. "What changed him?"

"God. And AA."

Wes nodded. "Good combination." They both watched as Nick continued to entertain the children. "I have to admit he seems to know what people—what each individual—needs. I've been watching him. A quick smile for the kids, a shoulder for the elderly who want to talk, a good word for everyone. And he seems genuinely interested."

"He's a good guy."

"Not according to Emily."

Kate shrugged. "They weren't good for each other back then. But that was the past, and Emily sometimes has trouble letting go of the past."

Wes kept his voice low and even. "What about you?"

"What *about* me? Do I have trouble letting go of the past? Sometimes. But not all the time."

"No, I mean, is he good for you?"

Kate was taken aback by Wes's bold question. She wasn't ready to make that determination. Not yet. She and Nick were just getting to know each other. Sure, she liked what she saw, liked even more what she didn't see. But she wasn't quite ready to acknowledge the possibility of a more in-depth relationship. Not yet. But Wes deserved an answer.

"He could be." She couldn't help but glance in Nick's direction. "Good for me, I mean."

"Even if he drives a wedge between you and Emily?"

Kate turned her full attention to Wes. "Nick's had nothing to do with any division forming between me and Emily. Trust me. Emily has been causing that all on her own."

"So what are you going to do?"

Good question. Kate surprised herself by voicing the first thought that came to her mind. "Probably have a big, hairy showdown with her."

"Sounds ominous."

"It might be. It all depends on how she reacts."

They remained silent for several moments before Wes spoke again. "You don't want to tell me what she's done now, do you?"

"No, not particularly."

"That bad?"

"Yes."

Wes shifted his gaze to Nick. "Does *he* know anything about it?"

"You mean Nick?"

"Of course I mean Nick. Does this problem between you and Emily involve him?" Wes turned his gaze away as if worried Nick might instinctively know he was the subject of their discussion. "I heard he was a person of interest in the deaths of Maia Bari and the guy she was with."

"Trust me. He had nothing to do with it."

"You sure?"

Kate suddenly grew tired of the messages that floated just below the surface of the conversation. She pivoted and faced her friend, balancing her fists on her hips. "It's not like you to be this . . . obtuse. Just say what's on your mind, Wes."

"What do you know about this guy?"

She tried not to roll her eyes like a teenager being grilled by a parent. "Gee, not much. I've only known him twenty years or so."

Wes crossed his arms, his posture screaming a message

she didn't want to hear. "Ever since he was your best friend's husband, right?"

"You too?" She couldn't help but sigh. "First my father and now you. Why have the men in my life suddenly decided that I've lost the ability to distinguish good from bad, right from wrong?"

Wes's face softened. "We're just trying to look out for you."

"I've been a grown woman for many years now. I appreciate the sentiment, but I'd also appreciate it if you'd trust me."

"You, I trust. Him?" He spared Nick a quick glance. "The jury's still out on him." He raised his hands to forestall Kate's next comments. "To his credit, he seems like a nice guy." They both watched as Nick leaned over and whispered something to a sullen little boy who cracked a brief smile in response. "I just hope it's not just a passing phase. . . ."

Kate placed her hand on Wes's arm. "It's not. Give him a chance and you'll see what I see."

He graced her with a smile and pulled her close for a quick hug. "Like I said, I trust you. And if you say he's changed, then I trust your judgment."

✯ ✯ ✯ ✯ ✯

The next twenty-four hours were filled with solace, solutions, and resolutions. After getting a tour of the stricken area, Kate remained at the church shelter, pitching in. She didn't realize how exhausted she was until she fell asleep after sitting down ostensibly to retie her shoe.

Nick and Wes colluded and presented a united front, insisting she go back to Wes's house and get some sleep. As much as she hated taking a break—a pointed reminder that she had a safe home to go to—she finally agreed and picked her way through the debris-strewn streets to Wes's house a few blocks away.

Anna greeted her with a hug, and Dani managed to shoot her a shy but sleepy smile of recognition.

"Wes called me. You look beat."

"I am," Kate admitted for the first time.

"It's perfect timing," Anna said as Dani leaned her head onto her mother's shoulder and released a yawn. "Miss Priss here is about to go down for her morning nap. It'll be quiet for you."

Kate stepped forward and planted a kiss on Dani's head. "Did the tornado frighten her?"

Anna shook her head. "She slept right through it. The three of us huddled in the closet, but she never woke up. The real challenge will be tonight when it gets dark. Babies and candles aren't a good combination."

"I have power at my place if you want to go there. It's not babyproof, but it is Buster-proof, and trust me, the two are very similar."

"That's okay. Me and the munchkin plan to camp out. Right, sweetie?"

Dani released a sleepy yawn. Kate found it infectious and stifled her own yawn.

"Nap time. Both of you."

Anna led Kate to the guest room, where she fell asleep. When she woke up, she was stunned to learn she'd slept for three hours. She emerged from the bedroom and found Anna in the living room, reading Dani a book.

"Sleep well?"

"It depends. Is it still today or is it tomorrow already?"

Anna laughed. "It's still Sunday. Wes called and the troops have arrived. You and Emily literally moved heaven and earth. You don't know how much everyone appreciates this."

Kate shrugged. "All I did was make a phone call and tell Emily what I saw."

"It was far more than that. It's just good to know we have a president who really cares."

☆ ☆ ☆ ☆ ☆

A president who really cares . . .

Anna's words haunted Kate for the rest of the day, even as she and Nick drove back to her house. The trip home was far less taxing than their initial drive because most of the roadways had been cleared. But the sense of turmoil that filled her mind was just as challenging.

"You're quiet," Nick commented as they hit the Beltway. "Tired or troubled?"

"Both."

"Me too."

"We did good. We helped channel Emily's power so that it did something incredible today."

"True."

Kate's moment of triumph flared and fizzled a moment later. "But it doesn't change what she did."

"Or what she might do again."

She pushed back in the passenger's seat. "That's the problem. I worry that the next four years will be a matter of doing everything I can to either mitigate the damages she causes or at least offset them so that I can live with my own conscience."

"She has no incentive to change."

"Then it's up to me to help her find the incentive."

GETTING NICK INTO THE WHITE HOUSE wasn't actually all that hard. Nick had already gone through the cursory investigation for his first visit the previous month. So Kate simply used the powers of her office as chief of staff to get him waved through.

However, getting Nick upstairs into the private residence was another matter, especially doing so without alerting Emily to his presence. But again, Kate had a solution that she hoped would work.

She dialed Emily's private number. "M, it's Kate."

The president sounded chipper as usual. "How are things down on the old homestead? Is your dad's workshop a complete loss? Or are we going to make it a tool-filled Father's Day this year?"

"Well . . . that's the thing. I decided to not go home. I'm not sure how much help I would have been. I probably would have gotten in their way. Instead, I decided I'd bring someone by to see you."

"Who?"

Kate smiled at the Secret Service agent who openly listened to the conversation. "You said you wanted him to visit more often."

"Buster?"

"That's the one. I just need for you to tell your agent to allow me to bring up a very important guest."

"Give him the phone."

Kate handed the agent her cell phone. "She wants to talk to you." While she waited—a plastic smile plastered on her face—she prayed that Emily wouldn't specify that she was expecting Kate and a dog rather than Kate and Emily's ex-husband.

The agent listened intently, then said, "Yes, ma'am. Thank you." He handed Kate back the phone. "The president says for you and your guest to enter and proceed to the third floor. She's in the sunroom." Only the slightest gleam in his eyes suggested that he knew exactly who Nick was but was unsure why the president was so enthusiastic about his arrival.

"Thank you."

Kate didn't drop her phony smile until the door closed behind them. Then she allowed herself to sag with relief.

"Gutsy move," Nick said.

"I'm not comfortable with this sort of obfuscation," she admitted. "It could have so easily blown up in our faces."

"But it worked."

"But it worked," she echoed. "For the moment . . . Buster."

"Woof."

Once in the private residence, she led him down the hallway and to the back staircase, where they climbed to the third floor. They wound their way past the tables and chairs that dotted the Central Hall and headed down the corridor toward the sunlit room ahead.

Emily caught sight of Kate first since Nick was a few steps behind her and not quite in view. "Hey, where's my little ma—"

Her look of amused anticipation dissolved when Nick came into view. "What in the world is he doing here?"

"An intervention?" he quipped. He stepped past Kate, surveyed the comfortable room, and dropped into an overstuffed chair. "Nice room." He pretended to examine the fabric of the chair's arm. "Pretty." He bounced slightly. "Comfortable." He shot her a grin that would disarm and charm any other woman in the world.

Except Emily.

Her usually expressive face remained blank. "What's he doing here?" she repeated.

"We've come here to talk to you."

Emily stared at her, and then something incredible happened. Something Kate had never seen before and never thought remotely possible. Emily's left eye twitched and she turned away.

For the first time ever in her life, Kate felt as if she had the upper hand with Emily. Emily—who could stare down angry protesters with a steely gaze. Emily—who relished arguments and ate unprepared debaters alive. Emily—who faced the toughest law professor at Georgetown with such confidence that the man began to question his own logic.

Emily had never twitched when facing those challenges, but she had now.

"You better sit," Kate said with as much charity as she could muster.

Emily sat, regaining her usual composure. "Can I get you something to drink? coffee? tea?" She smiled sweetly as she turned to Nick. "Arsenic?"

Kate ignored the gibe. "First, what you did in terms of disaster aid was—in a word—miraculous."

Emily straightened, a small ripple interrupting her otherwise emotionless expression. "You're the one who figured out the problem with the school construction. I'm just sorry it took a catastrophe of this proportion to uncover it. But I already have investigators looking into the situation. They'll ferret out exactly how this happened and how many heads are going to roll over it."

Kate pointed to her. "This. This is the Emily I want to work for and work with. This is just one of the great things you've done and an example of the things you can do in the future. But if we're going to continue working together, we have to straighten some things out."

"Like what?"

Kate sat, an action meant to minimize the threat that her words would contain. She knew full well that the best way to play the superiority game was to do it on selected levels.

She lowered her voice. "You should have never trusted Maia Bari." She made it sound like a statement of quiet fact, not an accusation. "If you hadn't foisted her on me and insisted she become part of the campaign staff, I doubt she would have ever gotten her hooks into Dozier and learned all about his financial irregularities. But you did and she did. And from there, she wouldn't have gotten the connections she needed to blackmail half of Washington. She wanted to bring the government down—you, Talbot, everyone. And you know it. And now she's dead."

Kate leaned forward, balancing her elbows on her knees. "I don't think it was an accident."

Nick drew attention to himself by shifting in the chair, getting into a more comfortable position. "I found it really hard to believe that one too."

"True." Kate turned back to Emily, who remained quiet. "Maybe you had her killed and Tim was simply an acceptable casualty in the line of duty. A dead Maia meant no more blackmail, no more threats to your power. No threats to Dozier and none to you in the future."

Emily looked shocked. "Me? I don't have people killed. You know that."

"True. But what I do know is that you gave her far too much access far too quickly. Were you trying to create a protégée?"

"A mini-me?" Nick said with a laugh.

Emily shot him a look that made his laughter fade into uncomfortable silence.

"No, I bet she had something on you. Something you couldn't bear to have released." A possible answer flashed in Kate's head, an image she instantly wanted to erase from her imagination. "Or was she just a threat to what you wanted your whole life—this presidency?"

Emily broke her silence, an indicator that Kate might have accidentally stumbled onto the truth. "Kate, she'd have destroyed this country. She had to be stopped—"

"It doesn't matter," Kate said, interrupting Emily. "Not anymore. She's dead, right? But what about me? When Dozier confessed to me, did that make you start worrying about me too? Were you concerned that I might not believe that you knew nothing about Dozier's problems?"

Kate rose to her feet, unable to keep her cool, professional demeanor any longer. "The funny thing is I did believe you. What I didn't believe was that Jack would give up his fortune so quickly, but you two were convincing."

Emily bristled visibly at the mention of Jack. She stood and straightened to her full presidential height. "Now, wait just a minute. I'll have you know that Jack Marsh is an honorable man who—"

"Sit down and shut up," Kate ordered, surprising herself with the strength of her command.

Emily didn't sit, but her posture and expression changed, sagging visibly.

"Jack Marsh was your lackey who flew to Panama and had the audacity to change the foundation records so that Nick is listed as the investment manager of one fund and *my father* for the other. *My* father!" she said, her voice reverberating around the room.

The look of utter shock on Emily's face appeared genuine, but Kate couldn't be sure. Not anymore. The president sagged back into her chair as if her knees had given out, making her look decidedly unpresidential. "He did what?"

"You heard me. Jack's trying to make it look as if both Nick and my dad are involved in financial improprieties, and that I'm planning to funnel the Pembrooke stock profits into an offshore account in my father's name. And Jack's doing it on your command, right?"

"Absolutely not." Emily regained her strength and proved it by rising from the chair and crossing over to the nearest window. She leaned her head against the glass and slapped the frame with her open hand. "That blithering idiot. I told him expressly not to do that. All we had to do was remove any connection between Dozier's foundation and Green World."

"Well, evidently he didn't listen."

She shrugged. "He's too protective."

Kate gawked at the description. "Protective?"

Emily turned away from the window and faced Kate. A cold gleam in her eyes signified that Kate had probably just lost the advantage of surprise and might be on the receiving end of some new and unsavory revelations.

"You better sit down, Kate." She glanced at Nick, who was beginning to rise from his seat. "And don't *you* get up. I'll have the Secret Service here in five seconds flat, and we'll see just how fast they take you down."

Nick settled reluctantly back into the chair, matching her cold stare with his heated one.

Kate refused to sit. There was no way she would give Emily the height advantage. No matter what.

Emily cocked her head at Kate's position. "Hmmm . . . toe to toe. Okay. I admire that." She drew a deep breath. "You've seemed to lose sight of the bigger picture and are concentrating too much on the smaller pieces. Jack described you as a liability, and I'm afraid I have to agree with him."

"Since when have you turned to him for advice? Last thing I heard, you hadn't seen him in years."

Emily offered her a sad smile. "Here I am worrying about how much you do know about me, and then I realize there's so much you don't know. Jack and I have been close for years. Since we were kids. I just never let you into that part of my life. But despite that, you still know too much,

Kate. Pure and simple. You know my strengths but you also know too much about my weaknesses. I've come to realize that I can't really trust someone who knows that much about me."

"You trust Jack Marsh. Sounds like he knows you better than I do."

"We're . . . a lot alike." Something crept into her expression that softened it, and Kate wondered if Emily and Jack had a far deeper relationship than she was willing to admit.

Emily kept her voice low and soft. "Don't make me go public with what I know."

"You mean with what you've trumped up," Kate said.

"I really regret that. The last thing I wanted to do was hurt you. I didn't need Jack to go rogue and create stupid lies. We'll have a talk about that the next time I see him. No, the beauty of *my* plan is that everything I have on you is true."

Emily offered her deadliest shark smile. "Your dad. How long has he been retired from Glaswell? Six years? I bet you didn't know his retirement included a deferred stock option deal. Or that Pembrooke bought out Glaswell's parent organization four years ago. Your father is due to make a nice bit of change when Pembrooke gets the drilling contract. That's real, Kate. Not trumped up. You'll be hard pressed to convince federal investigators, plus the press, that you knew nothing about it."

Kate opened her mouth, but no sound came out.

"And Charles Talbot might even be pursuaded to unburden himself and admit that it was you, not me, who called him and threatened him with dirt you'd dug up on him. Isn't that the very definition of blackmail? If you think about it, you helped a murderer avoid criminal prosecution. Bad girl . . ."

The blood rushed so furiously in Kate's ears that she could barely hear Emily when she turned and spoke to Nick.

"And you, scum of the earth, I haven't forgotten about you. How's the job going? Getting your feet wet? That's why I engineered that exact position for you. I figured you'd enjoy being a lobbyist. You schmooze well, Mr. Charm."

The expression that crossed Nick's face contained none of his legendary charm. "You know what my father always said: 'Flattery always comes before the flat iron.' Quit trying to get back into my good graces, Emily. Just spill it."

"Here you go. Better Energy Alliance, a division of Stern, White, and Hodge, whose parent company is . . . the Pembrooke Group."

"Coincidence."

"On its own, yes. But not combined with pictures of you and Madam Chief of Staff over there having intimate late night assignations. I have some rather lovely shots of you two, looking like you'd just come out of the bedroom, all rumpled and such. There's even one of you kissing. When those photos show up in the gossip columns, it'll look bad—the White House chief of staff fooling around with the president's ex."

Kate reached blindly behind herself and found a chair that she dropped into, her knees no longer willing to support her weight. After a moment, she managed to say, "I thought you said the last thing you wanted to do was hurt me."

"A good strategist works several moves ahead and covers all her bases." Emily came closer. "And I had to do it. This country couldn't stand the shock of what you know, what Maia knew, becoming public. That's right. You know too much, Kate. That's the bottom line. I really don't want to have to expose your sins to the public—showing them how you've disgraced me by taking advantage of your position for financial gain. Not only you, but your loved ones too. Your quest for personal pleasure has resulted in a romantic relationship with my ex-husband. A relationship that I'm afraid might have originated during my marriage to Nick, which would, of course, make you the other woman."

She could have stood next to Kate's chair, towering over her. But instead, Emily dropped to the couch, putting them on the same level. Instead of shouting, she spoke barely over a whisper.

"Don't make me say those things about you. Especially not about your dad. I actually like him."

Our Father, who art in heaven . . .

Kate said nothing.

"It doesn't have to be this difficult, Kate."

. . . hallowed be thy name.

"Don't throw this friendship away, not after all this time."

Thy kingdom come . . .

"Tell me you'll play it my way. Tell me you're still with me for the long haul."

. . . thy will be done, on earth as it is in heaven.

"Think of all the good things we can do. All the people we can help. Look at O:EI; it's the first real step to saving this world from our mistakes."

Give us this day our daily bread.

"Say the word and I can make all the bad stuff disappear." She snapped her fingers as if to demonstrate the strength and swiftness of her power.

And forgive us our trespasses, as we forgive those who trespass against us.

Kate finally spoke, forcing all emotion from her words, leaving them flat but factual. "You can't make the truth disappear. But remember, I know everything. All about the toll road program, the dirty tricks you played during the campaign, evidence showing that you and Jack stood to profit, just like Dozier. We even have proof that someone added my father's name and Nick's after the fact in an effort to discredit both of us. And despite all of your efforts to destroy the evidence, you failed. I still have all the documents in safekeeping." *Most of the documents,* she said to herself.

And lead us not into temptation . . .

"I have faith that my truth will not only offset your lies, it will destroy them."

Emily betrayed no reaction except for her white-knuckle grip on the edge of the couch's cushion.

"Stalemate," Nick muttered, almost to himself. He turned to Emily. "It's a stalemate," he repeated louder. "If you fire the first shot, we've got enough ammunition to hit back. Hard. You try to take Kate down, you'll go down with her."

Emily released a string of terse expletives, a clear sign that she realized her predicament. And didn't like it one bit.

. . . but deliver us from evil.

Kate knew there was only one thing she could do. The prospect should have felt frightening, but a sudden peace filled her, the sort of serenity that could only come from God. It was that sign she'd been looking for.

Pure and simple.

For thine is the kingdom . . .

"Emily?" She stood and faced the person who had been her best friend for over twenty years.

. . . the power . . .

The person with whom she shared laughter and tears, a woman who she had hoped could be America's greatest president.

. . . and the glory, for ever and ever.

"I quit."

Amen.

A NOTE FROM THE AUTHOR

Welcome back to the world of Kate Rosen and Emily Benton. As you've learned, the road of their relationship isn't particularly smooth, especially not after Kate has done some soul-searching. Is there any chance for recovery? That's up to them.

I know it sounds odd for me to talk about them as if they are real, but to me, they are. As a writer, you work very hard to create characters who become three-dimensional and realistic. If everything goes right, they almost gain lives of their own. I may plan scenes, set up plot points, but often, things simply . . . happen. The characters say something or do something I haven't planned, and suddenly the story takes a slight detour from what I expected. That's when you sit back and realize that you've been writing for four or five hours without a break, and it seems as if you've been sitting there for only minutes. We call that being in the zone—and it's a marvelous feeling.

This leads me to the admission that when asked "What's next for Kate and Emily?" all I can say is—it's up to them. I know what I think will happen, but you never know what surprises are around the bend when you're working with two other headstrong women who may have ideas of their own.

ABOUT THE AUTHOR

Born and raised in Birmingham, Alabama, Laura Hayden began her reading career at the age of four. By the time she was ten, she'd exhausted the children's section in the local library and switched to adult mysteries. Although she always loved to write, she became sidetracked in college, where the lure of differential equations outweighed the draw of dangling participles.

But one engineering degree, one wedding, two kids, and three military assignments later, she ended up in Colorado Springs, Colorado, where she met people who shared her passion for writing. With their support, instruction, and camaraderie, she set and met her goal of selling her first book. She now has published eleven novels, including the First Daughter mystery series, as well as several short stories.

The wife of a career military officer, Laura has moved with surprising frequency and has now returned to her native Alabama. Besides writing, she owns Author, Author! Bookstore and is the head of the graphics department for NovelTalk.com. When not at the keyboard of her computer, Laura can be found at the keyboard of her piano.